The gynecologist had confirmed what the little pink X's had told Sarah so clearly that night. She was going to have a baby next summer.

But it still seemed unreal. Like a very, very long bad dream. As she entered her apartment, Sarah dropped her purse and her "So You're Having a Baby" brochure on the coffee table. Then she dropped herself onto the sofa, like a puppet with cut strings.

Her half-focused gaze fell on the table where the mail still lay. She was unable to work up the energy to open it. A few bills, a dozen Christmas cards…

But now she saw that one of the cards was from Uncle Ward. The sight was strangely comforting. She reached for the card, wondering if her uncle had included one of his long letters chronicling the goings-on in his little mountain town. How lovely it would be to escape, even for a few minutes, into his world.

She sat up, wondering how much a flight to upstate New York cost. Uncle Ward and Firefly Glen had been a sanctuary once. Perhaps they could be the same now. She picked up the telephone. Surely somewhere in that gentle valley town, amid all that snowy silence, she could figure out what to do with her life.

Dear Reader,

Home. It's a small word to mean so much. And yet that one syllable holds the power to inspire writers and poets, philosophers and painters.

But what is it, really? A hundred people will give you a hundred different answers. It's a house, a city, a parent, a husband, a friend. It's where you retreat, sick and frightened, and come out brave and well. It's where you can finally take off your armor, lay down your sword and rest.

Sometimes the treasure of home is handed to you at birth, gift-wrapped with love and laid at the foot of your cradle. Sometimes, though, you have to search for it on your own.

Sarah Lennox, the heroine of *Winter Baby*, has almost given up searching. The child of a home that was broken and broken again, she has decided that, for her, *home* is a dream that will never come true. The closest she ever came to knowing that security was one magical summer in Firefly Glen, a tiny town high in the Adirondacks.

So when she finds herself pregnant and alone, that's where she turns. She needs a peaceful place to hide while she sorts things out.

But instead of being swaddled in solitude and silence, Sarah finds herself instantly caught up in the madness and mayhem and pure sparkling magic that make up Firefly Glen. And somewhere between building ice castles and visiting puppies in the local jail, she finds herself doing the one thing a confused, abandoned, pregnant woman should never do. She falls in love.

And, most surprising of all, she finds a home.

Because when you peel away all the poetry and the philosophy, that's what home really means—*love.*

Warmly,

Kathleen O'Brien

Winter Baby
Kathleen O'Brien

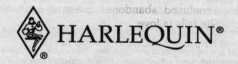

HARLEQUIN®

TORONTO • NEW YORK • LONDON
AMSTERDAM • PARIS • SYDNEY • HAMBURG
STOCKHOLM • ATHENS • TOKYO • MILAN • MADRID
PRAGUE • WARSAW • BUDAPEST • AUCKLAND

ISBN 0-373-71015-1

WINTER BABY

This edition published by arrangement with Harlequin Books S.A.

® and TM are trademarks of the publisher. Trademarks indicated with ® are registered in the United States Patent and Trademark Office, the Canadian Trade Marks Office and in other countries.

Visit us at www.eHarlequin.com

Printed in U.S.A.

To Renie, with a kiss to put in your hand.

CHAPTER ONE

SARAH LENNOX WASN'T SURPRISED the soufflé fell. It was difficult to focus on creating frothy dinner concoctions when you'd just discovered you were pregnant.

Minutes later, the soufflé began to burn, but she didn't get up to rescue it. Instead, she sat on the edge of the tub, letting the acrid odor of scorching eggs fill her nose while she stared stupidly at the little pink *x* on the test strip.

It must be a mistake. It *had* to be a mistake.

She wasn't going to have a baby. Not right now. She wasn't even getting married for another fifty-nine days. And she wouldn't begin having children until two years after that. That was the plan. The master plan. Ask anyone who knew her. Check any of her diaries since she'd been twelve years old. College. Career. Marriage. Wait two years just to be sure. *Then* children.

That was the plan. So this...this *nonsense* had to be a mistake.

But the counter was lined with these little strips, and they all had pink *x*'s on them. This was the fourth home pregnancy test she'd used tonight.

It was a mistake, all right. But it was *her* mistake, not the test's.

The master plan was toast, just like her soufflé. She was definitely, disastrously, terrifyingly pregnant.

In the living room, the stack of Christmas CDs she'd put on an hour ago clicked and shifted and began playing "What Child Is This?" *Cute. Very cute.* She felt a faint urge to get up and break the CD in two, but she didn't have the energy to follow through. Apparently shock and horror worked like a tranquilizer dart. She couldn't move a muscle.

When the doorbell rang, she was confused, momentarily unable to remember whom she'd been expecting. It rang again, then again, short and hard, as if whoever it was didn't much like waiting.

Her subconscious recognized that irritable ring. Of course. *Ed.* Her fiancé was coming for dinner. They'd had an 8:00 p.m. date. It was now 8:01, and he didn't like tardiness. He had a master plan, too—and, if anything, it was even more rigidly scheduled than Sarah's own. It had been one of the reasons she chose him in the first place. It was definitely one of the reasons she stuck with him, even though lately their relationship had been…a little rocky. Just a tiny bit unsatisfying.

Still, all relationships had their rocky moments. And Ed would make a good husband. She wasn't the type to run around breaking off engagements. She wasn't like her mother. When she gave her word, she meant it.

And now she had no choice. She was pregnant with

Ed's child. *Pregnant.* She made a small gasping sound, as if she couldn't breathe around the fact.

She stood numbly, instinctively sweeping all the tiny test strips and empty pink boxes into the wastebasket. For a long moment she stared down at the debris, which seemed to represent the bits and pieces of her shattered master plan. How solid could the plan actually have been, she asked herself numbly, if it had been so easily destroyed?

Ed had given up ringing and was knocking now. Sarah actually half smiled at the frustrated annoyance in the sound. Poor Ed. If he didn't like her being slow to answer the door, he was going to really *hate* the rest of his evening.

"Good God, what is that *smell?*" As Sarah opened the door, Ed started to signal his annoyance by one disapproving glance at his watch, but almost immediately his horror at the odor in the apartment superseded everything else. He wrinkled his aristocratic nose into a disgusted twist. "Sarah, for God's sake. Have you burned dinner?"

"I think so," she said. And then, because he was looking at her with an expression of complete incredulity, she realized that something else probably needed to be said. She wondered what it was. She felt as if she were speaking a foreign language. "I'm sorry?"

"Me, too," he agreed curtly. "I haven't eaten since breakfast." He sniffed the air again. "Have you turned off the oven?"

''I don't think so,'' she said, trying to remember. ''No. I don't think so.''

He narrowed his eyes. ''Are you all right?'' He didn't wait for her answer. He moved into the kitchen with the assured purpose of a man in charge in his own home. But it wasn't his home, Sarah thought suddenly. It was her home. Why did he feel that he was in charge?

Because somebody had to be. She obviously would burn the whole apartment complex down if somebody didn't take over. Already the kitchen was filling with smoke.

After he flicked the thermostat off and determined that dinner was completely ruined, Ed let the oven door slam impatiently. He punched the exhaust fan to High, then returned to the living room, closing the kitchen door tightly behind him. The Christmas CDs were still playing, and the gentle pine scent of her tree fought with the nasty burned smell of dinner.

''I'm sorry,'' Sarah said again, although she no longer felt very sorry. It was just a soufflé, after all. Why was Ed making such a big deal out of it? His handsome face couldn't have looked sterner if she had just charbroiled the original copy of the Magna Carta. ''Maybe we could order pizza.''

He looked at her silently, as if he didn't trust himself to speak. Sarah felt the beginnings of rebellion stir. Was burning dinner really such a sin? In the early days she had thought Ed's perfectionism was admirable, a sign that he possessed high standards. He expected a lot from others, but he required a lot of himself, too. For instance, Sarah knew that he would require himself to be a faithful, reliable husband, which was exactly what she wanted. What she needed. She had no intention of repeating her mother's mistakes.

After Sarah's father had been caught cheating, when Sarah was only eight, her mother had promptly divorced him. She'd spent the next several decades trying to find a replacement. But she was a rotten judge of men.

Sarah couldn't remember a time when she hadn't been determined to choose more wisely. She wanted someone sensible. Strong. Faithful. Someone with a plan.

Several times during the past few weeks, however, traitorous thoughts had crept in. He had sometimes seemed not admirable, but...pompous. Petty. Dictatorial.

Out of nowhere came a chilling thought. Someday he would turn that expression, that cold, unforgiving blue gaze, upon their child. Over a broken toy, a soiled diaper, a C in math. She felt a quick, primitive burning in her legs, as if they were straining to run somewhere far, far away—somewhere he couldn't find her. Or the baby.

But this was crazy. It must mean that her hormones were already acting up. She'd better pull herself together, or she'd never find the courage to tell him.

"Chinese. How about Chinese?" Ed liked Chinese food. Maybe he was just hungry. Maybe he'd be less tense after he ate something. She smiled as pleasantly as she could. "My treat."

"No." He sighed from the depths of his diaphragm. "Oh, maybe it's just as well. I really shouldn't stay very long anyhow. I've got a lot to do tonight."

He gestured toward the sofa, which was decorated with small needlepoint pillows that read "Peace on Earth" and "Joy to the World."

"Sit down, Sarah," he said somberly. "I have news."

"Oh," she said. She moved the pillows out of the way and sat. She looked up at him, trying to find the man she had fallen in love with, that handsome, twenty-eight-year-old former math teacher whose extraordinary maturity had made him the youngest high school principal in the state of Florida. That worthy man couldn't have disappeared overnight.

She smiled the best she could. "I have news, too, Ed."

He sat on the chair opposite her. "Let me go first," he said. "Mine is very important." He winced. "Oh, hell. I didn't mean it like that."

Somehow, still smiling, she waved away the insult. He'd know soon enough that her news was important, too. Life shattering, in fact. She tried to compose her face to look interested, but her mind couldn't quite focus on anything except the new truth inside her.

What would he say? How would he feel? How, for that matter, did *she* feel?

After a moment she realized he wasn't speaking.

She glanced over at him, surprised to see him looking hesitant. Ed was rarely at a loss for words. At Groveland High School, where they both worked—Ed as principal, Sarah as Home Economics teacher—Ed was legendary for his ability to subdue hostile parents. He smothered every complaint under a soothing blanket of verbiage.

He cleared his throat, but still he didn't begin. He looked around her tiny living room, then stood abruptly. "I can't breathe in here, with all this smoke. Let's go outside."

Sarah felt a new unease trickle through her veins. What was this news that he found so difficult to share? But she followed him out onto the small balcony that overlooked the complex swimming pool. The air was balmy, typical December weather in south Florida. The colored holiday lights looped along nearby balconies blinked rather desperately, as if reassuring themselves that it really was Christmas, in spite of the heat.

Ed went straight to the railing and leaned against it, looking down at the turquoise pool, where several of Sarah's neighbors were having a keg party. They were all dressed in Santa hats and bathing suits.

Sarah was suddenly eager to postpone whatever Ed had to say. Eager, too, to postpone her own devastating news. "Uncle Ward had hoped we could come spend Christmas with him in Firefly Glen," she said. "Wouldn't that have been lovely? White mountains and sleigh rides, and marshmallow roasts, and—"

"And four days snowed in with a bad-tempered, senile old man?" Ed shook his head. "No thanks."

Sarah stared flatly at the stranger in front of her. "I never said he was senile."

"Well, he's almost eighty, isn't he? Besides, I didn't have the time, you know that." Ed turned around, squaring his shoulders as if he had finally come to a decision. "Sarah. Listen."

She stood very still and waited. A drunken chorus of "Grandma Got Run Over by a Reindeer" wafted up from the party below, but she could still hear Ed's fingers drumming against the railing.

"All right," she said. "I'm listening."

"They offered me the job, Sarah. The superintendent's position. I'm going to California."

She didn't take her eyes from him. But she had heard the telling pronoun. *"I'm" going to California. Not we. "I."*

"Congratulations." She'd known he was applying for the job, a plum assignment as superintendent of schools in a small, affluent Southern California county. But she hadn't really believed he'd get it. He was so young. He'd been a principal only a couple of years. But apparently he had wowed them in California, just as he wowed people everywhere, with his good looks, his sharp mind, his glib conversation.

"Sarah, do you understand? I'm going to California. Next month. Maybe sooner."

"Yes, I understand." But she didn't, not really. "Are you saying you think we should postpone the wedding?"

He set his jaw—his square, well-tanned jaw...he really was so incredibly handsome—and licked his lips. "No. I'm saying I think we should call off the wedding."

"What?" She couldn't have heard him correctly.

He shook his head. "It's not working, Sarah. I know you've sensed that, too. You must have. It's just not the same between us. I know we haven't wanted to admit it, but I don't see how we can deny it any longer. And now, with me leaving..."

She waited. Her whole body seemed suspended in a weightless, airless space.

He looked annoyed, as if he had expected her to finish the sentence for him. "Well, now, with me leaving, it's the right time to just admit it isn't working, don't you think?"

"What's not working? What exactly isn't working?"

He made an impatient noise, as if he felt she were being deliberately dense. "*We're* not working. You've changed lately, you know that. You've been—well, to put it bluntly, Sarah, you've been bitchy for months. You criticize everything I do, for God's sake, at school and at home. And it's been weeks since you've wanted to make love, really *wanted* to. I know some of it is my fault. I've been busy. Preoccupied. Maybe I haven't been as thoughtful as I should. I know I forgot your birthday."

She closed her eyes on a small swell of nausea. *He* hadn't forgotten her birthday. His florist had. For every major holiday, anniversary or birthday, his florist had a standing order to send her white roses. Ed had never even asked her whether she *liked* white roses. Which she didn't.

She hated white roses, especially hothouse ones, which never quite opened and had no real scent. Why hadn't that told her something, right from the start?

"Anyhow, it's obviously not going to work. I'm sorry, Sarah. But this seems like the perfect time to make a clean break. Don't you think so? With me leaving. Next month. Maybe sooner."

She felt herself trembling with shock. And beneath the shock, but rising...something that felt like anger.

"No, actually, I *don't* think so. Remember I said I had news, too? Well, here it is. I'm pregnant, Ed. I'm going to have a baby. Next July." She smiled tightly. "Maybe sooner."

For a moment, he reacted as if she had produced a gun and aimed it at his heart. He blinked. His mouth dropped open. He felt blindly with both hands for the metal railing behind him.

But he recovered quickly. He straightened to his manly six-four, a full foot taller than her own height, as if he could intimidate her into withdrawing her accusation by sheer size. He narrowed his eyes, closed his jaw and squeezed the railing so tightly his knuckles grew white.

"That's ridiculous," he said through clenched teeth. "It's simply not possible. I have never had unprotected sex with anyone in my entire life. Never."

She lifted her chin. "And I have never had sex with anyone but you," she said. "So obviously we're part of that small but unlucky percentage for whom the *protection* wasn't quite infallible."

He was shaking his head. "Impossible," he said firmly. "Simply impossible." After a moment, his face changed, and he moved toward her, his eyes liquid with a false pity. "Sarah. If this is some pitiful attempt to hold on, to try to keep me from going to California—"

When he got close enough, she slapped him. The sound rang out in a momentary lull in the partying below. Several Santa hats looked up toward her balcony curiously.

Ed rubbed his cheek, which was probably stinging. It was definitely red. "Good God, it's true." He looked bewildered. "It's really true?"

"Yes, you bastard," she whispered furiously. "Of course it's true."

He worried his lower lip, his unfocused gaze darting back and forth unseeingly, as if he were scanning his mind for options. "Well, no need to panic," he said softly. She knew he was talking more to himself than to her. "It will be all right. There are lots of ways to fix this. It's not even very expensive anymore."

For a moment she thought she was going to be sick. Morning sickness already? At night? But then she realized it was pure, unadulterated disgust. *Fix this?* As if she were a bad bit of plumbing.

"Get out." She pulled the sliding glass door open behind her with a savage rumble. "Get out of my house, and don't ever come back."

"Sarah, calm down." He reached out to touch her shoulder, but she jerked away. "This isn't the end of the world. Let me help you. At least let me write you a check—"

"Get out."

He moved through the door, but at the threshold he paused again. He was trying to look concerned, but under that fake expression she glimpsed the truth. He was relieved that she was throwing him out. Relieved that he could scuttle away from the problem and still blame her for being unreasonable.

"I want to help you deal with this," he said. "I'll pay for whatever it costs. But remember, I won't be here for long. I'm heading out to California next month, maybe—"

"I know," she said. "Maybe sooner. As far as I'm concerned, it's not soon enough. Or far enough. *Now get out.*"

A WEEK LATER, the gynecologist confirmed what the little pink *x*'s had told her so clearly that night. Sarah was going to have a baby next summer. Probably late June or early July. *Congratulations.*

But it still seemed unreal. Like a very, very long bad dream. As she entered her apartment, Sarah dropped her purse, her mail and her *So You're Having a Baby* brochure on the coffee table. Then she dropped herself onto the sofa, like a puppet with cut strings.

Her answering machine was blinking. One call. It was probably Ed, who had left one message every day this week. Each time he said the same thing. "I've looked into it, and your insurance will cover the procedure. I'll write you a check for any out-of-pocket expenses. But you need to hurry, Sarah. The sooner the better, as I'm sure you know."

She pulled her feet up underneath her and rested her head on the softly upholstered arm, hugging her "Peace on Earth" pillow to her chest. Maybe she ought to call him back. Surely two people who were close enough to create a baby ought to be able to discuss what to do about having done so.

And perhaps Ed didn't really mean what he was suggesting. He was shocked, just as she was. Maybe even a little frightened, though he'd never admit it. Neither of them was acting quite rationally.

Maybe she should call him. It was only six. He would be at home. His schedule was as familiar to her as her own. She could pick up the telephone right now. Yes, she should probably call, try to talk calmly.

But she didn't move. She felt suddenly exhausted, as if she hadn't slept in weeks. She didn't want to talk to Ed. She didn't want to talk to anyone. He had already planned to leave her, she reminded herself. He had already decided he didn't want her. She felt her mind recoiling, rejecting the overload of emotion.

Her half-focused gaze fell on the coffee table, where the week's mail still lay where she'd dropped it as she came in every day, unable to work up the energy to open it.

A few bills, a dozen Christmas cards.

But now she saw that one of the cards was from

Uncle Ward. His brief return address was written in
his familiar arrogant black scrawl: Ward Winters,
Winter House, Firefly Glen, NY.

The sight was strangely comforting. She reached
for the card, wondering if Uncle Ward had included
one of his long, witty letters chronicling—and sometimes sharply satirizing—the goings-on in his little
mountain town. How lovely it would be to escape,
even for a few minutes, into Uncle Ward's world.

The envelope was bulky. There *was* a letter. She
settled back to read it, smiling her first real smile all
week, suddenly hungry for the sound of her uncle's
voice.

The letter was filled with rich, amusing stories and
with vivid, tempting descriptions of the beautiful
snowy winter they were having. She came to the end
reluctantly.

> ...And I can't seem to make anyone see rea-
> son about the damned ice festival. Greedy poli-
> ticians, all puffed up and self-important. I guess
> I'll have to take matters into my own hands. But
> what about you, Sarah? Aren't you ready for a
> real winter? Florida! Bah! What do palm trees
> and cockroaches have to do with Christmas? If
> your stick-in-the-mud fiancé won't come, come
> without him. I'd like that even better, actually.
> This Ed guy sounds as if his life view is a little
> constipated.

Sarah caught herself chuckling. Ward was actually
her great-uncle, and, while Ed had been wrong to call

him senile, he'd been right to call him bad tempered. Ward was crusty and sardonic and demanding, but he was also tough and practical and wise. And entirely right about Ed.

She sat up, wondering how much a flight to Upstate New York cost these days. She didn't feel quite as exhausted anymore. Maybe a dose of Uncle Ward was just exactly the bracing tonic she needed.

And maybe his quaint and quirky Firefly Glen, with its white mountains, its colorful architecture and its silly, small-town squabbles, was just the sanctuary she needed, too.

Firefly Glen. She had spent one summer there, back when she was thirteen. Her mother and her husband had been fighting through a nasty divorce, and she had been packed off to Uncle Ward while the grown-ups settled important matters, like who would get possession of the Cadillac and the mutual funds.

Her memories of that summer were emotional and confused, but they were surprisingly happy. Long, green afternoons walking with Uncle Ward in the town square, hearing rather scandalous stories of Firefly Glen's history. Talking with him late at night in the library of his fantastic Gothic mansion, huddled over lemonade and popcorn and chess, and feeling understood for the first time in her life.

He was acerbic and affectionate, hot tempered and honest, and she had adored him. In August, her mother had collected her—in the Cadillac, of course. Her mother was very good at divorce, and would only get better with each failed marriage. Sarah's life hadn't allowed another long visit, but to this day, when she wanted to speak the truth—or hear it—she had called her Uncle Ward.

He and Firefly Glen had restored her then. Perhaps they could do the same now. She picked up the telephone. Surely somewhere in that gentle valley town, amid all that snowy silence, she could figure out what to do with her life.

CHAPTER TWO

AT EIGHT-THIRTY on Christmas Eve, both downtown streets of Firefly Glen were wet with an icy sleet, the shining asphalt crisscrossing at the intersection like two ribbons of black glass.

The temperature on the bank clock said twenty-nine degrees, but the garlands strung between the streetlights had begun to swing and twinkle, which meant the mountain winds had found their way through Vanity Gap and into the Glen. Sheriff Parker Tremaine, who was headed toward the large red-brick City Hall at the end of Main, huddled deeper into his fleece-lined jacket and decided that the real temperature was probably more like two below.

Still he took the street slowly. Every couple of minutes a car would crawl by, and the driver would wave or honk or even pull over to offer Parker a ride. But Parker would shake his head and wave them on. Call him crazy, but he wanted to walk.

He liked the cold, liked the swollen bellies of the clouds overhead—they'd probably deliver snow by morning. He liked the pinpricks of sleet against his cheeks and the tickle of wool against his ears.

He liked the peace of the hushed streets. He liked the way the stained-glass windows of the Congregational Church beamed rich reds and blues into the darkness.

Most of all, he liked knowing that most of the 2,937 "Glenners," whom he'd been hired to protect, were safely tucked in for the night. The rest, the Fussy Four Hundred, as they were known in the Sheriff's Department, were gathered in the assembly room of City Hall for an ice festival planning session.

Parker, who had just responded to a prowler call at the park—a false alarm, of course—was a little late to the meeting, which had begun at eight. By now the planning session had probably escalated from civilized discussion to hotheaded shouting, and Bourke Waitely was undoubtedly brandishing his cane like a weapon.

But the image didn't make Parker hurry. As long as he got there before nine, he'd arrive in time to forestall any actual violence.

And when it was all over, he'd be off duty, and Theodosia Graham, who owned the Candlelight Café, had a hot, thick slice of pumpkin pie waiting for him.

"You're one damned lucky man, Tremaine."

Realizing he'd spoken out loud, Parker had to laugh. The chuckle formed a small white puff in the icy air, like a visible echo.

Lucky? Him? That was pretty damn funny, actually.

He was the thirty-four-year-old divorced sheriff of a tiny Adirondack town that gave bad winters a new meaning, and he was looking forward to spending

Christmas Eve alone with a seventy-five-year-old spinster and a piece of pie.

Plus, apparently he'd begun talking to himself on the sidewalk, which back in Washington, D.C. would have scared all the other pedestrians into crossing the street.

Who in his right mind would call this lucky? He looked at himself in the window of Griswold's Five and Dime. The only guy out here, shuffling along in a freezing rain, no wife waiting at home, no kids dreaming of sugarplums, not even a girlfriend dreaming of a diamond. The textbook illustration of a loser.

So what the hell did he have to be so smug about?

Nothing. He grinned at the guy in the window. Nothing except for the fact that, after twelve years of exile, he was home again. He had ditched a career he hated, even though everyone told him he was crazy to give it up. And the beautiful, bitchy wife he couldn't please had finally ditched him, though everyone had told him he was nuts to let her go.

But he didn't care. He liked being alone, and he liked being the sheriff of Firefly Glen. In fact, he was so damn pleased with his life that he decided he'd give Theo Graham a great big sloppy Christmas kiss.

"Sheriff! Sheriff, come quick! It's an emergency!"

Parker looked over toward the emphatic voice. It was Theo. She had climbed down onto the front steps of City Hall, and she was leaning forward into the wind, her sweater wrapped tightly but inadequately around her bony shoulders.

He loped up the icy steps carefully, wondering

what the problem was. Could he have misjudged the timing? Could Bourke Waitely actually have thumped someone with his cane? God, he hoped it hadn't been Mayor Millner. Alton Millner would slap Waitely in jail just for the fun of it.

"What's happened, Theo?"

"It's Granville Frome," Theo said as they hurried through the doors. "He was boring everybody to tears with tourism figures, you know how he is. So Ward Winters called him a greedy little pea-brain, and before you could say 'stupid old coot' Granville came around the table and knocked Ward to the floor. They were still down there, wrestling like a couple of crazed teenagers, when I came out to look for you."

Parker shook his head. Ward Winters was usually smarter than that. Everybody in Firefly Glen knew that Granville Frome, who owned half the downtown property, wasn't a greedy little pea-brain. Frome's brain was much bigger than a pea, and his ego was considerably larger. And his temper was bigger still.

The scene inside was pure melee. So many people were standing around, waving their arms and shouting, that Parker had a hard time finding Ward and Granville. Finally he pushed his way through to the center of the room, where he saw the tangle of flannel and denim, long, bony limbs and mussed silver hair that constituted the two elderly combatants.

Granville's grandson, Mike Frome, was leaning over the two old men, begging his grandfather to stop and plucking at any arm or leg that stood still long enough. Mike looked up as he saw the sheriff enter the room, and Parker could tell that the teenager had received a shiner for his efforts. Poor kid. He'd look like hell by morning.

"Sheriff! I've been trying—"

"Greedy son of a bitch!"

"Cave-dwelling Neanderthal!"

"Oh, God, Granddad, stop. Please, just stop!" Mike looked harried and embarrassed. "He won't listen to me, Sheriff."

"He probably can't hear you." Parker pointed to a couple of other men. "Sam. Griffin. Give us a hand here."

It was a struggle, but the combined efforts of the four relatively young males finally pulled the two old scrappers apart. And then it took all four of them to keep them separated—two on Ward, two on Granville. The old men glared at each other, their chests heaving and their arms still straining to land one more punch, until gradually their breathing slowed.

Parker, who was in charge of Ward's right arm, felt the slow return of common sense. The shoulder relaxed slightly, and the fist dropped to the old man's side.

"Oh, all right, damn it," Ward Winters said gruffly. "You can let go now. I won't kill the stupid son of a—"

"You couldn't kill me if you tried, you pathetic old bastard!"

The four guards tightened their grips as Granville Frome tried to lunge forward once again. Parker glanced over at Mike, who held his grandfather's left shoulder in a determined clutch. "Mike, can you get him home?"

Mike nodded. He turned to Granville. "Grandmother is going to be really mad," he said. "You promised her you'd behave if she let you come tonight."

Ward Winters made a scoffing noise. "I should have known you'd let your wife tell you what to do, Granville, you pitiful little—"

Parker let his hold on Ward's elbow tighten painfully. "Enough," he said firmly, and Ward subsided with a low, unintelligible muttering.

Parker turned to the crowd. "This meeting is over, folks," he said, raising his voice to be heard over the din. "The weathermen are calling for six inches by sunup. Might be a good idea for everyone to head on home now."

No one resisted, but still it took a while. Goodbyes between friends were slow, with warm Christmas messages sent home to loved ones. Between enemies, parting was even slower, with all parties vying to have the last word. And then it took forever for coats, scarves, hats and mittens to be divvied up and donned.

While Ward and Parker stood there, about ten women—all between the ages of sixty and eighty— stopped to be sure Ward was all right. Parker had to smile as he watched the ladies fuss over the old guy, smoothing his thick shock of wavy white hair, tenderly brushing dust from the sleeve of his blue flannel shirt and offering to deliver everything from aspirin to chicken soup in the morning.

Ward, whose lanky good looks had attracted women like this for most of his seventy-seven years, brushed them all off brusquely, but Parker noticed that a subtly flirtatious charm lay beneath the gruff exterior.

Add that to his mansion and his millions, and it was no wonder the ladies were enchanted. Roberta Winters, Ward's wife, had died last year, and the women of Firefly Glen were lined up at the gate, hoping for a chance to be the next Mrs. Winters.

Parker wished them luck. But he had a feeling that Ward would be single for a long time. There weren't many women in Firefly Glen—or in the entire world, for that matter—who could compete with Roberta Winters.

"So tell me the truth," Parker said as he and Ward ambled out of the nearly empty meeting room. "Why are you so hell-bent on stopping the ice festival?"

Ward winced as he shoved his hand into his glove. "That blasted fool damn near broke my wrist."

Parker let the silence stretch, waiting for his answer. Finally Ward turned to him with a scowl. "Why do I want to cancel the festival?" He growled under his breath. "Because I don't want a bunch of morons crawling all over my town, clogging my streets and my air with their dirty cars. I don't want the café crammed with their slobbery children. I don't want to have to fight through a noisy horde of them to buy a stamp at Griswold's. I don't want to find them tramping across my lawn taking pictures of my house—*my private house!*''

He pulled his muffler tight around his neck, achieving an amazingly rakish look for a man his age. ''And I damn sure don't want them to move here. I don't want them thinking that pretty patch of woodland over by Llewellyn's Lake would be the perfect spot for their tacky new mansion.''

Parker chuckled. ''You know, Ward, two hundred years ago the land where Winter House stands was probably forest, too.''

''I don't care.'' Ward waved his hand, then winced. His wrist must really be hurting him. ''I don't want them mucking up my town.'' They were passing the one bar approved by the cautious city council, and Ward jabbed his forefinger toward its sign irritably. ''Look at that! *Cricket's Hum Tavern?* What the hell kind of name is that? Ever since we've started bringing in the tourists, we've become so damn cheesy I could just throw up.''

He started reading the signs as they walked. ''Frog's Folly Children's Fashions. Candlelight Café. Black Bear Books. Duckpuddle Diner.'' He made a face. *''Duckpuddle Diner?''*

''Yeah, I thought that one was a little much myself.''

''Well, if we've already sunk to Duckpuddle Diner, can Sweet Sally's Smut Shoppe and the Lorelei Landfill be far behind?''

Ward wasn't really expecting an answer, and Parker didn't give him one. He knew it was a legitimate debate, whether the town leaders should go looking for growth and prosperity or whether they should concentrate on keeping Firefly Glen safe and clean—and *small.*

The argument had been going on for two hundred years, and it wasn't going to be solved tonight.

Besides, it was cold, it was late, and the two of them were basically on the same side of the debate anyhow. The Tremaine clan had been living in Firefly Glen just as long as the Winters family, and Parker's love for this town was every bit as possessive and protective as the old man's could ever be. Maybe more—because Parker had tasted life away from Firefly Glen, and he had found it bitter.

They reached Ward's car just as the church bells rang out ten o'clock. Both men stood quietly, listening to the clear tones echo in the crisp silence of the Christmas air. The first few drifting flakes of snow fell slowly around them.

"You're a good man, Parker," Ward said suddenly. "I'm glad you decided to come home. And you've been a good sheriff, even if you were one of those damn political appointees, which are usually just about worthless."

"Thanks." Parker smiled, surprised. Even that backhanded compliment was uncharacteristically effusive for his crotchety friend. Had the sweetness of Christmas bells softened the old man up, or had Granville Frome landed a big one to Ward's head?

Anyhow, it was ironic that Ward should say such a thing, on this same night when Parker had already been feeling so lucky. "Me, too. I like it here. I wasn't sure, when I first came back. You know, after being in Washington. And I knew how Glenners felt about political appointments. But I like being the sheriff."

"Yep. I thought you did." Ward sighed. "That's why I think it's a damn shame your own brother-in-law would be such a son of a bitch as to run against you."

Parker frowned, completely confused. His own brother-in-law...run against him...for what? He squinted. "What are you talking about?"

"About that snake Harry Dunbar." Ward pointed toward the front window of the stationery store, which was run by Parker's younger sister, Emma Tremaine Dunbar. "Sorry, son."

And right there in the window, next to the display of Christmas cards and smiling Santas, was a sign. A campaign poster, to be precise.

Vote Dunbar For Sheriff, it said in red, white and blue letters. Because It's Time For A Change.

SARAH GUIDED HER RENTAL CAR slowly, making her way through the sharply twisting curves of Vanity Gap without a lot of confidence. This wasn't at all like driving in Florida. The narrow path was closely bordered by rugged, ice-capped granite walls, and though the road had obviously been cleared lately, new snow was already falling, obscuring the tarmac.

Now and then the granite walls would part, giving her a dizzying view of the steep mountainside that brought on a fierce wave of morning sickness. She tried to keep her eyes on the road, her breakfast down and her courage up. But what, oh, what had made her think she could handle this?

She had hoped to get here in time to spend Christmas with her uncle, but the details had swamped her. Arranging for a six-week leave of absence from her teaching position hadn't been easy, and then the minutiae of closing down her apartment—stopping mail and electricity, farming out plants, throwing out food and saying goodbye to friends—had seemed to take forever.

Still, she had managed to free herself by New Year's Day, which had felt like a good omen. The perfect time to be making a new start.

She had landed at the Albany airport this morning with fairly high hopes, but now, after two hours of mountain driving, she was beginning to wonder whether she should have stayed in Florida. What exactly had she accomplished by running away? And why here, so far from home and everything she understood? What if her memories of Firefly Glen were romanticized by time and youth? What if it was just a grim, bleak, cold little hole in the mountains?

All of a sudden, like a spectacular surprise designed by a movie director, her car finally broke through the gap, revealing the valley below.

Sarah pulled onto the overlook, letting the car idle as she stared, utterly enchanted. Firefly Glen lay before her like a toy village arranged on a coffee table, too perfect to be true.

It was a clear, crisp morning, the sun round and winter-white. The snow glistened like crushed diamonds on the branches of trees, the rooftops of houses and the steeples of the churches. That tall one, on the eastern edge of town—that was the Congregational Church, Sarah remembered suddenly. The golden bells in that steeple had rung out the hours here for more than two hundred years.

The whole village was heavily wooded, as if it had nestled itself into these mountains back in the 1700s without disturbing a single leaf. On the western border of town, the Tallulah River winked in and out of white-frosted elms and hickory pines like a ribbon of silver sequins.

The entire scene exuded beauty, permanence and peace. Sarah leaned her head against the car window, overcome by a strange sense of longing. It would be good to belong to a place like this.

But she didn't. She wasn't sure she belonged anywhere anymore. Suddenly she felt intensely isolated here on this mountain, removed from the simple charm of Firefly Glen, exiled from those solid, cozy homes with soft gray plumes of smoke rising from their red-brick chimneys.

Alone. She fought back stupid tears and uncomfortable nausea with equal determination.

It's hormones. Just hormones, she reminded herself bracingly. Everyone knew that pregnant women were irrationally emotional. She had to stop giving in to it, stop this maudlin self-pity. She was alone on the mountaintop only because she had stopped to appreciate the view.

But the nausea...

That was very real.

She stumbled out of the car and lurched over toward the trees, her boots crunching on snow. In spite of the freezing air, sweat beaded on her forehead and upper lip. She leaned against the smooth white bark of a birch, closed her eyes and concentrated on taking deep breaths.

To her dismay, she heard another car approaching. She held her breath, hoping it would go on by, but it didn't. It paused, slowed, and then, tires rolling over the snow, eased onto the overlook.

It was a rather large black SUV that dwarfed her small rental car. Firefly Glen Sheriff's Department, the gold lettering across the side panel announced. Two people were in it, a male driver, and a female passenger next to him.

The driver had rolled down his window and leaned his head out.

"Everything okay here?"

"Yes, I'm fine," Sarah called, glad to discover that it was almost true. The wave of nausea was passing. It would return, she knew, but for now the relief was blissful. She smiled at the man, noticing the gleaming gold star on his black leather jacket.

The sheriff himself. She tried to remember any stories her uncle might have told about this man, but came up blank. She moved closer to the Jeep, to demonstrate that she was safe and unharmed...and harmless. "I'm really fine. I was just enjoying the view."

He smiled back. Even from this distance, she could tell it was a dynamite smile, white and wide and charmingly cocked toward one side. For just a flash of an instant, she forgot she was a recently ditched, slightly desperate, pregnant schoolteacher. For one lovely second her stomach did a very different, very pleasant little flip, the kind it used to do when she was a teenager.

"It's nice, isn't it?" He glanced toward the Glen below them, then returned his smile to her. "We look even better up close," he said, apparently completely unaware of any double entendre. "So. Are you headed our way?"

She nodded, knowing that underneath the friendliness he was appraising her, as any good sheriff would, deciding whether she was a problem that needed controlling. "In a few minutes."

"If you'd like, we can follow you." He waved a hand toward the winding mountain road. "Make sure you're okay."

But she didn't want to do that. Her stomach was settled for now, but what if it started acting up again once she was back in motion? She couldn't imagine herself screeching to a halt, tumbling out of her car and getting sick on the snowbanked side of the road— all right in front of the horrified eyes of this man.

It had nothing to do with how good-looking he was, she assured herself. In her condition, she was hardly in the market for any man. It was just—well, it just wasn't the first impression she wanted to make on the residents of this town.

"I'll be fine," she assured him. "Really. I don't want to hold you up."

"I'd hate for you to get lost," he began, but suddenly the woman next to him broke in.

"For heaven's sake, Parker, maybe she doesn't want a sheriff's escort. It's one road, less than a mile. A straight shot. No forks, no detours, no nothing. Even a woman can handle that."

Sarah looked curiously toward the female who was speaking, but the shadows in the SUV were too dark to make out much. One of his deputies? She wasn't taking a very subservient tone for a subordinate.

The sheriff shook his head and tugged at his ear in frustration. He looked a little embarrassed. But he was still smiling. "It has nothing to do with whether she's a man or a woman, Emma."

"Oh, really?" The female voice was equal parts amusement and sarcasm. "Is that so?"

With a sigh, the sheriff turned back to Sarah. "I'm sorry. I certainly didn't mean to...to be patronizing...I mean, to imply..." He gave up, chuckling helplessly. "Well, anyway, welcome to Firefly Glen."

Then, with a smile, he shifted his Jeep into reverse and prepared to exit the overlook.

He paused in a shaft of sunlight that spotlighted the most amazingly gorgeous man Sarah had ever seen. Black hair, blue eyes...and that smile so sexy it had the power to transform a beleaguered woman into a giddy teenager. But, she saw now, it also had warmth. Warmth enough to make a total stranger feel suddenly befriended.

"I'm Sheriff Parker Tremaine," he said. "And if you need anything at all while you're visiting our town—"

The woman, a pretty twenty-something with hair as dark as the sheriff's, leaned back, letting out a laughing groan. "Oh, brother. Dudley Do-Right."

The sheriff shook his head. "Sorry. This is my sister. She's a little crazy. Recently escaped. I'm taking her in." He lifted his right elbow to fend off a friendly blow from the woman. "But don't let her scare you away. Most of us down there in the Glen are perfectly sane."

EMMA HAD ATTRACTED quite a crowd with her story, and Parker thought if she didn't shut up pretty soon he really was going to toss her in jail.

Not that they had any room in the jail. Suzie, his part-time clerk, had turned the one holding cell into a replica of the Bethlehem manger, complete with papier-mâché cows and a baby-doll Jesus that, if anyone touched him the wrong way, said in a rather disturbing, machinelike voice, "Betsy needs a new diaper."

He had hoped that Suzie would take it down now that the new year was here, but she had bristled at the suggestion. Suzie, a seventeen-year-old high school junior, was gunning for an interior design scholarship to NYU, and she expected her manger to clinch the deal. She wasn't letting anyone dismantle a single straw of hay until she had good pictures for her résumé.

So Parker really had no choice but to let Emma keep regaling the customers of the Candlelight Café with her reenactment of Parker's rescue on the mountaintop.

"But won't you let me escort you down the mountain, miss?" Emma's voice was a syrupy, annoying imitation of Parker's own. "I am the valiant Sheriff of Firefly Glen. I can protect you."

Parker growled. Even though Emma was now twenty-six and about to celebrate her first wedding anniversary, she would always be his annoying little sister. They had lost their parents in a car accident three years ago, and the tragedy had been one of the reasons he'd decided to come back to Firefly Glen. He hadn't liked the idea of Emma here without any family at all. But the move had certainly left him at the mercy of her irrepressible teasing and, even worse, her incessant matchmaking.

"Damn it, Emma, give it up. I just asked the woman if she needed help. It's my job, remember?"

Emma grinned and tucked into the pumpkin pie Theo Burke had just placed in front of her. "Yeah, but if she'd been a three-hundred-pound logger with a face like a gargoyle, I'll bet you wouldn't have stopped." She turned to her audience. "This lady was gorgeous. Petite, honey-blond hair, great body. Dudley Do-Right here was practically drooling on his boots."

Parker held out a napkin. "Shut up, Emma. Don't talk with your mouth full."

While she chewed, somehow he diverted the conversation, subtly leading Theo and the other customers in a debate about the ice festival, a subject that was always good for a distraction. Eventually the others wandered off, and he breathed a sigh of relief.

Emma could be a royal pain. But he had to admit—at least to himself—that she had been right about one thing. The woman on the overlook had been a knockout. He found his thoughts circling back to their encounter, over and over. She'd been underdressed for the weather, with only a green turtleneck sweater, jeans and a pair of boots. But the sweater had outlined a body that was darned near perfect. And her face had been more than pretty. He remembered the vulnerable curve of her cheek, almost as soft as a child's. It made an interesting contrast with the strength he had glimpsed in her hazel eyes, the hint of determination in her chin.

Fascinating. He wondered who she was visiting. But that was the advantage of living in such a tiny town. Sooner or later, he'd run into her.

"What's the matter with you, Emma Tremaine?" Theo Burke had appeared at their side, holding a second piece of pie for Parker. He grimaced. After a sugar rush like this, he'd have trouble staying awake all afternoon. But Theo would be hurt if he didn't eat it. And besides, it was the food of the gods.

Emma looked up questioningly, her mouth still full of pie.

"Trying to get Parker interested in this woman on the mountain." Theo scowled. "You don't want to hook him up with another out-of-towner, do you?"

Emma shrugged, tossing her dark brown bob, the same haircut she'd had since high school. "Well, we've got to get him hooked up with someone, don't we?" Her blue eyes, so like Parker's own that it was like looking into a mirror, began to dance. "I'm not getting any younger, Theo," she said plaintively. "I want to be an aunt."

Theo narrowed her eyes, considering. Though she herself was a spinster, she had appointed herself the official town matchmaker, and she took her job seriously. "Still, there must be a suitable woman here in the Glen—"

Down the next row of tables, someone dropped a plate with a splintering crash. Theo didn't bother to finish her sentence. She rushed over, ready to comfort her inconvenienced customer and to chasten her clumsy employee with one quick, deadly look.

Parker and Emma shared an amused glance. Theo Burke was famous for treating her customers like royalty. The Candlelight Café lived up to its name. Every table really did have an ivory taper set in a silver candlestick. And real linen, too. Theo trained her teenage waiters to what she called "French standards." It amused the customers, but it kept them coming back. Where else could you get five-star service with your French fries?

"Seriously, though, Parker—" Emma toyed with

the last bit of piecrust on her plate ''—aren't you interested in ever getting married?''

''I've been married,'' he said calmly, drinking his coffee. ''It wasn't that much fun.''

''Yeah, but you married a bitch.'' Parker gave his sister a quizzical look, and she bristled defensively. ''Well, I'm sorry. But you did. The way she acted when you decided to come back to the Glen! Man, was she ever a witch.''

Parker put his coffee cup down. ''Well, you can't really blame her. Tina liked being married to a member of the Secret Service. It impressed her friends. And she thoroughly enjoyed having affairs with all the cutest politicians in Washington.'' He grinned at his sister. ''Apparently she couldn't work up much enthusiasm for cheating on the sheriff of Firefly Glen.''

Emma eyes were as dark as mud. ''I'd like to find that woman and—''

''Let it go, Emma,'' Parker said lightly. ''A lot of it was my fault, too. She didn't start out being a bitch.''

That was true. He remembered how hypnotized he had been by Tina's exciting body, her cover-girl face—the sophisticated pampering she'd showered on him, purring and seducing and flattering.

And he'd never forget how hot they had been for each other. Or how alarmingly fast that heat had burned itself out.

''That's partly why I'm not eager to try it again.'' He heard the sober note in his voice, and he was sure

Emma recognized it, too. "Not unless I'm sure. I would have to be one hundred percent positive it's the perfect woman."

Emma's expression was suddenly wistful, her earlier effervescence dissipated. "I don't think that's possible, Parker," she said softly. "Nothing's ever really perfect."

He could have kicked himself. Though Emma never outright acknowledged it, he knew something was wrong in her marriage. She'd married Harry Dunbar, Parker's deputy sheriff, just last year, and for a few months, things had seemed fine. But lately Emma's natural buoyancy had flattened out. Something was definitely wrong.

Harry had been out of town since before Christmas, visiting his family in New York City. Emma hadn't gone with him, something Parker couldn't understand. Their first Christmas, and they spent it apart?

And there was the problem of the upcoming election. Apparently Harry had decided to run against Parker, which made for a damn sticky family situation. Harry had been pretty ticked off last year when, after the old sheriff's death, the governor had appointed Parker to take over. Harry had fully expected to get the nod. After all, he'd been the deputy sheriff here for years.

So it was not really a shock to discover that Harry planned to oppose him in the election. He might win, too. Harry had lived in Firefly Glen all his life—a real plus with the voters. Some people around here considered Parker a traitor. It was okay to go off to college—everyone did that—but you were supposed to come right back. Parker hadn't. He'd stayed away for eight extra years, getting his law degree, being a "big shot" in Washington. A member of the Secret Service. "Putting on airs," Mayor Millner had called it once when he thought Parker wasn't listening. Glenners didn't care for "airs."

Obviously Harry hadn't consulted Emma about his decision. Rumor had it that Emma had ripped down Harry's campaign poster the minute she saw it. She had apologized to Parker, and her repressed anger was obvious. He wondered what she had said to Harry.

But she wouldn't talk about it. In fact, she still insisted everything was fine. And when Harry wasn't around, like today, she was so much her normal playful self that Parker could forget.

"I know nothing's perfect," he said, reaching across the table to lay his hand over Emma's. He was horrified to discover that it was trembling. "But we don't have to settle for anything really *bad,* either, Emmy."

She looked up and tried to grin. It was such a failure that Parker suddenly wanted to find Harry Dunbar and beat him senseless. "I mean it. We have a right to be happy," he said tightly.

"Then get married and make me an aunt," she said, banishing her gloom with an obvious effort. "That's what would make me happy."

CHAPTER THREE

AFTER HER ODD but appealing encounter with the sheriff, Sarah's mood changed completely, and she entered the township of Firefly Glen with a light heart and a happy sense of New Year optimism.

She hardly recognized the place. Winter had completely transformed the summer playground of that visit so long ago. Carrot-nosed snowmen stood sentry at each corner of the town square where she and Uncle Ward had once played Frisbee and licked their melting ice cream from sticky fingers. And the leafy green maples where the Frisbee had finally gotten stuck were now just delicate brown skeletons against the dove-gray sky.

For a lifelong Southerner like Sarah, the sight was pure magic. She drove slowly, drinking in every detail. The shopkeepers here obviously didn't feel that the arrival of January meant that Christmas decorations must come down. Windows, doorways, streetlights and storefronts were looped with deep green pine garlands threaded with velvety red ribbons. The large tree in the center of the square shone with huge red balls and small twinkling white lights.

And to Sarah's surprise, the placid serenity she had imagined as she stood on the mountain looking down had been merely an illusion. What a world of teeming life these few blocks held, in spite of the freezing cold and the snow that still fell lightly.

The sign she'd passed on the way in had proclaimed that Firefly Glen had 2,937 residents. Surely every one of them was out here today, bundled up in puffy blue coats, cherry-red knitted hats, green-and-navy-checkered mittens and bright yellow mufflers.

As she watched one little toddler struggle to walk, as stiff-legged as the Michelin Man in his padded snowsuit, she cast a doubtful look at her own light gray wool-blend coat, which lay across the back seat of the rental car. It had been the best she could find at the department stores in Tampa, but she suddenly realized that it wasn't going to be nearly warm enough for the rigors of a New York winter.

She thought of the long, twisting walk up the path to the front door of Uncle Ward's medieval mansion. In that flimsy coat, she'd be frozen solid before she had a chance to rap the massive brass knocker. They might not find her until spring.

She began searching the names of the stores she passed, looking for something that might save her.

Adirondack Outerwear. Yes, that sounded perfect. Gratefully she slipped the car into one of the designated parking spaces. Clenching her teeth against the sharp bite of wind, she darted into the store, hoping her charge card could handle the extra expense.

A sweet-toned little bell announced her arrival, but no one came to greet her. In fact, at first sight, the store seemed deserted, the coats hanging abandoned on circular racks, the multicolored mittens lying in neat, forgotten rows under empty glass countertops.

But as Sarah made her way toward the back, she realized that she was not alone. Something was going on at the back of the shop, near the cash register. All the salesclerks—and several people who looked like customers, as well—were clustered around the counter.

A sales meeting? It didn't sound like it. In fact, as she stood, wondering, the voices grew louder. It quickly became clear that she had stumbled into some sort of fracas. One person was waving a newspaper, and about four other people began talking at once.

Feeling like something of an intruder, Sarah considered trying to sneak out again. But her curiosity got the better of her. What, in an idyllic hamlet like this, could be making everyone so hot tempered?

She fingered a few coats not far from the action, shamelessly eavesdropping. She couldn't help being curious about the people here. The anecdotes in Uncle Ward's vivid letters had made her feel as if she knew them.

"It's libel, I tell you. It's actionable. I can prove damages—"

"He can't do this! I won't make it through the winter without the profits from the festival!"

"Damn it, Tremaine, if you can't do something about that bad-tempered old hermit—"

Tremaine? Sarah looked up, wondering if it could be the sheriff she'd met on the mountain. It was hard to see through the crowd, but finally the agitated people shifted, clearing the way. And there he was.

Sheriff Parker Tremaine, his gold star still resting on the soft black leather of his jacket, was the man at the core of the debate, the authority to whom they all appealed. No question it was the same man. Same wavy, dark hair, same startlingly blue eyes. Same tip-tilted smile on the same generously chiseled lips she had admired once before. Apparently he wasn't exactly terrified of the annoyed crowd around him.

Sarah caught her breath. She had found him fairly eye-catching before, but obviously seeing Parker Tremaine from the neck up didn't tell the whole story. As she watched him leaning back against the cashier's counter, listening to the escalating complaints, Sarah finally got the full effect of his long, lazy limbs and tight, narrow hips.

He was even better looking than Ed, she realized. And yet, he had a kindness in his expression that Ed hadn't ever exhibited. Even more appealing, he seemed comfortably indifferent to his looks. His jacket was well-worn, fitting his broad shoulders with a fluid familiarity. His hair was just wavy enough to be unruly, but she saw no sign that Parker cared. Where Ed had always been obsessively gelling or spraying, Parker's hair was merely cut and combed and then ignored. But the result was an unintentional sexiness, as if that slight disarray invited someone to smooth it into place.

Her hands unconsciously stroked the silky fabric of the coat she held. Yes, she concluded, Parker Tremaine wore his sex appeal the same way he wore that shiny badge on the breast of his black leather jacket— lightly. As though both of them were fun but ultimately unnecessary.

She hadn't realized she was staring until she saw that Parker was looking right at her. Even from this distance, she could tell that there was a pleased recognition in his gaze.

Maybe she could help. In a way, she owed him. He had offered to rescue her on the mountain, and he had, without realizing it, actually done so. She hadn't needed a jump start or a can of gas or a new tire. But she had needed that smile, that simple gesture of welcome. He had rescued her confidence, her optimism. He had given her the courage to make it that last mile down the mountain.

She spoke up quickly, just loud enough to be heard over the clamor of voices. "Excuse me? I'm sorry to interrupt, but is there anyone who might be able to tell me about this coat?"

Everyone turned toward her, apparently shocked to discover that there was a witness. Sarah felt herself flushing, slightly uncomfortable at being the center of attention, but then she caught Parker Tremaine's eye one more time, and he was giving her that special smile. She smiled back, but she felt the flush deepen.

"I'm sorry. May I help you?" Two salesclerks came over instantly, chagrined. The rest of the people dispersed edgily, talking to one another in lowered tones, as if wondering what imprudent comments this stranger had overheard.

Sarah pretended to listen to the saleswoman extolling the virtues of Polarweave technology—something about storm cuffs and synthetic insulation and temperature ratings—but she was really watching as Parker Tremaine made his escape through the confused crowd.

As he passed her, he winked conspiratorially in her direction. "Thanks," he mouthed, and she found herself grinning stupidly back, as if she really had done something heroic.

"Damn it, Tremaine, you can't get out of here without promising you're going to do something about that selfish old bastard."

One of the men from the crowd, a seventy-ish, self-important type with a red face and a snub nose, had followed the sheriff to the door and was obviously not going to give up easily.

Parker sighed, pulling on black leather gloves as he shouldered open the shop's front door. A blast of freezing air hit the front of the store, driving the older man back, as the sheriff had no doubt expected it to do.

"I'll take care of it," Parker said firmly as he zipped up his jacket and prepared to exit. "This festival is going to take place even if I have to lock Ward Winters in the county jail until spring."

Ward Winters?

But Sarah was too shocked to say a word. And with a melodic ringing of door bells, Parker Tremaine departed, leaving her standing there, with an expensive black Polarweave coat in her arms and a stupid, disbelieving smile fading from her lips.

FOR THE THIRD TIME, Emma Tremaine Dunbar sat down in the back office of her stationery store, The Paper House, to proof the copy for the Kemble baby announcement.

She prayed that the front door chimes didn't sound. It seemed ridiculous to hope for bad business, but she couldn't afford to get called away again. She had promised Harry that she'd close early. He wanted to have lunch at home together. He wanted to have a "serious talk."

But this announcement had to get to the printer today, or the Kemble family would be justifiably furious. If only she thought Harry would understand. He liked the money her store brought in, but he seemed to think it took care of itself. He didn't accept that Emma should ever be busy when *he* needed her.

Darn. There were three typos. She swiveled to the computer, punching in the keys as fast as she could, trying to call up the Kemble file. She glanced nervously at the clock overhead. It was one. She was already late.

The door chimes rang out. Emma stifled a groan, mentally begged the file to open more quickly, then stood up to return to the sales floor.

But this time it wasn't a customer. It was Harry.

He wasn't in uniform. Harry didn't work on Monday. His days off were Monday and Tuesday, about which he complained bitterly, blaming Parker for de-

signing an unfair schedule. Emma had pointed out
once that Parker's own schedule was even worse—he
didn't even get two days off in a row—but Harry
didn't care. Whenever anything displeased him these
days, it was always Parker's fault.

Or Emma's. She looked at Harry's tight face and
wondered why he was still so unhappy. Last year had
been so different. Back before Parker had moved
home and snagged the job Harry had wanted. Before
the other bad news, before they had discovered that
they...

Well, just *before*. They had been happy then. They
had laughed—a lot. Now she couldn't remember the
last time Harry had even smiled.

And yet, in spite of his frown, he looked so darling
today, in that brown suede jacket she'd given him for
his birthday, which matched his brown hair perfectly.
Her heart did a couple of hot little thumps, thinking
how much she loved her husband—and yet how little
she seemed to be able to comfort him.

"I knew I'd find you here," he said stiffly. "I knew
you'd forget I had asked you to come home for
lunch."

"I didn't forget," she said, vowing not to take offense. "I had customers."

He looked around the empty store, commenting silently on its emptiness.

"And then I had an order to proof." She felt her
patience giving out on her. "Come on, Harry. You
aren't always able to get home on time, either. Do I
give you this kind of grief about it?"

He tightened his lips. "I don't think you can really equate the two, do you? I think enforcing the law might be just a little more significant than sending out invitations to Birthday With Bozo."

Emma stared at him helplessly. She wanted to go up to this sour, embittered man and grab him by his suede collar and shake him until he told her what he had done with her real husband. Or else she wanted to go up and kiss him until he thawed, until he remembered that he was special, no matter what had happened to make him feel so insecure. Until he remembered that she loved him, and she always would.

But she'd already tried those things, more or less. And they hadn't worked. They'd only driven him deeper into his emotional hole. Apparently he didn't want to get better. And he didn't like it that she seemed to be able to move on, to put together a happy life in spite of the grim disappointments they had endured this past year.

Her strength didn't sustain him. It only made him feel even more inferior.

But she wouldn't be weak just to please him. She wouldn't drown with him, no matter how much she loved him.

"Well, we're together now. How about if I lock the door, and we can have our conversation here? What did you want to talk about?"

He raked his hand through his hair. "You know what. The poster. I want you to explain to me why you took it down. I want to know why you aren't willing to campaign for your own husband. I want to know why, when the income from my career supports you, too, you can't do even that one little thing to help me win.''

Emma's heart was beating rapidly. Stalling, she arranged herself on the edge of the nearest table, careful not to dislodge the large sample books of cards and invitations. She took a deep breath and gave Harry a steady look.

''That's not a conversation,'' she said. ''That's an interrogation.''

''I don't care what you call it. I want some answers.''

''So do I.'' She folded her hands in her lap, to help her resist the temptation to choke him. ''I want to know why you'd put me in the embarrassing, distressing position of having to choose between my brother and my husband.''

Harry narrowed his eyes. ''And I want to know,'' he said, his voice acid, ''why that choice should be even the slightest bit difficult.''

The urge to shake him grew stronger. Was it possible he really didn't understand this? That his self-absorption had become so complete that he couldn't imagine what she was feeling?

''Because I love you both, you idiot. Because you and Parker are the two most important people in the world to me. I can live with the fact that you are competing for the same job. But I will not be forced to take sides.''

''You're already taking sides. If you don't publicly

support me, it makes me look bad. Everyone will know what that means."

"I disagree," she said, still striving to be rational. "I think it makes you look good. It shows that you're not eager to make this campaign any more uncomfortable for your family than it has to be. It makes you look as if you're sensitive to your wife's dilemma. *Even if you're not.*"

He made an angry gesture. "Oh, so now I'm not sensitive, either?"

"Harry, for heaven's sake—"

To her dismay, the front door chimed, and a customer walked in. Oh, God, she had forgotten to lock the door. The tension of living with this new Harry was making her absolutely crazy.

It was a middle-aged woman. A tourist. You could tell by her deep copper suntan, something you never saw on the faces of locals. She was dusting snow from her shoulders, oblivious to the fact that she was shaking it onto the Valentine's display Emma had just begun to assemble, where it would melt and ruin everything it touched.

The woman patted her big, teased helmet of preposterous yellow hair, transferred her huge designer purse from one hand to another and scanned the store avidly. "Have you marked down your Christmas cards yet?"

Emma stood politely. "Yes," she said. "I'll show you where they are. Just give me a minute to—"

But Harry was already gone.

THE COAT HAD COST her three times what she could afford, but as Sarah trudged up the winding path toward Winter House, which sat at the top of a small, snow-covered hill, she decided it was worth every penny.

Though it was only about two in the afternoon, the temperature had begun to drop, and the light had taken on a bluish cast, as if twilight were impatiently pressing against the sun. The falling snow was thicker now, and with every step Sarah's feet sank into several inches of fresh white powder.

Looking up toward the mansion, Sarah saw that it, too, had been transformed by winter. In that long-ago summer, to the thirteen-year-old Sarah who had harbored here, Winter House had seemed like a happy, honey-colored, sun-kissed castle. The hill it stood on had been kelly-green, and the surrounding lush parkland of oaks had softened the mansion's asymmetrical lines.

It was different now, in this stark setting. It was more like some mysterious, silent abbey—dark and complicated and vaguely forbidding. For the first time, she could see that the mansion had been aptly titled. Even if its owners had been named Smith, this would have been Firefly Glen's Winter House.

It was a typical nineteenth-century Gothic mansion of fawn-colored stone. Its eccentric, disorderly silhouette of crenellated towers, steeply pointed arches crested with fleur-de-lis, wide oriel windows, turrets, spires and gables stood out boldly against the low, oppressive pewter sky.

Rising from its bare and snow-covered hill, it looked like the ultimate temple of winter: cold and hauntingly beautiful.

When Sarah finally reached the huge oak doors, which were decorated with bold iron strap hinges and a brass lion's mouth knocker, she almost expected it to swing open with a creak, revealing a shuffling, half-mad hunchback.

Instead, the door was answered by a charming woman of about sixty-five, with silver hair impeccably groomed, pink lips, sparkling brown eyes, and a trim figure displayed to advantage in a shirtwaist dress patterned in giant yellow tulips, as if in defiance of the weather.

At the sight of Sarah, the woman smiled sweetly and swept the door wide.

"Oh, how wonderful, you must be Sarah. Ward has told me so much about you. It's just marvelous to meet you. Just an absolute delight. Come in, come in. You must be freezing. Give me your coat—what a lovely coat. Your uncle will be so happy. I'm Madeline Alexander, dear, a great friend of your uncle's."

Apparently without drawing a breath, she whisked Sarah's coat away, hung it on a large oak hall stand and kept talking.

"Yes, a very great friend. In fact, dear, I'll tell you a secret," she said as she led Sarah by the arm through the enormous, wood-paneled front hall, moving so briskly that Sarah barely had time to register the ribbed, vaulted ceiling and thick tapestries draped along the walls. "I'm probably going to marry your uncle Ward someday."

Sarah hesitated without thinking, pulling the older woman to an abrupt stop. "What?" Her uncle's letters had never even mentioned anyone named Madeline.

Madeline smiled peacefully. "Well, he doesn't know it yet, of course. And you don't need to mention it to him—it would only upset him." She patted Sarah's shoulder with a beautifully manicured hand. "It'll just be our little secret, all right?"

Sarah began walking again, unsure what else to do. Madeline seemed quite in control of the situation, and completely at home in the mansion. "Your uncle is in the library. He does love the library, doesn't he? Although I think it's rather gloomy. Those stained-glass windows may be quite valuable, but they do strange things to the light, don't they? Right here, dear. I keep forgetting it's been so long since you've visited. You probably don't remember where the library is."

But Sarah did remember. The library had been her favorite room, too. She and her uncle had spent many a happy hour here, lost in deep, philosophical conversations over a game of chess. Uncle Ward had been the world's best listener, and his young, unhappy great-niece had had much she wanted to say.

Suddenly she was so eager to see her uncle that she wanted to burst through those doors and wrap her arms around him. She felt a burning behind her eyes, thinking of him living in this huge, strange mansion, all alone now that Aunt Roberta was gone. She wanted to hold him close, to apologize for letting Ed stop her from coming to Aunt Roberta's funeral. And she wanted to thank him for extending his friendship, opening his haven—on that long-ago summer, and again today, when she was almost as vulnerable as she had been at thirteen.

But that was probably just the hormones acting up again. With effort she restrained herself. Effusive boiling over of affection wasn't Uncle Ward's style. If such feelings were ever to be shared between them, it would be more subtle. Indirectly, through a seemingly impersonal discussion of art or literature or theater, they would make their emotions understood.

So Sarah hung back, letting Madeline, who obviously relished acting as mistress of the mansion, throw open the ornate doors and announce her formally.

It took a moment for Sarah's eyes to adjust to the light, what little there was. Red and yellow stained-glass windows made up one whole wall of the library, and the winter sun was just barely strong enough to penetrate. The result was that everything—leather-bound books, mahogany tables, Oriental carpets and people alike—seemed washed in a watery golden glow.

Sarah had been expecting to see her uncle enthroned here in lonely splendor. But as her vision cleared she saw that at least four other people were in the room.

Two women of approximately Madeline's age

perched in the window seat, pouring tea from a tea set that probably was silver but glowed an eerie bronze in the strange light. Her uncle sat in his usual chair—his throne, Aunt Roberta had always teasingly called it. It was a heavy, carved monstrosity with serpent arms and lion's claw feet.

And in the chair beside him sat another man. This had been Sarah's chair, that summer. The chair of honor. The chair of the chosen chess partner, the lucky confidant, the favored friend.

She squinted, unable to believe her eyes. But it was true. The man who sat in that chair today was the sheriff of Firefly Glen. The man who, just half an hour ago, had threatened to put her uncle in jail.

CHAPTER FOUR

SARAH WENT FIRST to her uncle, surrendering in spite of herself to the overwhelming impulse to envelop him in a tight hug. For a long moment, she remained there, silently drinking in the comfort of his wiry strength, his familiar scent of soap and leather and pipe tobacco. Oh, she was so glad she had come. She hadn't felt this safe in a long, long time.

He accepted her embrace with uncharacteristic patience and warmth, as if perhaps he, too, had found the years apart too long and lonely. But just when she began to fear she might dissolve into overemotional tears, he patted her back briskly and chuckled in her ear.

"If you don't let go soon, Sarah, my love, you'll ruin my reputation as a prickly old bastard. And then I'll have to beat the Alexander sisters off with a stick."

Sarah grinned and pulled away, finally remembering her manners. Turning, she faced the others. "I'm sorry," she said, smiling. "Hello."

Madeline took over. "Oh, my dear, you mustn't apologize. Of course you want to say hello to your uncle, after all these years. It's just the sweetest thing. Well, now, I'd like you to meet my sisters. Flora and

Arlene, Flora's the eldest. I'm the youngest, of course—'' this with a flirtatious double blink in Ward's direction. ''I know they'll be happy to pour a cup of tea for you. You do like tea, don't you? It's just the thing on such a nasty day.''

The two women over by the stained-glass window immediately began clinking cups and saucers and pouring steaming, aromatic liquid. The sisters were every bit as lovely as Madeline, though they couldn't match her rippling stream of charming chatter. They didn't, in fact, seem to try. They merely beamed at Sarah and nodded their heads in agreement that, yes, it was delightful finally to meet her.

''And the guy with the badge over there,'' Sarah's uncle said from behind her, ''is Sheriff Parker Tremaine. Tremaine, this is my niece. Keep away from her. I haven't had a long visit with her in fifteen years, and I don't plan to share her visit with anybody.''

''Hello, Sarah.'' Parker, who had stood at Sarah's arrival, smiled that cockeyed smile she remembered all too well. ''I was hoping I'd get a chance to say thank you in person. Your niece and I have already met, Ward,'' he added blandly. ''She saved my life about an hour ago.''

''She did what? How?'' Ward looked irritated. ''No, don't even tell me. Sarah, I'm going to have to ask you not to fall in love with Tremaine here. It would be just too boring. Every other female in the Glen already has beaten you to it. Hypnotized by the badge, I guess. You know women. Anything that sparkles.''

Madeline made a small, offended noise. ''Not *every* woman, Ward,'' she sniffed, but the old man just rolled his eyes and ignored her.

''Besides,'' Ward went on, obviously enjoying himself, ''he's kind of a half-ass sheriff, and lately he's been annoying the hell out of me. But he's a passable chess player, so I haven't thrown him out. Yet.''

''Actually, I think you should hear this story.'' Parker Tremaine was clearly undaunted, as amused by the bickering as her uncle was. He tossed a wink at Sarah. ''It's a good story, Ward. You'll love it—it's all about you. See, your niece rescued me from a lynch mob. That's right, a lynch mob, ready to string me up in the town square. And you know why? Because I haven't slapped you in jail yet.''

''Ha! Put *me* in jail?'' Ward raised his shaggy black eyebrows. ''You and whose army?''

''The Chamber of Commerce army, Ward. Every one of the Firefly Glen innkeepers, shop owners, ski renters and hot chocolate vendors who had planned to get rich from the ice festival. They think you're trying to destroy them financially, and they don't plan to lie down and let you do it. I'm pretty sure the words 'libel' and 'punitive damages' were mentioned.''

So that was what it had all been about, all those tense faces and strained voices at the clothing store.

Sarah looked over at her uncle, perplexed. She wondered what he'd done.

"Oh, what a bunch of babies," Ward said, waving his hand in a symbolic dismissal of the entire argument. "It was just a couple of little letters to the editor. Just one man's opinion. This is America, isn't it—even this far north? Since when did it become libel to express your opinion?"

"I'm pretty sure it's *always* been libelous to imply that there's something dangerously wrong with the Glen's tap water."

To Sarah's surprise, her uncle looked sheepish, an expression she didn't remember ever seeing on his rugged face before. "Well, mine tastes funny, Tremaine, and that's a fact. Try it. Tastes like hell."

"It's always tasted like hell. It's the minerals. You know that. And honestly, Ward. Ten newspapers? Including the *New York Times?*"

"Well, I didn't think they'd *run* it," Sarah's uncle said, his voice a low grumble.

"Tea, Ward?" Madeline chirped merrily. Ward glared at her, but she kept bustling around, gathering up his cup and saucer, tsking and fluffing his napkin. Sarah couldn't tell what had set the older woman into such a dither. Was it because the topic of the ice festival upset her, or was she just tired of being left out of the conversation?

"Flora, do pour Ward a fresh cup. His is cold. Do you think it might be a little chilly in here? I do." She shivered prettily. "I think we might have let the fire burn down too far. I'll fix it. I just love a good strong fire, don't you?''

Brass poker in one hand, Madeline opened the heavy metal screen that covered the flaming logs and began stirring carelessly. The fire surged in a whoosh of sound, one of the bottom logs collapsed, and embers flew out like red and orange fireworks.

Just as Madeline turned away, one of the embers settled on the bright yellow tulips of her flowing skirt. Sarah noticed it and felt a faint stirring of alarm, but before she could say a word, the frothy fabric began to blacken and curl. A lick of flame started traveling with hideous speed up the back of Madeline's dress.

''Oh!'' Madeline was turning around, trying to see what was happening. She was clearly too rattled to do anything sensible. With a whimper of fear, one of her sisters tossed a cup of tea over the flame, but it was half empty, and managed to extinguish only one sizzling inch of fabric. The rest still burned.

Sarah began to run. Ward began to run. But miraculously Parker was already there, gathering up the skirt in his hands and smothering the flames.

It was out in an instant. Just as quickly as it had begun, the crisis was over. Half-crying with nervous relief, Madeline collapsed helplessly into Ward's waiting arms. She murmured weak thanks to Parker, but she didn't lift her face from Ward's shoulder and so the words were muffled and, it seemed to Sarah, just slightly grudging.

It was as if Madeline resented the fact that Parker,

not Ward Winters, had stepped forward to be her hero.

But Parker didn't seem to care. He accepted Madeline's thanks, and that of her sisters, with a comfortable lack of fuss, as if he did such things every day. Marveling at his indifference to his own courage, Sarah stared at the sheriff. He was still down on one knee, his hand resting on a lean, muscular length of thigh, graceful even at such a moment. His careless waves of black hair fell over his broad forehead as he checked the carpet for any live embers.

Sarah swallowed against a dry throat. Madeline might prefer her heroes to be silver haired, craggy faced and over seventy. But if Sarah had been in the market for a hero, *which she wasn't,* Parker Tremaine would have been just what the fairy tale ordered.

A minute ago, he had joked about how she had saved his life. But he had *really* saved Madeline just now. With his hands. His bare hands—

She looked at those hands. Blisters had begun to form on the palms. Everyone was clustered around Madeline, oohhing and aahing over her near escape. Why wasn't anyone worrying about Parker?

She touched his shoulder softly.

"Sheriff," she said, trying to force out of her stupid mind any thoughts of fairy tales, to think only of ointment and bandages, aspirin and common sense. "Come with me, and I'll find something to put on your hands."

LUCKILY, PARKER KNEW where the first-aid supplies were kept at Winter House. Madeline, who was glued to Ward's shoulder, was making a hell of a racket. Sarah Lennox, inquiring politely where the bandages were stored, was no match for her.

Parker knew he didn't really need a bandage. The damage to his hands was minimal—just one small blister on each palm. He got more torn up chopping wood every week or two. But Sarah looked so sweetly concerned he just couldn't resist. And besides, it would give him a couple of minutes alone with her, something he'd been hoping for ever since he first glimpsed her on the mountain this morning.

He had fully expected to meet her again sooner or later. Firefly Glen was too small for any two people to avoid each other for long, even if they were trying. But what a piece of luck that she should be related to his good friend Ward.

"The supplies are upstairs," he said, cocking his head toward the doorway, inviting her to follow him. "I'll show you."

Back before indoor plumbing, the bathroom had been a small bay-windowed bedroom adjacent to Ward's own suite. When the mansion had been updated to include all the modern amenities, this room and several others had morphed into bathrooms and walk-in closets.

As a result, it looked like the bath in some fantastic monastery. It was painted Madonna blue, with a ribbed, domed ceiling forming a Gothic arch over the claw-footed bathtub. The bay windows were blue and gold stained glass.

Sarah smiled as Parker opened the door. "I'd forgotten how amazing this house is," she said. "When I was here as a kid, I was a little afraid of it. I was always getting lost."

"I'll bet. I still do. I'm convinced the place was designed by a lunatic." Parker unlatched the medicine chest with the tips of his fingers, revealing a well-stocked supply of ointments and bandages. He held out his hands and smiled. "Okay, then. Be gentle."

Sarah smiled back and, as she leaned forward to assess the damage, he could just barely smell her perfume. Nice stuff. Sweet and modest, but with a hidden kick to it. A lot like the impression he got of Sarah herself.

Not that he'd know anything about that. Not really. Not yet.

"Oh, dear," she said, running the tips of her fingers across the pads of his palm, tracing the outline of the biggest blister. "Does it hurt a lot?"

He couldn't decide whether she'd be more impressed if he suffered agonizing pain stoically, or if he professed himself too tough to feel pain at all. So he settled for the truth. "It's pretty minor. Stings a little. I used her skirt to do most of the work. The worst of the fire never got to my hands."

Guiding his hand toward the basin, Sarah turned on the water and let its soft, cool trickle run over his palm. The pain stopped immediately, and he had to admit it was something of a relief. She kept his hand there, cupped within hers almost absently, while she scanned the labels of the available ointments.

"She was lucky you were nearby." Sarah frowned at the cabinet, as if she didn't see what she wanted. "At least you knew what to do and weren't afraid to do it. I think the rest of us were paralyzed with shock."

"Oh, I don't know," he said. "Ward was only a step or two behind. And I'm not at all sure Madeline wouldn't rather have waited for him."

She glanced up, and their eyes met in the mirror. She had great eyes—hazel, with deep flecks of green. And they seemed to have so many moods. On the mountain, he would have called them sad. Vulnerable. But then, in the shop, he'd been struck with how perceptive they looked. Now they were uptilted, dancing with amusement in a way he found absolutely adorable.

"I noticed that, too," she said with a small laugh. "Incredible. Madeline's clothes are on fire, and she's thinking about romance?"

"She's in love." Parker allowed Sarah to place his other hand under the spigot. "You know how that is, I'm sure."

Until he saw the guarded expression fall over Sarah's face, he hadn't even realized what he was asking. But she knew. She had instinctively sensed the question behind the question.

Are you already spoken for? Should I back off—or is it okay to take another step forward?

Well, heck, of course she knew. She was beautiful, smart, sexy, interesting. She probably saw that question in men's eyes every day. And, judging from the way the amusement had flicked off behind her eyes, she didn't much like it.

But because he was a fool, and because he suddenly itched to know, he pressed. "Come on. Admit it. Hasn't love ever made you do anything really, really stupid?"

"Of course," she said tightly, turning off the water and reaching for the nearest hand towel. She took a deep breath, and finally she smiled again. "But I think I can safely say, Sheriff, that if there's a man in this world worth setting myself on fire for, I haven't met him yet."

Parker laughed. "Good," he said. He was absurdly satisfied by her answer. What was going on here? Was he flirting with Ward's niece? That would be dumb.

But he hadn't been this fascinated by a woman since the day he met Tina.

Well, everyone knew where *that* had landed him. In six years of hell, and then in one ugly, pocket-draining day of divorce court. You'd think he would have learned his lesson.

Still…Sarah Lennox was inexplicably intriguing. Maybe it was that hint of her uncle's determination in her jaw, so at odds with her fragile femininity.

Or more likely it was just his own hormones growing restless. He had actually enjoyed his year of celibacy. It had been a relief after Tina, a time of emotional and physical R and R.

But maybe, just maybe, a year was long enough.

Wow. He pulled himself up with an embarrassed

yank. That was damn cocky. And way off base. Sarah Lennox didn't look at all like the kind of woman who would find it fun to share the sheets with some relative stranger during her winter vacation. Even more to the point, while she was friendly and polite, she hadn't shown signs of being one bit overwhelmed by his manly dimples.

Not to mention how Ward would react if Parker started exercising his hormones again with the old man's favorite great-niece. Ward might be in his late seventies, but he was still plenty tough enough to scatter pieces of Parker's body all over a tri-county area.

Parker returned reluctantly to reality. While he and his ego had been taking that stupid mental flight, Sarah had already smoothed on the ointment. Now she was ready for the bandage. She gingerly placed a snow-white square of sterile gauze against the first blister, then started winding a strip of bandage around his hand to keep it in place. She seemed completely focused on her task, eyes down, lower lip clasped between her teeth intently.

Parker felt a little silly. It was just a blister, for Pete's sake. And he was damned glad that Emma couldn't see him. He probably looked like an over-eager lapdog, holding out his blistered paws so Sarah could make them better.

But he had to admit it was kind of sweet.

"Tell me," she said as she tied off the bandage. "What's really going on with my uncle and the ice festival?"

She let go of his hand and began on the other one. Parker flexed his fingers for a moment, testing the bandage, before he answered. He didn't want to upset her. But maybe she could help him make Ward see reason.

"He's putting up some serious opposition this year. Some of the merchants in town think he's damaging them financially. They're pretty steamed up over it."

Sarah looked thoughtful. "But I thought Firefly Glen has always had an ice festival. I remember my uncle telling me about it when I was just a little girl. He made it sound charming."

"Yeah, he and Roberta used to love it. They were even king and queen one year, back when they were first married. But the festival keeps getting bigger. New events are added, bringing in more and more tourists. Ward's been grumbling for years now, saying it's going to ruin the Glen."

"Is it?" Sarah looked up from her work, her eyebrows arched in a serious query. "That would be tragic."

She sounded sincere. Maybe she understood, Parker thought. Maybe she already felt a little of the magic of this peaceful valley. After all, she lived in Florida, a tropical paradise that wobbled on the same environmental tightrope.

"I don't know," he said honestly. "It could. All you have to do is look at some of the big tourist spots around here to see how tacky and congested things could get. But I guess it's human nature. If you're a businessman, you always want more business."

He sighed, feeling as conflicted as he did whenever he tackled this conundrum. "Anyhow, this year the city council voted to open some of the events to outsiders, and to advertise big time. I think, for Ward, that was just the last straw. He's making it his mission to ensure that the festival fails."

Sarah was finished with his hands. He held them up, eyeing the white gauze skeptically. He looked like a prizefighter, taped and ready to don his gloves. His deputies would get a good laugh out of this. They already liked to tease him about being a "city kid," even though he was born and raised right here in the Glen. Those years in Washington had really cost him.

Sarah put her supplies carefully back in the cabinet. She lowered herself to the edge of the large white tub and looked up at him, her expression more somber than ever.

"He actually wants it to fail? That must make a lot of people very angry," she said.

He nodded. "It does."

"How angry?" Her voice was quiet. "Do you think my uncle is in any danger?"

What should he say? He didn't think so. He knew these people, had known many of them all his life, and they weren't wicked. They weren't violent. They were, for the most part, people who valued solitude, people who revered nature, people who believed in individualism. That was why they had chosen to live in such a place, where nature was raw and beautiful, so dangerous it taught you courage, so powerful it taught you humility.

But he couldn't be sure. He had experienced enough to have learned that you never *really* knew how far a person would go if you pushed him. And Ward was definitely pushing.

"I can't be sure," he said carefully. "I don't think so, but I'd be a whole lot happier if Ward would back off a little. It's true that love makes people do some pretty weird things. Well, so does money."

Sarah studied his face for a long moment, as if she were trying to read between his lines. Finally she took a deep breath and stood, smoothing her honey-colored hair back with one steady hand. She was only about five-four, and she probably didn't weigh a hundred and ten pounds dripping wet, but she looked like a force to be reckoned with. She also looked sexy enough to make Parker's palms tingle where she had dressed them.

"I see," she said. "Then maybe it's a good thing I came when I did."

Parker couldn't have agreed more.

IT WAS NINE O'CLOCK. Snow had been floating outside the library windows for hours. Sarah and Ward had long ago fallen quiet, in that lovely way good friends do, when comfortable intimacy has no need of words.

Plus, the chess game had reached its climax. Sarah had just realized that her uncle's king was only two pawns away from her undefended queen.

But then the telephone rang.

Its metallic trill was jarring, an ugly crack running through the glassy silence. Though the phone actually had been sitting on the table beside Ward's chair all along, Sarah stared at it as if it had landed there from outer space.

Ward didn't seem to share her confusion. He answered it without skipping a beat, taking her pawn with an evil grin even as he said, "Hello?"

Then, to her surprise, he held the phone across the chessboard. "It's for you."

Sarah's heart thumped uncomfortably in her throat. For her? Who could it be? She mentally scanned the few possibilities. She had told the school, of course, in case her replacement teacher had questions. And her mother, on the off chance that she and Husband Number Four would worry.

And Ed.

But Ed wouldn't call. Would he? She had left a curt sentence on his answering machine. *I'm going to stay with my uncle for a while.* And then, almost an afterthought. *I know you'll be gone by the time I get back. Have a nice life.*

So it couldn't be Ed. He was officially off the hook, and he'd probably take the fastest jet he could find to California, thanking his lucky stars she hadn't made a scene. Of course, someday they would have to talk. She didn't want any money from him, but still…someday there would be issues of what to tell the baby. And would Ed want to know when the baby was born? Would he want information, pictures, visits…*rights?*

She knew she had taken the coward's way out, leaving that message. Perhaps in their future lay unpleasant negotiations with lawyers, difficult conversations with their families, wrenching decisions about a thousand little things. But not yet. Please. She wasn't ready yet.

She must have looked frozen, because Ward frowned, tilted his head and gave her a quick, assessing glance. Then, before she could will her hand to reach out, he brought the telephone back to his own ear.

"Sarah's not available," he said in a voice of gruff authority. "I said she's not available. If you'd like, I'll take a message."

He listened a minute, muttered another syllable or two, then pressed the disconnect button and lay the phone facedown on the end table.

"That was Ed," he said casually, his gaze on the chessboard. "He still sounds constipated. Your move."

Obediently Sarah studied the pieces, but she couldn't help smiling. Oh, how she loved this tough and wonderful old man! She could just picture Ed right now, staring in outraged disbelief at the dead receiver. He wasn't accustomed to being thwarted. He liked being the boss—at work, and, she realized now, even at home with her.

In a twisted way, he probably would actually have enjoyed fatherhood. All that power, all that sheer physical superiority.

She shuddered slightly, thinking of it. She stared down at her doomed queen and came to a decision.

"You know, it may be inevitable, but I don't feel

like surrendering tonight.'' She looked up and gave her uncle a crooked smile. "Let's finish this tomorrow.''

He leaned back in his chair, stretching so broadly it made the old wood and leather creak. "Good idea. I think we both could use some fresh air," he said. "Feel like taking a walk around the lake?''

She darted a glance at the windows. "It's still snowing, isn't it? Won't it be awfully cold?''

Ward laughed as he headed across the room, making for the hallway, where the coats and hats were kept. "Of course it's cold, Short Stuff. That's the point, isn't it? Otherwise you'd be back in Florida, working on your suntan and bickering with your boyfriend.''

He was right, of course. The minute they stepped outside, she knew it. Here was a new world, a world of such mysterious beauty that Ed and his temper immediately faded to total insignificance. Even her pregnancy seemed merely a simple, uncomplicated truth, one small detail in the huge, unstoppable rhythms of nature. She couldn't worry. She couldn't plan. She could suddenly do nothing but admire this amazing, magnificent landscape.

With a strange sense of excitement, she curled her fingers inside the cashmere-lined gloves her uncle had loaned her. "I love it," she said, tucking her arm through his. "And I love *you*.''

He made a low growl in his throat. She had violated one of his basic rules—No Mushy Stuff. But then he chuckled, forgiving her. "Come on. You ain't seen nothing yet."

They walked slowly, their feet sinking into the brand-new snow with soft crunches. Though slow, fat flakes fell all around them, it was easy to find their way. The moon was huge and blue, so close it seemed to be pressing its face against the treetops, peering in at them, trying to make contact.

"There's the swinging tree," Ward said, pointing to a gigantic cottonwood, its gray, ridged bark bright in the moonlight. No rope-and-plank swing hung there tonight. "Remember? That means the lake's not far now."

During Sarah's summer here, they had walked around Llewellyn's Lake almost every day. Afterward, she'd seen it in her dreams a hundred times, reliving the green-and-gold hours of laughter, the kites, the picnics, the scarlet cardinals blinking between the trees, the clumsy ducks clamoring for crusts of bread.

But when they finally reached the lake, she could hardly believe her eyes. It was frozen solid, a hard, vast expanse of blue and white and gray, as if a chunk of moon had fallen to the earth. They stopped at the edge, between two snow-heavy pines, and stared over its eerie contours.

"See that little white light over there?" Ward pointed toward the north. "Brighter than the others—straight across the lake from us? That's the light at the end of Parker Tremaine's dock. Just in case you were curious."

Sarah could barely make it out. It winked in and out of snowflakes. She turned to her uncle with a quizzical smile. "Curious about what?"

"About where the sheriff lived." His voice was bland, but Sarah noticed he didn't meet her gaze. "It's not one of the Season houses. But it's a respectable spread anyhow. The Tremaines have been around the Glen forever. They're good people." He paused. "He's a good man."

Sarah took a deep breath—then wished she hadn't, as the freezing air burned into her lungs. She coughed slightly, hugging her uncle's arm a little tighter. "You wouldn't be thinking about matchmaking, would you, Uncle Ward?"

"Matchmaking?" He sounded indignant. "Hell, no. Why would I do that? You're getting married on Valentine's Day, right? Nope, I just thought you might like to know where the sheriff lived. You know, in case there's ever any trouble."

She pressed a little closer, using his strong body to block the wind. "What kind of trouble? You mean about the ice festival? Surely it won't come to that."

"Well, now, you can't tell. One of those greedy apes in town might decide I'm too much of a nuisance. Take Bourke Waitely. He owns the hotel, and he's got a temper like a wet weasel. Smells like one, too. He might get some dumb idea that he could stop me."

She stared out at the lake. The snow was letting up, and moonlight flashed off its icy surface.

"I don't really know many of the details," she ventured carefully, "but would it be so terrible if you let the festival proceed? I mean, rather than risk getting anyone so angry that…" She sighed. "I just want you to be careful."

When he didn't answer, she looked up at him, her concern deepening. Snow dusted his broad shoulders and sparkled against his navy blue ski cap. He looked as if he belonged in this harsh landscape. Tough and rugged and alone.

And yet, though he looked almost the same as he had fifteen years ago, the truth was that he was getting older. He wasn't as invincible as he once had been. She found that she couldn't bear the thought of any harm coming to him.

"The year Firefly Glen was incorporated," he said suddenly, his voice edgy and bitter, "there were only fifty residents, all loggers and trappers. Simple people. And there was one tiny path scratched through the mountains, just wide enough for a wagon. But then a bunch of New York millionaires decided the Glen was the perfect place to escape from the crowds and the dirty air. And before you could say *hell no,* they were everywhere, building mansions just like the ones they were so eager to get away from."

He clicked his teeth irritably. "They even had to cut a new road through the pass just so they could fit all their fancy furniture and gew-gaws. That's why the loggers named it Vanity Gap, because it was the hole those rich fools squeezed their egos through."

Sarah chuckled. She'd heard the story before, but she never tired of it. It always amused her to hear her uncle's indignation, as intense and righteous as if he'd been one of the original loggers himself—when, in fact, he was a direct descendent of one of those pesky millionaires.

"And what exactly does this have to do," she said, nudging him gently, "with the ice festival?"

"Oh, I don't know. I guess it's just more of the same. More change." He sighed heavily. "Too much change. You know, your aunt hasn't been gone a full year, but I wonder whether she'd even recognize some things around here today. They're building a new subdivision in the woods where I asked her to marry me."

He squared his jaw hard. "I look around, Short Stuff, and I wonder how long it will be before there's nothing left. Nothing left from before."

"I know how much you must miss her," Sarah said quietly, beginning to understand her uncle's fierce opposition to change. "I miss her, too. She was always so happy. She made everyone around her happy, too. You two had the most beautiful marriage I've ever seen."

"She was too damn good for me, and that's the truth." Ward finally turned to Sarah. "Listen. It's none of my business, but I've just got to say something. Just this one thing, and then I'll shut up, I promise."

"You don't have to," Sarah broke in, anticipating where he was heading. "I already know what you're going to say."

Ward looked grim. "I doubt it. You don't use words like this."

She chuckled. "Really, I *do* know. And it's okay. I'm not going to."

He tilted his head. "Not going to what?"

She smiled. "I'm not going to marry a constipated son of a bitch who doesn't give a flying flip about anything except himself."

Ward whooped with laughter. He gathered her up into his arms and swung her around until she felt lightheaded, just as he had done when she was only thirteen. "Well, darn it, Short Stuff. Why the hell didn't you say so?"

CHAPTER FIVE

"YOU TELL YOUR UNCLE I want to know how he likes that book," the tall, slim, silver-haired owner of Black Bear Books said as she handed Sarah her change. "Tell him he's overdue for a visit. I've been keeping hot chocolate ready for him ever since Christmas."

Sarah smiled. She'd been in Firefly Glen only three days and she was already getting used to this. Every spinster and widow in town seemed to have a line out, hoping to catch her rich, rugged Uncle Ward. As soon as they realized Sarah was Ward's great-niece, these women turned relentlessly chummy. They tucked little treats under her arm and whispered little messages into her ear, all sent with love to the owner of Winter House.

Somehow Sarah managed to get out of the shop without committing her uncle to anything. She'd learned that, too—the women might be angling for him, but Ward had no intention of getting snagged on any of those sugary hooks.

Sarah wasn't due back at Winter House until lunchtime, so she walked slowly, browsing the shop windows. It was cold, but the air was crisp and clean, and the sunlight was neon-white. She'd had to buy a

pair of sunglasses. Naively, she had never guessed
that a cold New York sun shining on snow was every
bit as blinding as a hot Florida sun reflecting off the
water.

Shifting the load of Ward's novels to her other arm,
she paused at the entrance to *Bewitching Stitchery*. A
nursery display had been set up in the window, with
a beautiful rainbow of yarns cascading over the lacy
canopy of a gleaming white cradle.

The colors were enticing, and Sarah was tempted
to go in. She hadn't ever knitted much—there was
little need for sweaters and mittens in Florida. But
suddenly she could imagine what fun it would be to
create pale pink booties, or baby-blue blankets, or
soft, doll-sized caps with fuzzy pompoms on top.

She had her hand on the doorknob before her better
judgment pulled her back. That idyllic nursery in the
window was just fantasy. And Sarah didn't have time
for fantasy. This vacation was supposed to be an op-
portunity to face reality calmly. A chance to sort
things out and make some tough decisions.

Like…what on earth did she think she was doing?
Was she strong enough to meet the challenge of single parenthood? She didn't feel strong. She felt downright cowardly. She couldn't even bring herself to tell
Ward. How was she going to tell her co-workers, her
friends? *Her mother?*

And, when the truth was admitted, then what? She
had arranged a six-week leave from Groveland High
but was she really going back? What was the point

in that? As soon as her contours began to change she would undoubtedly be fired.

And yet, if she didn't go back to Florida, didn't go back to teaching—what *would* she do? How would she support herself and this new life, too?

She felt a tightening of anxiety in the pit of her stomach, a sensation that was becoming all too familiar. She hadn't realized she was still holding on to the knob until the door lurched under her hand and another customer rushed out of the store, clutching bulky shopping bags stuffed with packets of blue and green yarn.

Surprised, Sarah backed up, but her feet slipped on a patch of ice that coated the sidewalk. She had no experience with ice. As if in slow motion, she sought her footing, but she had on the wrong shoes, and there wasn't enough tread to help. The armload of Ward's books unexpectedly tilted her center of gravity. Her arm grabbed for the rapidly closing door—and missed.

She fell helplessly into an undignified heap on the icy sidewalk.

The exiting customer was horrified.

"Oh, I'm so sorry. I didn't see you there! Oh, dear. Let me help you up."

Sarah tried to smile, though her elbow was already aching and she knew she looked ridiculous. "It's nothing. My own stupidity. Don't worry, really. It's nothing."

But as she tried to pull herself to her knees, something in her stomach protested. A white knife of pain shot from her ribs to her hips. Startled by the intensity of the pain, she froze.

"Are you all right?" The woman looked worried. She dropped her bags. "Have you broken something?"

Stay calm, Sarah told herself. She had probably just strained a muscle. She tested her legs and found that she could, indeed, find her way to her feet. But the pain was still there, intensifying as she straightened up completely.

Her mind throbbed, too, registering a formless, wordless fear. She put her gloved hands across her stomach numbly, not even thinking to help as the other woman picked up the scattered books and handed them to her.

She took the books. Her fingers were trembling.

The woman clearly wanted to go, but apparently something in Sarah's face stopped her. "Gosh. I just—are you sure you're okay?"

Sarah nodded numbly. "I'm fine. But could you tell me—" She paused. "Is there a doctor nearby?"

AN HOUR LATER, as she redressed behind the cheerful, soft blue paisley drapes at the ob-gyn's office, Sarah had begun to feel silly.

Not that the obstetrician, a surprisingly young, auburn-haired beauty named Heather Delaney, had said anything to embarrass her. Dr. Delaney had been nothing but soothing and supportive. The office staff had worked her in immediately, and the doctor had checked her out thoroughly, finally pronouncing that the baby was just fine. It was merely a strained muscle. It probably would be better in a couple of days.

But Sarah felt stupid anyhow. She knew that she had foolishly overreacted. She'd panicked at the first small mishap. She'd let the first twinge of pain send her rushing to the doctor, who, in spite of her warm, professional bedside manner, probably thought Sarah was a hypochondriac.

She was buttoning up her green corduroy jumper, arranging the ivory turtleneck sweater beneath, when Dr. Delaney came back into the room, holding a small piece of white paper.

"If you need something for pain," the doctor said, "this should help." She smiled. "Though of course you probably already know that the less medication you take, the better. The baby gets a dose of whatever you swallow, whether it's alcohol or aspirin."

Sarah smiled back. "I don't need anything," she said. "It doesn't really hurt all that much. I was just—" She tugged on the sleeves of her sweater self-consciously. "I guess I'm just so new at this. Everything about it scares me."

Dr. Delaney leaned against the edge of the counter, which was filled with parenting magazines, tissues and silver jars of mysterious instruments. Though Sarah knew the doctor had a waiting room full of patients, she acted as if she had all day to address Sarah's concerns.

"It's pretty overwhelming, isn't it? The idea that you're responsible for creating anything as complex as a human being, somehow insuring that it comes out perfect.'' She chuckled. ''But you know what, Sarah? The baby is definitely in the driver's seat on this one. And believe me, he knows what he's doing. All you have to do is make sure you don't interfere.''

Sarah laughed, imagining this determined little being, intently steering his way into existence. Into her life. What a delightfully fantastic image! It made her feel strangely lighthearted about the whole thing for the first time since she had glimpsed that terrifying little pink x on the test strip.

''Wow.'' She raised her eyebrows. ''You mean I'm not the boss here, Dr. Delaney? In a way, that's kind of scary, too, isn't it?''

''You bet!'' The doctor grinned. ''Because from what I hear, the little darlings are pretty much in control for the next twenty years or so.'' She wadded up the painkiller prescription and lobbed it into the gleaming silver trash can in the corner. ''But you really have to call me Heather. Everyone does. And I'm a good friend of your uncle's, so—''

''You are?'' Why on earth hadn't Sarah thought of this possibility? She obviously hadn't fully absorbed just how *small* a small town really could be. ''Oh, I see. I hope you'll—'' She wasn't sure how to put this. ''Dr. De—I mean, Heather. I—I hope you won't mention that I've been here. You see, I haven't told my uncle about the baby yet.''

Heather's green eyes widened, and she looked younger than ever. Her skin was as pale and flawless as if it had been made of ivory satin. But her gaze was intelligent and probing. ''I'm a doctor, Sarah, not the town gossip. But do you mind telling me why you haven't said anything to Ward? I've known him all my life, and I'd be willing to bet he'll be absolutely thrilled.''

Sarah threaded the straps of her purse around her fingers. This was the difficult part. It was going to be the difficult part for rest of her life, admitting that she had made a terrible mistake, a mistake she and her child were going to have to pay for forever. How could she explain it to others when she hardly understood it herself?

And how could a woman like Heather Delaney understand what a muck-up Sarah had made of her life? After watching her for a mere twenty minutes, Sarah already knew that Dr. Delaney didn't make mistakes. She was serene and beautiful, focused and professional, educated and successful. She wouldn't in a million years have allowed a faulty condom to derail her life plans.

But, as the sages always said, it wasn't the falling down that was the problem. It was the *staying* down. The mistake was made. Sarah's job now was to face the consequences. And to do it with at least some semblance of grace.

She straightened her shoulders and met the doctor's serious gaze steadily.

''I am going to tell him. Soon. But it's complicated. As you may have guessed, this pregnancy was unplanned. My fiancé and I just broke off our relationship. He's very angry that I intend to keep the baby.''

Heather frowned gently. "I'm sorry," she said simply. "That must be difficult."

"Yes. It is." Sarah cleared her throat. "I need a little time to get used to it privately before I share the news with other people. Having a baby alone is a huge responsibility. I honestly don't even know how *I* feel about it yet."

The doctor's frown smoothed out, transforming slowly into a wide, engaging smile. "Oh, I think you know, Sarah." She laughed softly. "I think you know exactly how you feel about it."

For a second, Sarah didn't answer, surprised by the absolute confidence of the other woman's voice. Then she tilted her head. "Really? What makes you think so?"

"The fact that you're here." Heather shrugged, undaunted by the chill in Sarah's tone. "Tell me. What went through your mind when you fell? How did you feel when you thought you might have harmed the baby?"

Sarah swallowed, remembering. "Terrified," she said. "Panicked."

"And why were you so frightened?"

Sarah put her left hand over her stomach. She stared down at the bare hand, with its naked line of untanned skin where Ed's ring used to be.

"Because I thought I might lose the baby. Because I thought this—this miracle—might be taken away from me."

She shook her head, almost unable to believe the words she was saying, or the sudden clarity that was sweeping through her like rain, cleaning out the fog and the fear.

Sarah looked up, and she knew her surprise was registered on every feature. She could hardly see around the sudden rush of warmth behind her eyes. "Because I can't imagine the rest of my life without this baby."

When her gaze cleared, she saw that Heather Delaney was grinning, and that her lovely green eyes held a hint of moisture, too.

The doctor held out her hand. Still feeling slightly weak with the unexpected emotion, Sarah did the same.

"Congratulations, Ms. Lennox," Heather said, shaking Sarah's hand with a firm, bracing warmth. "You're going to be a mother."

THE FIREFLY GLEN Sheriff's Department was a fairly modern red-brick annex attached to the east side of City Hall. It looked kind of silly, actually. The architect had decided to get creative with the roofline, which tilted up against the bigger building like a tired youngster leaning against its mother.

But Parker wasn't complaining. About a hundred and fifty years newer than City Hall, the department was comfortable and up-to-date. And it was generously proportioned, especially considering the fact that Firefly Glen had almost no crime.

Four deputies, one secretary and a part-time file clerk shared the large main area, which was flanked by Parker's office on one side, and the holding cell on the other. More than fifteen hundred square feet total. There should have been plenty of room for everyone.

But the way Harry Dunbar and Parker were getting along these days, Yankee Stadium itself probably wouldn't have been big enough for both of them.

Parker had taken to scheduling the two of them in different places, on different days, as often as possible. He didn't want to hear Harry talk to Emma on the phone anymore. He didn't think he could stand listening to Harry's cold, distant tone without wanting to plug the son of a bitch. Who the devil did he think he was, treating Emma like that?

Unfortunately, creating distance hadn't been possible today. Their new budget was due at City Hall tomorrow, and it would take both of them to prepare it. Consequently, by four-thirty in the afternoon, the air in the Sheriff's Department stank of tension.

Suzie, who had come in after school to dismantle her manger, sized the situation up the minute she opened the door.

"Oh, great," she said, dropping her electric-purple backpack on her desk in disgust. "Both tigers in the same cage. I guess it'll be a laugh a minute around here." She adjusted her eyebrow ring. "You know, I could have had a job at the Sweet Shoppe," she reminded them.

Harry ignored her, but Parker looked up from his paperwork with his best attempt at a smile. "I'll be glad to write you a reference," he offered.

Her only answer was the trademark Suzie Strickland withering glare. She stalked into the holding cell and began her work. For the next hour or so, they heard only an occasional muffled curse and the now-familiar electronic lament, ''Betsy needs a new diaper.''

Parker and Harry continued to work side by side, crunching department budget numbers, without saying a word. When a call came in from Theo Burke, it was almost a relief.

Parker asked a few questions, then hung up and turned to Harry. ''That was Theo. She says she's got burglars in her basement.''

''No kidding.'' Suzie stuck her head out of the cell and laughed sarcastically. ''I knew she had bats in her belfry, but—''

Parker waved her back into the cell. Suzie's first job had been at the Candlelight Café, but her sarcastic tone had never quite met Theo's exacting standards, so she'd been fired. Apparently the rejection still rankled.

He turned to Harry. ''Can you check it out?''

Harry closed the file he'd been working on and stood. ''Sure. Fine.'' He grabbed his jacket and headed for the door.

''Good riddance,'' Suzie muttered as the door swung shut behind him. She peered around the barred cell door. ''That man has some serious attitude going. What is *with* him, anyhow?''

Parker didn't look up. He wasn't going to discuss this with Suzie. There was a slim chance he might not have to discuss it with anyone. After the one aborted attempt to put a campaign poster in Emma's shop window, Harry's campaign had seemed to stall. Almost three weeks had gone by, and he hadn't announced anything officially yet. Maybe he had changed his mind.

"Well, okay, fine." Suzie's voice was huffy. "*Don't* answer me."

"Don't worry. I won't."

The peace didn't last long. Within twenty minutes, Harry was back. And he had Mike Frome and Justine Millner, the mayor's gorgeous eighteen-year-old daughter, with him.

Parker raised his eyebrows toward his deputy.

"The burglars," Harry said succinctly. "I caught them wedged between rows of canned tomatoes. They apparently weren't expecting company. They weren't dressed for entertaining, if you know what I mean."

Oh, good grief. Parker transferred his gaze to the teenagers. Mike met it bravely, but he was struggling, redfaced and miserable. Justine looked down at her hands, modestly weepy and winsome.

At that moment, Suzie rounded the cell corner again, awkwardly dragging two large mannequins behind her. "Could somebody please take Mary and Joseph back to Dickerson's for me? I promised I'd return them today, but I can't do the whole thing alone."

She broke off, finally noticing the other kids. Parker could see that she read the nuances accurately. Suzie, for all her posturing, was actually smart as hell.

"Oh, brother," she said, scanning Justine Millner's

graceful slump and disheveled hair. She snorted rudely. "I *swear,* Mike Frome. You are so *lame.*"

"Suzie, back to work." Parker intervened quickly, taking pity on Mike, whose flush had deepened to a deep maroon. "Haul those mannequins over to Dickerson's for her, will you, Harry? I'll take care of our burglars."

Harry agreed readily. Harry wasn't a fool, either. He knew that busting the mayor's daughter was not the kind of job that won you any medals. He was obviously happy to let Parker do the dirty work.

Finally Parker was alone with the terrified teens. He let them stew a minute, shuffling papers around on his desk and making notes on his calendar. Finally, as Justine began to fidget, he swiveled his chair and faced the guilty pair.

"So, you and Justine were down in Theo Burke's storeroom after hours." He gave Mike a hard look. The kid worked for Theo, for God's sake. He knew that the old woman owned a dainty but perfectly lethal handgun. And she knew how to use it. "What kind of dumb pills have you been taking, Frome?"

"I know, sir," Mike said, hanging his head. "I know. But I was just—I mean we were just—"

"I know what you were just," Parker said. "You were just hunting for your retainer."

Mike looked bewildered. He glanced over at Justine, but that was no help. She had decided to cry. Probably dissolving into charming weeping had been her strategy for every tough situation she'd ever encountered. Mike looked back at Parker. "My retainer?"

Parker shook his head. Had he been this dense when he was eighteen? Would he ever have chosen a spot like Theo Burke's storeroom to romance his girlfriend? Had he ever been horny enough to find industrial-sized cans of stewed tomatoes an aphrodisiac?

Oh, well, hell yes, he had. All teenage boys were exactly that horny.

But this one was about to be in big trouble, unless he started thinking a little faster. Justine had begun to cry noisily, which, if she didn't muffle it quick, was going to annoy Parker so much he'd change his mind about saving her spoiled and, to his mind, somewhat overrated ass.

"That's right. Your retainer." Parker stood, walked over to the sink along the far wall and plucked a paper towel from the dispenser. He held it out toward Mike. "Sadly, you left your retainer in a paper towel in the café's break room. You were almost home before you realized you'd accidentally thrown it away with the night's trash. Right? You didn't want to bother Miss Burke, so you came back to look for it. I can call and explain that to her right now."

Mike was finally catching on. He took the paper towel, retrieved his retainer from his pocket, and folded it up carefully. "But…" He put his arm manfully around Justine's shoulders, though he cast Parker a rather endearing, imploring look. "What about Justine?"

"Justine wasn't there. I think Justine was home doing her schoolwork, don't you?"

Justine, who apparently had been listening intently even through her tears, beamed a beauty queen smile Parker's way, the tears miraculously drying. "Oh, thank you, Sheriff! Thank you so much! I'm going to tell my dad he shouldn't vote for Deputy Dunbar! I don't know why anyone would vote for him anyhow. He's so strict about stuff. He was downright mean tonight."

"Right. Okay, then, we've got that settled." Parker had to work at staying professional. "I'll call Theo. Mike, you stay here in case she wants to talk to you. Justine, you have a car, right?"

"Yes, sir, I do. My dad's BMW is outside." Justine was dabbing at her eyelashes, making sure the tears hadn't caused any makeup damage. "You're so sweet, Sheriff. I know my dad donated money to Deputy Dunbar's campaign, but I'm going to tell him he should vote for you instead." Justine smiled radiantly toward Parker once more. "You *aren't* a lousy sheriff."

Mike groaned under his breath. "Justine," he begged.

"Well, he's not," she insisted. She leaned over and kissed Mike, then checked her lipstick with her forefinger. "Bye-bye. See you tomorrow."

Parker and Mike watched her go in silence, locked in their own thoughts. Mike, with the single-mindedness of a teenage boy, was undoubtedly lamenting his aborted seduction and wondering when he'd get his next chance.

Parker's thoughts were a little murkier. The mayor was aligned with Harry against him? Well, how about that.

This was what he got for being so moronically self-satisfied with his life recently, he thought. He'd been imagining himself the heroic town lawman, beloved by all, opposed by none—presiding over his idyllic little hamlet with even-handed justice.

Then, on Christmas Eve, the truth had hit him like a shovel. His own brother-in-law was running against him. And now the mayor—and God knows who else—was contributing to Harry's campaign.

Heck, with a war chest like that, Harry might even win.

"I'm really sorry about what Justine said, Sheriff," Mike put in tentatively. "She doesn't think sometimes." He breathed a lovelorn sigh. "But she sure is pretty, isn't she?"

Parker started to make a caustic comment, but who was he to criticize? He'd actually been fool enough to *marry* his mistake.

"Yes," he agreed. "Very pretty. But maybe you two ought to slow down a little, huh? You wouldn't want to find yourself standing in front of a preacher with Mayor Millner's shotgun in your back."

Mike frowned. "No," he said slowly, as if he found it hard to process the mixed signals his hormones and his common sense were sending him at the same time. He looked at Parker sadly. "But she's gorgeous, you know?"

Suzie made a rude sound from the cell. Both males looked over, surprised. Parker had forgotten she was still here. Clearly Mike had, too.

"Hey, Mike," she called out. "Do you know what Vanity Gap is?"

Mike threw the cell a dirty look. "Yes, weirdo. I know what Vanity Gap is. It's just outside town. It's that road between the mountains."

"Nope." She poked her head out. Her glasses were crooked, and her dark, lanky hair was covered in straw. "It's that space between Justine Millner's ears."

Mike growled and made a pretend lunge, but Suzie darted back into the cell, chuckling evilly.

Parker almost laughed himself, but he managed to turn it into a severe throat-clearing. "Well, maybe we'd better call Theo now."

But Mike hadn't stopped feeling bad about the election. "You know, it's just a rumor," he said. "About Deputy Dunbar running against you. Maybe it isn't even true. You know how rumors are."

Though he knew Harry's campaign was far more than rumor—he'd seen the poster with his own eyes—Parker grinned. "Around here they're as reliable as sunrise. I don't think they've been wrong in two hundred years."

"They're definitely not wrong about Justine," Suzie's disembodied voice rang out.

Mike squinted, then set his jaw, determined to ignore her. "It's mostly about the ice festival, I think. You know, the way old man Winters is trying to get it canceled? Justine said her dad is really mad. He says the festival is super important to people around here. He says you should find a way to make Mr. Winters stop making trouble, like lock him up or something."

Parker chuckled. "Mayor Millner always was a little fuzzy about how the Constitution works."

Mike looked confused, which didn't surprise Parker. The day the teacher covered the Bill of Rights, Mike had probably been obsessing about Justine's tight red sweater.

But he also looked worried. Touched by the boy's sincere concern, Parker patted his shoulder reassuringly. "Hey, don't worry about it. Deputy Dunbar can run if he wants to. It's called democracy. Now come on, let's explain things to Theo before she comes down here and shoots us both."

"AND TEN. And hold it. Excellent, ladies. Excellent. *Hold it!* You can do it!"

Could she? Sarah realized her leg was shaking as she tried to keep it elevated in a donkey kick, the same donkey kick the aerobics instructor was somehow holding so effortlessly.

Amazing how out of shape you could get in just a month.

"And relax! Okay, ladies, very good. Let's take five."

Sarah collapsed in a damp heap on the floor of the

gym. She had to be kidding. It was going to take a lot more than five minutes to get her jellied muscles under control again.

"She's tough, isn't she?" Heather Delaney, who had been right next to Sarah for the past half an hour, smiled sympathetically. It was some consolation to Sarah that the exquisitely toned Dr. Delaney was breathing rather fast herself.

Sarah closed her eyes and groaned. "If this is 'low impact' aerobics, I'd hate to see the hard stuff."

Heather shook her head. "As your doctor, I'd have to forbid it. Her advanced class is only for Amazons and eighteen-year-olds."

The two of them wandered out into the anteroom, where chilled juices and warmed towels were available. For a community center exercise class, the setup was fairly ritzy—and these little niceties reminded Sarah that this definitely wasn't your average community.

As her uncle was always pointing out, though it had started out as a community of loggers and trappers, for more than a hundred years now Firefly Glen had been a favorite hideaway for millionaires. Apparently millionaires even *sweated* in splendor.

"*There* she is!" Heather pointed toward the door, which was just shutting behind two new arrivals. "Well, it's about time. Come with me, Sarah. I want to introduce you to Emma Tremaine. She's supposed to be my best friend, but somehow she always manages to leave me to face the donkey kicks alone."

Sarah smiled and started to follow, but within a fraction of a second the name finally registered.

Tremaine. And not one Tremaine, but two. The sheriff and his sister.

CHAPTER SIX

EMMA LOOKED SO MUCH like Parker it was startling. Where he was tall and uncompromisingly masculine, she was petite and feminine. But otherwise, they could have been twins. Same dark hair, same blue eyes, same charismatic vitality that could reach across the room, or across a snowy mountain, and *make* you notice them.

Good genes. But dangerous. You had to handle that much sex appeal carefully. You couldn't just let it loose in a crowded room.

Like this one. Sarah noticed that several of the women milling around stopped talking and stared at Parker, who wore a marvelous blue muffler that was probably the exact color of his eyes and a black leather jacket, which fit like a supple second skin.

Sarah swallowed raggedly, suddenly miserably aware of her sweaty, tousled hair and her total absence of makeup. And her brand-new exercise clothes, which she'd let the salesclerk talk her into, and which she belatedly realized were *much* too green and *much* too tight.

But it was too late now. Heather was striding toward the Tremaines, and Sarah could only follow, praying that the warm towel she draped over her shoulders covered the deep, ridiculous vee of her neckline. What had she been thinking? This shade of green looked positively radioactive. She looked like that shiny, feathery green thing her uncle attached to his fishing hook. What had he called it? *A lure.* Good God, she looked like a lure.

As they drew closer she could hear Emma talking. Or not *talking,* exactly. More like yelling very quietly.

"Damn it, Parker, I've told you a hundred times to stay out of this!"

Parker jammed his hands into his pockets. "Make sense, Em. What am I supposed to do? Just sit back and let him talk to you like that?"

"That's right." Emma was scowling fiercely. "I told you—this is between Harry and me."

"Em—"

But finally the Tremaines noticed they had company. Emma looked over sheepishly. "Heather." She made a visible effort to compose herself, finally removing her heavy silver-wool coat and hanging it up. "Hi. Sorry I'm late. I had to stop by the department and see Harry for a minute."

"No problem." Heather smiled smugly. "I told Svetlana the Sadist that you'd be glad to do an extra fifty donkey kicks after class as makeup." She ignored Emma's groan. "Meanwhile, I'd like you to meet Sarah Lennox. She's Ward's great-niece. Remember he told us she'd be visiting for a few weeks?"

Sarah sent the other woman a mental thank-you. She appreciated the smooth implication that they had met through a common connection to Ward rather than across the obstetrician's examination table.

Emma seemed to have sloughed off her temper. She grinned broadly. "Of course! The damsel in distress!" She put out her hand enthusiastically. "I see you made it down the mountain."

Sarah laughed. "And I see you escaped from the mental hospital."

"What? Oh, that's right. He told you I was a nutcase that day, didn't he? Well, Parker's all talk," she said, tossing her brother a narrowed glance. "He doesn't really want to lock me away behind bars. He'd rather bundle me up in bubble wrap, so I never get bumped or bruised. Isn't that right, Parker?"

"That's right, Em." Parker seemed to be recovering from their tiff more slowly. His handsome face still looked tight and worried. But he gave Sarah a fairly dazzling smile anyhow. "Hi," he said. "I've been meaning to call you, to thank you for the first-aid."

"Oh, no. It was nothing," Sarah said stiltedly, tugging on her towel. "I was glad to help."

"Are you the one who taped up his hands?" Emma looked delighted. "I was *wondering* who did that. Usually Parker is way too macho for a bandage. He'd rather just bleed all over the furniture like a *real* man."

"Emma." Parker's voice was quiet iron. "Don't you need to go in there and get some ass-kicking?"

Emma scowled at him. "Donkey-kicking," she

corrected icily. "I need to go *do* some *donkey-kicking*."

"Well, don't let me stop you," he said politely. He turned back to Sarah. "Actually, I really was hoping you'd be here."

Out of the corner of her eye, Sarah saw Emma elbow Heather. "Told you," Emma whispered loudly to her friend.

Sarah felt herself flushing, but she refused to speculate on what Emma might have meant. She dabbed at her face with the towel calmly. "Really? Did you need to talk to me?"

"Yeah." He looked around, noticing as if for the first time the room full of damp, spandex-wrapped women, many of whom were watching him from behind their sparkling water bottles. "But not here. What about tomorrow? Maybe we could have lunch?"

"That would be fine," she said, thinking it through hurriedly. "I could make sandwiches. Uncle Ward is having lunch with Madeline tomorrow, so we could have the house to ourselves."

Emma choked, and Sarah sensed that even Heather was smiling curiously.

Damn. She felt ridiculous. This was like junior high school, when a cute boy stopped by your locker, and every word became a double entendre, and your friends giggled mercilessly, till you wanted to crawl right into that narrow metal compartment with your books and slam the door behind you.

But she wasn't in junior high school. She was a

grown woman. A very grown-up, very *pregnant* woman. However much Emma or Ward or *anyone* would enjoy playing matchmaker here, she was not looking for a boyfriend. As the little pink *x* proved, she had already had one boyfriend too many.

"I meant, I thought perhaps you'd rather he weren't around. I'm sure you want to talk to me about him." She hoped she didn't sound too defensive. "About the problems with the ice festival?"

"Sure," Parker said easily. "Among other things. See you around noon, then."

As the three women walked slowly back toward Madame Svetlana's torture chamber, Emma was practically humming with excitement. "Did you see his face, Heather? Absolutely amazing. I haven't seen Parker this revved up about anyone since the divorce, have you?"

Heather shrugged. "I haven't been monitoring his heart rate, Em," she said. "And neither should you. Stop meddling."

"I'm not meddling." She turned toward Sarah earnestly. "I'm really not. I'm just thrilled that he's finally interested in somebody."

Sarah couldn't help smiling at the openhearted eagerness she saw in the other woman's face. Obviously there was a lot of love running deeply between brother and sister.

"I'm afraid you're misreading Parker's interest, Emma. He's only interested in finding an ally to help rein in my uncle. That's it. Honestly, it's nothing personal."

Emma shook her head. "I *never* misread Parker. I know him too well. It's personal, all right. And I'm delighted. He's been alone too long. A whole year. But his divorce was tough on him. She was such a—"

Emma caught Heather's eye and swallowed the word she'd been going to say. "Anyhow, ever since Tina, Parker's decided he's got to have the perfect woman, the perfect marriage, the perfect life. I keep telling him, there's no such thing. But he won't gamble. He says it's the perfect woman or nothing."

She dropped her towel on the floor, turned and eyed Sarah with a friendly speculation. "And apparently, Miss Sarah Lennox, *you're it*."

IT WAS EASY, when living at Winter House, to settle into a lazy, luxurious rhythm, to pretend you were one of those earliest millionaires to settle in Firefly Glen.

No problems your money couldn't solve. No worries, no responsibilities, no tomorrow. Just the sweet smell of wood smoke in the fireplace, the warm cinnamon taste of morning tea in a Sevres cup, the smooth spill of your satin robe against your arms. And, in a couple of hours, lunch with a handsome man whose sister thought he liked you.

Sarah leaned back against the headrest of the silk chaise and stared at the ceiling. It was her favorite feature, out of the hundreds of interesting quirks in Winter House's eccentric design. The beautiful ceiling was only half painted. The left half was crowded with floating cherubs and simpering angels. The other half was as blankly white as new snow.

During her first visit, Sarah had asked her uncle about the ceiling, and he had said it was a grown-up story. He had promised he'd tell her when she was older.

Well, she was older now. She'd have to remember to ask him this time.

Sarah's lunch with Parker was set for noon, so when someone rang the doorbell at ten o'clock, she assumed it must be for her uncle. She stayed where she was, sipping tea and watching the snowflakes, until the rapping became a pounding, and she realized her uncle wasn't going to answer it.

Tightening the sash of her long robe, she hurried to the door, a little embarrassed to be caught lounging this late in the morning. But this deep, silent snow was like a blanket wrapped around the house, lulling her into a slower pace, the same way it urged the wild animals into hibernation.

It was Parker. And he didn't look lulled by the snow, or anything else. He looked crisp and official. And out of sorts. He was in full uniform, his badge gleaming in the sunlight. And why was he so stilted? Gone was the languid ease of the friendly small-town sheriff. Instead his lanky body was ramrod alert, the official posture of any ticked-off big-city cop.

Something was wrong. She checked the grandfather clock in the foyer, wondering if she'd mistaken the time. But the clock was ticking steadily, and it really was only ten in the morning.

"Parker," she said, confused. "I wasn't expecting you—"

"I'm not here for lunch," he said tersely, glancing past her into the hall. "In fact, thanks to your Uncle Ward, I probably won't be having lunch at all today. Where is the bullheaded son of a—"

"I don't know," she said quickly. "Maybe getting ready for his date. I haven't seen him—"

"I'm right here, Tremaine." Her uncle's voice thundered out from the staircase behind her. Sarah swiveled, her hand still on the doorknob. Ward was coming down the stairs, fully dressed in a thick black fisherman's sweater and gray corduroy slacks.

He was smiling. The expression had a disturbingly smug quality, Sarah thought, watching him uneasily.

"Well, let the man in, Sarah, and for God's sake shut the door. The sheriff has something to say, and I'm not going to let it snow all over my hallway while he says it." Ward moved toward the gold parlor. "Want a cup of tea, Sheriff? We've got some herbal nonsense that is supposed to calm your nerves. Looks like you could use it."

"What do you think you're doing, Winters?" Parker had come in, but he wasn't moving toward the parlor. He was standing in the hall, just over the threshold, his feet planted squarely on the checkered marble tiles as if he were a piece in a chess game. His shoulders were stiff, snow dusting them like epaulets. "What are you trying to accomplish by this foolishness?"

Ward stopped and gave Parker a sly grin. "What

foolishness? Oh. Could you possibly be referring to the small issue of the sleighs?''

"The sleighs?'' Parker looked surprised, and not pleasantly so. "Damn it, Winters. Have you done something to the sleighs, too?''

"Not really. I rented them, that's all.'' Ward sauntered into the gold parlor, apparently confident that Parker would follow.

Which the sheriff did, his eyes narrowed and his jaw set into hard right angles. "You *rented* them? What do you mean? *All* of them?''

"Every last one.'' The older man grinned. "It took a while, but I tracked down every sleigh in a hundred-mile radius, and I rented the darn things. Just for one week in February, of course.''

"The week of the ice festival.''

"The man's quick.'' Ward turned to Sarah with a rakish tilt of one eyebrow. "He may look like the half-wit sheriff of a pokey little town, but he's always thinking. *Of course* the week of the festival, Tremaine. It's the only week that matters.''

Parker ran his hand through his dark hair and let out a deep, exasperated exhale. "It won't stop anything, you know,'' he said in a tired voice. "They'll bring some in from *two* hundred miles away, if necessary. Or they'll dig them out of people's barns. They'll build new ones. Believe me, they'll manage.''

"Maybe.''

"And even if you stopped the sleigh rides completely, so what? It's stupid, Ward. The rides are just icing. The festival can go on fine without them.''

Ward shrugged. "Maybe," he repeated. "But it'll annoy the hell out of Bourke Waitely, which is reason enough for me."

Parker cursed under his breath, and Sarah felt compelled to intervene. "Wait," she said, moving into the room to stand between the two men. "I don't really understand. You seemed upset from the moment you arrived, Parker. If you didn't know my uncle had rented all the sleighs, why are you here?"

Ward was busily pouring himself a cup of tea. With his back to the others, he said, "Probably because of the billboard. Right, Tremaine?"

Parker just nodded, pinching the bridge of his nose with his thumb and forefinger.

Ward chuckled. "Tell her, Tremaine. Tell her about the billboard."

Parker looked up, his blue eyes weary. "Why don't you tell her yourself?"

"Well, modesty wouldn't allow me to do it justice." Ward arranged himself comfortably in one of the biggest satin armchairs and smiled up at Sarah. "It was quite an inspiration, if I do say so myself."

Parker growled under his breath. "Your uncle, who may just be the biggest fool in the Western Hemisphere, has put up a billboard at the edge of town, on an empty but rather conspicuous lot."

"That's *my* lot, by the way," Ward interjected, his forefinger raised warningly. "A man can do what he wants with his own property, can't he?"

"I know," Parker said. "We already checked that out. Anyhow, your uncle has put a ten-foot picture of himself across that billboard. Must be the worst picture ever taken of him. He looks like the ugliest, meanest old coot you'll ever see. And above it, he's printed, Last Seen In Firefly Glen. Do Not Attempt To Apprehend.''

''Damn, I'm good!'' Ward laughed. ''It's a thing of beauty, don't you agree, Sarah? Simple. Effective. Ten little words, and every one of them true. Best of all, there's not a thing Bourke Waitely or any of those money-grubbing sellouts in this town can do about it.''

''Don't be too sure about that,'' Parker put in grimly. ''Mayor Millner's looking into it even as we speak. There are ordinances. Zoning. Height restrictions—''

''I comply with every one of them,'' Ward said, waving his hand dismissively. ''Damn, man, don't you think I looked into all that? I'm not stupid.''

''Well, you're sure *acting* stupid.'' A slow, heavy vein was throbbing in Parker's jaw. ''For God's sake, Ward, use your head. I don't know whether you're just trying to piss off Bourke Waitely, or whether you've just plain lost your marbles, but a lot of people down in that town are boiling mad. And I'm not going to be responsible if a mob of them decides to march up this hill some night and stuff one of those sleighs right down your throat.''

''Okay.'' Ward looked bored. ''You're not responsible. Now was there anything else you wanted?''

Parker stared at the older man for a long moment, apparently caught in a strangely inarticulate impotence. Then he slapped his hat against his thigh, muttered something short and furious under his breath and wheeled around to head for the door.

Sarah cast one pleading look at her uncle. She met nothing but his bland, poker-faced answering stare. With a sigh, she, too, gave up and rushed out of the room.

Her robe was whirling around her legs, and her bare feet made small slapping sounds as she ran lightly across the hallway. She caught Parker just as he was opening the door.

"Wait," she said, grabbing his arm. "Please. Tell me. You mentioned a mob. It hasn't come to that, surely. Has it?"

He shook his head, more in frustration than in denial. Anxiety squeezed at Sarah's throat. She wished she could follow Parker outside, so that they could talk in true privacy. Standing here at the door was no good. Snow was already falling on his shoulders, and cold air rushed in through her inadequate satin nightclothes, making her shiver uncomfortably.

Her sloth this morning had been a mistake. She should have dressed early. She should have been prepared for anything, the way she always had been back in Florida.

"I don't know." Parker sighed. "They're mad, Sarah. And they have reason. He's way out of line here."

"Can't you control them? I mean, you *are* the sheriff."

He tossed her an irritable glance as he efficiently

turned his collar up against the cold. "Sorry. My uniform didn't come with a magic wand to wave over angry mobs and turn them into flocks of geese."

"I didn't mean that. I just meant, surely they'll listen to you. Surely they'll back off if you tell them they should. His behavior may be childish, but he hasn't done anything illegal, has he?"

Parker slid first one hand and then the other into soft, black leather gloves. "Well, you can bet that Bourke Waitely and all the other lawyers in town are finecombing the city code book right now, trying to prove that he has. They want him neutralized. And that's Bourke's own word."

"Neutralized?" Sarah frowned. "That sounds a little threatening."

Parker zipped up his jacket with a frustrated metallic growl.

"Right," he said tightly. "*Now* you're catching on."

EMMA LIT A PATCHOULI CANDLE, put Dean Martin on the CD player and dimmed the lights. Yes. That was perfect. *Yes.*

Then, five minutes later, *no.*

She blew the candle out and raised the lights. It was too much pressure—it would just make things worse. But she left the music. Corny old Italian music was Macho Harry's embarrassing little sentimental secret. For the first six months of their marriage, he had warbled "That's Amore" in the shower every morning.

But not lately. Emma touched Dean Martin's smiling face on the CD case. "Come on, Dino," she whispered. "I could really use some help here tonight."

Tonight was the night. Tonight, come hell or high water, she was going to make her husband notice her. Make her husband *want* her. Make her husband be a husband.

But how?

She'd thought about buying one of those black leather teddies Ginger sold down at Sweet Dreams, the lingerie shop that was directly across the square from Emma's paper store. But she had decided against it. She didn't mind a little playful costuming now and then. In fact, the night they'd gone to a Halloween party dressed as Mulder and Scully from *The X-Files,* the sexual tension had been terrific. Harry had kept her awake all night, protecting her from aliens.

But that was *before*. This was *after*. And, given the current state of their love life, the teddy was risky. What if it didn't work? What if Harry still walked away and flicked on the television? How demeaning would that be? She could just picture herself standing there, tricked out like a two-bit dominatrix. She'd probably feel like killing him.

So she'd settled for her prettiest pink underclothes and Harry's favorite dress. When she heard Harry's car come up the driveway, she knocked back the rest of her wine for luck, and poured herself a second glass. She added another ice cube to his Scotch and water, and arranged herself with what she hoped was casual sensuality on the sofa.

"Hi." She looked up from the magazine she'd brought over as a prop. She pretended to glance at her watch in surprise. "Gosh, it's late, isn't it? You must be starving. I've kept a plate of roast beef warm in the oven. Do you want it now, or after you change?"

Harry tossed his coat over the arms of the hall tree. "Neither," he said, dusting the snow from his hair. "I knew the city council meeting would go on forever, so I grabbed a sandwich at the café."

Emma counted to ten silently, hoping she would keep her big mouth shut. He could have called. He could have spared her the effort of fixing a meal no one would eat. Not to mention he could have invited her to join him at the café. Just a few months ago, he would have.

But she mustn't say any of that. Nagging wasn't exactly an essential ingredient of any love potion she'd ever heard of.

Harry took his wet boots off and propped them in the corner next to the coats. Their house was too small to have a mudroom, so they had created a mud corner. He straightened wearily, twisted his back until his spine released a cascade of small cracking sounds, and sighed.

"Is your back bothering you?" Emma folded her magazine. "Come sit over here. I'll massage it."

Harry shook his head. "No, thanks. I'm fine. It's just those god-awful metal chairs at City Hall." He moved over to the CD player and punched the power button. "Do you mind if I turn this off? I've got a headache."

Okay, that was enough. Emma stood, forcing herself to stay relaxed. She went to Harry and put her arms around him, ignoring his subtle stiffening.

"Poor guy," she said, resting her cheek against his chest. Though he didn't return the embrace, it still felt so right. If only he knew how much she loved him, loved the familiar contours of his body, the jut of his collarbone against her temple, the thump of his heart under her hand. "It must have been a tough day."

"Not really. Just long."

She tried not to be discouraged, but she knew this mood. Passive, unreachable, yet steadfastly contrary. He would disagree, politely but firmly, with whatever she said. If she mentioned that it was Thursday, he'd say, no, it's just the day after Wednesday.

Even worse, though she had begun to softly knead the tense muscles along his spine, he remained completely wooden. She might as well have been hugging a life-size doll.

But she refused to take offense. She refused to give up. It had been three months now since they had made love. If he defeated her tonight, those months could stretch into four, then a year—and then what? He'd be like a boat whose tethers had been sliced, drifting further and further away from her on a tide that would never turn.

She kept rubbing softly. Her hands knew him so

well. She knew what he liked. She knew where the little kinks of tension were hiding.

"Emma, stop it." Harry put his hands on her shoulders. "I know what you're trying to do here."

"Good," she murmured, her face half-turned into his chest. She let her hands drift toward the small of his back, then down, over his belt, grazing the tight curve of his very sexy rear. She nuzzled him, encouraged by the skitter of his heartbeat. "Then help me do it. This kind of thing is usually a duet, you know."

"Stop it." He pushed a little with the heels of his hands, forcing her away from him. She lifted her head and looked at him. His face was so tense the muscles practically screamed. "Damn it, Emma, stop it. You know this is pointless."

She took a deep breath, but she was at her limit. *"Pointless?"*

"That's right. You know what the doctor said. It's never going to happen, Emma. We can't have a baby." He tightened his mouth. "No, correct that. *I* can't. I can't give you a baby, no matter how hard I try. You heard what he said."

"Yes, I heard him say that we probably can't have children." *Oh, Harry.* How could she want to strangle him and make love to him all at the same time? "But I *didn't* hear him say that we can't have sex."

For a minute she thought he might give in. He looked at her with such longing in his gaze that she was sure he couldn't resist. But, after only a few seconds, he muttered an oath under his breath and pulled away.

"What?" All the frustration she'd been smothering came roiling to the fore. This was so wrong. It was one thing if he had lost interest in her. That would be terrible, even heartbreaking. But she was strong, and she would survive it if she had to.

But when he so clearly still wanted her, how could he let this business about his sperm count come between them? As if she gave a *damn* about his sperm count!

"Harry, for heaven's sake. Stop making this so complicated. You are my husband. Not my baby-making machine."

He was facing the fireplace. "I know that you don't understand why it's complicated, Emma. Maybe that's because you're not the problem. I am."

"You certainly are." He was so unbelievably blind. And she was so damn mad. "I'm going nuts, Harry. I love you. I want to have wild and crazy sex with you. I'm talking about panting, sweating, up-till-dawn sex. Remember that? Believe me, babies have absolutely no place in this picture."

He shook his head. "I'm sorry. It's just not that simple for me."

"Well, it is for me. I'm only twenty-six years old, you know. I'm not quite ready to become a nun."

He didn't answer her. She clenched her fists, so frustrated that she was starting to feel slightly light-headed. Wasn't there anything she could say that could break through his shield of self-pity?

"I'm warning you, Harry. Maybe you should see someone. Talk to someone. Because if you don't work through this—if you don't stop pushing me away, then—"

He gave her a tired glance. "Then what?"

She set her shoulders. "You know what. If you won't make love to me, sooner or later I'll go looking for someone who will."

It was, of course, a lie—a deliberate jolt of electricity designed as a crude kind of shock therapy. She wanted to scare the apathy right out of him. She wanted to shock him straight into her bed.

Instead, he shocked her.

"Maybe," he said slowly, "that isn't such a bad idea."

"I'm counting on it," Harry Shorter was about to say more. Then he paused. "Besides—" he threw her a strange look—"you don't stay pretty *this* long, baby."

Kelly still felt the words like a blow. Just now, looking back in his grossly unfair remark, she forced a smile.

CHAPTER SEVEN

PARKER LIKED WORKING AT NIGHT. He liked working alone. He could get about ten times as much done when he wasn't distracted by Harry's sullen tension, Suzie's sarcasm, or the endless phone calls from the Fussy Four Hundred.

Not that he was exactly *alone* tonight. He actually had six companions, though they were all asleep. Suzie had turned the holding cell into a temporary pet store.

Yep, he thought, smiling to himself. He now worked in a zoo literally as well as figuratively. And he had no one but himself to blame.

Suzie had come in one day last week, practically in tears, her arms full of puppies. Apparently she had decided to raise a little "easy" money for her college fund by breeding her female golden retriever. The results had been five adorable, but not quite pure-blood, puppies. After several weeks of trying to be patient, Suzie's mother had finally thrown a fit and threatened to send the animals to the shelter.

Parker had been fool enough to feel sorry for the girl. Consequently, all five puppies, and the mother dog, now called the holding cell home. Suzie planned to trot potential customers in and out of here every day next week.

First the nativity, now this. He clearly wasn't ever going to get his cell back. Good thing there was no crime in the Glen. Unless, of course, Parker's own criminal stupidity counted.

When he heard the light knock on the front door, which he kept locked at night, he assumed it was the dispatcher, coming in to take over the graveyard shift. But, to his amazement, when he opened the door he saw that it was Sarah Lennox.

She was so thoroughly bundled up against the fifteen-degree freeze he almost didn't recognize her. The pale oval of her face peeked out from a dark green hood, and her honey-colored hair was escaping in wisps that looked even softer than the hood's golden cashmere lining.

What was she doing, coming down to the Sheriff's Department after dark? It was supposed to snow soon. Almost everyone was at home by a roaring fire.

"Hi," he said, too surprised to be very suave. Then he had a sudden troubling thought. "Is anything wrong? Is it Ward?"

She smiled. "No. Nothing's wrong." She shivered a little and bit her lower lip. "May I come in?"

Apologizing, he stood back and let her enter. She brought cold air with her, and something else, too. He sniffed the tantalizing aroma, trying to identify it. Perfume? No. *Food*.

Chinese food.

As she paused, scanning the office, apparently

looking for a spare surface, he finally noticed that she
was carrying a large brown bag with the logo of the
local Chinese restaurant stamped on it—*The Firefly
and the Dragon.*

His favorite.

It was too good to be true.

"I guess I've been working too long," he said,
awestruck. "I'm hallucinating. I actually think I saw
an angel walk in here holding my favorite takeout."

She laughed. What a pretty laugh she had! It had
a cool sparkle, like a clear, sun-shot creek. It was a
laugh you could wash yourself in and clean away the
grime of the day.

"No hallucination," she said. "It's real food. I
asked around. Apparently in a small town everybody
knows everyone else's habits." She dug in the bag
and pulled out a small container. "There's even a
piece of pumpkin pie for dessert."

"Wow." He closed his eyes for a moment, imagining how good it would taste. Then he opened them,
met hers and smiled. "But why?"

It was a simple question, but a fair one. They
hadn't exactly parted this morning on the friendliest
of terms.

Her answering smile was a little sheepish.

"It's an apology. For this morning. I should never
have said that about how you should control the people around here. It was rude, and it was ungrateful. I
do understand that you are trying to protect my uncle,
and I wanted you to know that I appreciate it, even
if he doesn't."

Parker didn't respond for a moment, marveling that anyone could be so humble and generous. He tried to imagine his ex-wife apologizing with such simple dignity about anything. But why would Tina ever say she was sorry? She wasn't. Tina didn't waste time regretting any of her sins. She was too busy committing new ones.

"That's okay. Just please warn your uncle that he'd better not get caught so much as jaywalking around here for a while. Or he and I will end up playing chess through the bars of a holding cell."

"I know," she said. "I have told him. It doesn't seem to sink in. Frankly, I'm stumped. I just don't know what to do."

"Do *anything*. Get him therapy. Drug his tea. Tie him up."

She smiled ruefully. "Put him in jail?"

"It's crossed my mind."

"I thought it might have. So I brought you a book, too." Sarah looked just slightly mischievous now. "I got copies for both of us." She held out a small paperback, a current self-help bestseller. *Make Anyone Do Anything—A Primer of Persuasion.*

He had to laugh, but he took it. "Thanks," he said, riffling the pages, catching the occasional psychobabble buzz-phrase. "I'm not sure the book's been written yet that can outsmart Ward Winters, but I'll give it a try."

"Me, too. We can compare notes later." She gave the bag of Chinese food one last nudge to make sure it was secure on the table. "Well, enjoy. I guess I'd better get back before it starts snowing."

"What?" He frowned. "You aren't going to stay and eat?"

"Oh, no." She looked uncomfortable. "You obviously have a lot of work to do. I'd just be a distraction."

A distraction. Well, she had that right.

It was ridiculous how often in the past couple of weeks he'd found himself thinking about her. Dumb stuff, like whether her hair was as soft as it looked. Whether that determined chin of hers meant she had her uncle's stubborn streak. Why she had looked so fragile, so sad, up there on the mountain that day. Whether she was always kind to strangers, the way she'd been when she tended to his blisters, or whether she had singled him out for special treatment.

And then of course there were the X-rated thoughts, the kind he hadn't had about anybody in a long, long time.

Yeah, she was a distraction, all right. If she only knew.

"I was almost finished with work anyhow." But he wasn't convincing enough. That two-foot stack of files on his desk probably didn't help. She was already putting her gloves back on. "Really, Sarah. You'd be doing me a favor. It's not much fun eating alone."

She was shaking her head, smiling politely, but, as if it had been a choreographed ballet of persuasion, at that very moment the dogs decided to wake up.

The soft, scuffling sound of clumsy puppy feet on shredded newspaper came first. Sarah looked toward the sound curiously. And then the master stroke—a series of the cutest little baby yelps imaginable.

Parker smiled. Hadn't he been clever to say yes when Suzie brought the puppies in? He might just have to buy one himself out of sheer gratitude.

"I'll show you," he said, answering her unspoken question, "if you'll stay."

She hesitated, but the puppies were clamoring now. They probably smelled the Chinese food, the little beggars. They were getting big enough to want more than mama dog had to offer.

"I didn't really buy enough food for two," she said doubtfully, but he could tell she was hooked.

"That's okay. I've got some leftover pizza in the refrigerator. You like green peppers? At least I think it's green peppers." He grinned at her. "It's green something."

She screwed up her nose. "Yum," she said. "Parker, I really should—"

"Please." He took her right hand and, holding her gaze with his, began easing off her glove. *Go slow, go slow,* he reminded himself. But it was hard. Something about her made him want to go fast. "Please stay."

She didn't stop him. He got both gloves off and dropped them onto the closest desk. Then he reached up and slipped his hands inside her hood. Slowly he eased it away from her head. Without it, she looked suddenly naked. Vulnerable.

He smiled reassuringly as he touched the top button of her coat. ''Why don't you take that off?'' The puppies were going crazy now, slipping and jumping and yipping for attention. ''There are some guys over there who seem pretty eager to meet you.''

She tilted her head. ''Are you sure you haven't already read that book I brought you? You seem pretty good at getting your own way.''

But she wasn't really annoyed. He could tell. She took off her coat, draped it over Harry's desk, then turned to him, her hands on her hips and a small smile on her lips. ''Okay. Show me. And they'd better be every bit as cute as they sound.''

He took her hand. ''They are.''

He felt pretty safe making that promise. And she clearly wasn't disappointed. When he unlatched the door and brought her around the corner, she let out a short gasp of delight.

''Oh, Parker,'' she breathed. ''Oh, how darling.''

Then she went down on her knees and was immediately swarmed by five pale blond fur-balls, all huge tongues, oversize paws and yelping excitement.

She didn't seem to mind the muss and the slobber, their paws clawing at her soft green sweater or their little teeth tugging at her shoelaces. She laughed and cooed and cuddled each one of them in turn. And from the quiet corner of the cell, mama dog looked on without the slightest bit of anxiety.

Parker watched, too, and as he did a liquid warmth seeped into his veins, a sensation he only dimly recognized as desire, because it came so gently, so comfortably, as if it was a perfect match for his own blood, as if it belonged there.

But once inside him, the feeling grew, flooding him with its light. He couldn't take his gaze away. He couldn't move at all. He could barely breathe.

When one of the puppies tried to climb up the front of her sweater, licking her throat as if she were made of sweet cream, Sarah flung back her head, eyes shut, lips curved in an innocent pleasure.

He couldn't stop himself. He bent over that blind, smiling, beautiful face. "Sarah," he said softly.

She opened her eyes, and they were full of laughter. "What?"

He didn't answer. He touched her chin. And then, before either of them could think better of it, he kissed her.

It wasn't a long kiss. It wasn't pushy or intrusive or threatening. And yet he felt the delighted smile fade from her lips as if his kiss had been a frost, forcing the petals from the rose.

He pulled away, of course. It would have been impossible to persist in the face of such a reaction. It was a bit of a shock, actually. Ordinarily his kisses weren't greeted as if his lips had been dipped in poison.

She lowered her head and stared down at the puppies. Her whole body had gone strangely still.

"I'm sorry," he said. "You just looked—cute. I didn't mean to make you uncomfortable."

"You didn't. Really." She set the puppies back down carefully. She managed to extricate herself, and she got to her feet. "But I was thinking—I just remembered that my uncle will be waiting up for me. I really should get going."

He didn't move as she slid past him, exiting the cell as if she feared he might try to lock her in. He still didn't move as she hurried to Harry's desk and scooped up her coat and gloves.

Slowly he pulled the cell door shut to keep the puppies in. He leaned against it, deliberately passive, watching her from a safe distance without making any sudden movements. He couldn't figure out exactly why she was so skittish, but he knew he had been clumsy, like a poacher crashing and stomping through a silent, untouched wood.

He kept his voice light. "Too bad. No Chinese, then?"

"I'd better not," she said, fumbling with her gloves in an awkward haste. "I'm sorry. It's just that I had completely forgotten about Ward."

She couldn't quite get the gloves on.

"Sarah," he said gently, as she threaded her fingers incorrectly for the second time. "Sarah, it was just a kiss."

"I know," she said, smiling at him with an intensity that was obviously manufactured. "It isn't that, really. I just don't think I should leave my uncle alone too long."

The buttons closed. The deep green hood swallowed her up once more. And then, with a polite exchange of goodbyes and small, firm click of the door, she was gone.

A puppy snuffled, scratching at the cell door.

"It's okay, buddy," Parker said softly. "We goofed, that's all. We'll get another chance." The puppy whimpered, as if he didn't have much hope that Parker would do any better the next time.

Parker glanced over at the paperback Sarah had left. *Make Anyone Do Anything.*

He chuckled under his breath. "I think you're right, little fellow. I think we'd better read this book after all."

ON SUNDAY AFTERNOON the temperature rose to fifty degrees, and the whole town of Firefly Glen came out to celebrate.

The square was a bustle of color—teens playing, mothers swinging babies, people walking dogs. The thermometer might drop to zero again by morning— weather up here was apparently famously unpredictable—so everyone wanted to make the most of this gift, this smiling hour of stolen spring.

In the Candlelight Café, Theo was serving Heat Wave Sundaes for fifty cents. Half the town was here. Sarah and Ward waited twenty minutes for a booth, and when they were finally seated, Sarah was dismayed to discover that she had an uninterrupted view of Sheriff Tremaine and his gorgeous brunette date, who sat at an adjoining table.

Of course he looked wonderful, in a casual blue cotton shirt with the sleeves rolled up to the elbow. Must be his day off. And he was smiling *that smile* at his date, who obviously was eating it up with one of Theo's silver dessert spoons.

Sarah studied her sundae, cutting into it with slow, surgical precision so that she didn't have to watch.

Just her luck. She had spent the past two days trying not to think about him. Trying to forget the flare of heat she'd felt when he kissed her. She had snuffed it instantly, of course, but for a split second there in the jail cell his sex appeal had sliced into her like a warm, sharp knife sinking into soft butter.

She might as well quit kidding herself that, as a pregnant woman facing major life decisions, she was beyond the tawdry urgings of mere physical desire. Apparently some deeply female part of her didn't realize that she was pregnant. Or didn't care.

So all right, denial was no longer an option. But self-control was.

And she'd start by refusing to look at him. She filled her mouth with sweet, oozing whipped cream and focused on her uncle, willing herself not to possess any peripheral vision.

"That's all right, Theo." A woman's voice broke into their conversation. "We can sit here, with Ward and Sarah. There's plenty of room."

Sarah turned at the sound. Madeline Alexander stood at the edge of their booth, wearing a shirtwaist dress covered in huge red roses and red earrings the size of Easter eggs.

But that was just typical Madeline. The real surprise was that she had three little girls in tow, lined up behind her like ducklings. The girls looked to be about eight years old, and they wore bright blue uniforms and beanies that read, Firefly Girls: Troop 637.

"They didn't have a table big enough for all of us," Madeline explained while she moved things around to accommodate the new situation. Sarah slid over, as it became clear that Madeline intended to sit with Ward, leaving the Firefly Girls to share Sarah's side of the booth. The girls looked embarrassed but obedient as they piled in, elbow to elbow, the last one half-hanging off the edge of the seat.

"Sarah, I'd like you to meet my girls. Well, not *my* girls really, but I'm their troop leader. This is half of our troop. The other girls are over there, see them? Hi, girls!" She raised her voice. "Girls! Girls, over here! Say hello to Sarah!"

If Sarah had hoped that Parker might depart without noticing her, those hopes were dead now. Half the customers in the café turned at Madeline's sunny outburst and the answering clamor of responses from the girls, who sat at a table nearby.

"Hi, Sarah!"

"Hello, Sarah!"

Amid the hullabaloo, Parker caught her eye. "Hello, Sarah," he mouthed silently, adding a wink for good measure.

Darned if she didn't blush. *Good grief.*

"Sarah, you're the very person I need," Madeline gushed as soon as the girls subsided, as if she couldn't bear a silence. "I need your help desperately. Tell her she simply must agree to help us, Ward. I know you don't approve of the festival, but you must tell her how important the costumes are to the girls.''

Ward shrugged. ''I haven't got any idea what you're talking about.''

''Well, you know one of our assistant troop leaders has gone out of town. Her parents are sick or something. So now we don't have enough help. And with the festival coming up—and the costumes...oh, it's such a disaster!'' She sighed, waving her hands in the air to illustrate the chaos she faced. ''And I know you are a good seamstress—after all, you do teach Home Ec, don't you? Oh, please. Do help us, Sarah!''

Amazed that Madeline was discussing the festival so openly in front of Ward, Sarah looked at her uncle. He didn't look angry. He looked bored. And he refused to meet her eyes, the coward. But everyone else at the table was staring expectantly at her—Madeline with damp, desperate melodrama, and the three little girls with owlish curiosity.

''All right,'' Sarah said weakly. ''I'll be glad to do what I can.''

''Oh, thank you, Sarah.'' Madeline, the social maestro, called out merrily to the rest of the troop. ''Girls! Girls! Sarah is going to be our new troop leader! Say 'thank you, Sarah!''''

A new chorus went through the café. By now the adult customers were grinning and joining in. A couple of people were clapping. Parker was openly laughing, though his date seemed less amused.

Sarah put her face in her hands helplessly. Why had she thought this was a sleepy little snow-shrouded town where she could hibernate until she decided how to handle her dilemma? She hadn't had a minute's real solitude since her plane touched down in Albany.

The little girl who had scooted into the booth right next to Sarah suddenly poked Sarah's arm rather insistently.

Sarah looked over with a smile. The girl was a pudgy, freckled redhead whose beanie was perched so high on her springy curls that it looked as if it might tumble at any moment. Sarah had noticed—as teachers always do—that she didn't seem to be very chummy with the other girls.

"Thanks, Sarah," the little girl said, as if by rote. Then she got down to business. "Are you going to eat that cherry?"

Sarah plucked the cherry out of her sundae and handed it over.

Madeline tsked and frowned in their direction. "Eileen O'Malley, if you keep eating everything in sight, you're never going to fit into your snowflake costume for the festival."

A couple of the other girls tittered, and Sarah felt her hackles rising on Eileen's behalf. But the spunky little girl seemed unfazed. She simply returned Madeline's glare and popped the cherry into her mouth defiantly. Madeline sighed and turned back to Ward.

The little girl munched quietly for a few seconds, then looked up at Sarah.

"Don't you think it's totally dumb," Eileen said, "for the *Firefly* Girls to dress up as *snowflakes?* It doesn't make one bit of sense, does it?"

"I don't know." Sarah made a show of considering it. Eileen looked deadly serious, as if this issue was her litmus test, and Sarah realized that she wanted to pass, if only to offset Madeline's cruel remark about the little girl's weight. "Snowflakes and fireflies. It does seem odd. But maybe firefly costumes were just too hard to make."

"Or maybe Mrs. Alexander is just a mean old poop." Eileen had spoken under her breath so that she couldn't be heard across the table. When Sarah didn't chastise her, she grinned suddenly, abandoning her grievance. "But that's okay. Are you going to lick that spoon?"

As Sarah handed her spoon over, she had a funny thought.

Her baby was going to be a girl. She knew it—somehow she just knew it. A little girl, maybe a lot like this one, full of spunk and laughter and loads of common sense.

And with that thought came a revelation. The baby wasn't an abstraction, a predicament. She wasn't a dilemma waiting to be solved. She was a person waiting to enter the world, where she would live and love and eat ice cream, laugh and cry and probably fail geometry.

And Sarah could hardly wait to meet her.

"IT'S LIKE RIDING A BICYCLE, damn it." Ward glared at Sarah, who was wobbling toward him on the ice. "You don't ever forget."

"Yeah? Well, tell that to my ankles," Sarah responded shortly, struggling as hard as she could to stay erect.

Why had she let her uncle talk her into this? She couldn't ice-skate. She was a Floridian, for heaven's sake. Maybe her brain dimly remembered using the indoor skating rink during her summer vacation here fifteen years ago, but her body had total amnesia on the subject.

Too bad Heather had assured her that a few spills wouldn't hurt the baby. Exercise is good, the doctor had said. The spills are worth it, as long as they're not from a ten-story building.

"Come on, come on. You can do it."

Ward was skating backward, holding both her hands, urging her on. The show-off. He looked so annoyingly dapper and fit in his parka and muffler and ski cap. Whereas she looked like an idiot. Her rear end was white with ice shavings, from all the times she'd landed on it, and her nose had started to run from the cold.

"No—I—can't." She tried to free her hands, but that was a mistake. The movement upset her precarious balance, and she began to weave and sway. She felt like a cartoon character with rubber legs that kept stretching in different directions.

And then, of course, she went down.

Ward laughed and skated a fancy figure eight around her. When she tossed a handful of snow at him he sped off, one hand tucked behind his back like a racer. He looked like a man half his age.

She, on the other hand, didn't dare try to rise to

her feet. She was only a couple of feet from the bank, so she crawled on all fours toward safety.

Suddenly, there was a face just inches from hers. A golden, furry face with a huge tongue hanging out.

"What—?" The tongue darted out to touch her nose, and then she knew. It was one of the puppies she'd seen in the jail cell last week. He started dancing around her, grinning with pleasure. Apparently he thought she was a kindred spirit, down on all fours like an animal herself.

She couldn't help grinning back. He was almost unbelievably cute. But he was so little he must be freezing. She picked him up and scanned the perimeter of the lake, knowing that Parker had to be nearby.

He was. He was sitting on the bench just a few yards to her left, watching the pair of them. His dark blue jacket and black corduroy pants blended into the bench so well she hadn't noticed him.

She cuddled the puppy close to keep him warm. He accepted her embrace without resistance, nibbling happily at the string of her mitten. Then she climbed awkwardly to her feet and walked stilt-legged through the snow.

She plopped down next to Parker with absolutely no grace. But she was too relieved to be on solid ground to care. "I'm trying to decide how embarrassed to be. How long have you been here?"

He grinned. "Long enough to know you won't be taking home the gold next year."

She had to laugh. She nodded toward her uncle, who was waving at them from the far side of the lake.

"Hans Brinker out there is pretty disappointed in me."

Parker tilted his head. "Somehow I doubt that," he said. He tugged at one of the puppy's ears playfully. "So. What are you going to name him?"

"Me?" She looked down at the puppy, who had lost interest in her mittens and had started chewing on his own paw, as if he'd never seen it before. "You want *me* to name him?"

"I think you should," Parker said. "He's yours."

"Mine?" Sarah looked down at the puppy in horrified amazement. "He can't be *mine!* I can't own a dog. I don't even live here. I mean, I will be going back to Florida in a few weeks."

"Oh?" Parker looked politely curious. "I've never been to Florida. They don't have dogs there?"

"You know what I mean. I live in an apartment. I'm never there. I can't have a dog." She looked down at the puppy, who had decided to gaze up at her adoringly. "Why don't you keep him?"

"Can't," Parker said apologetically. "I already bought one of his brothers." He watched as the puppy began licking Sarah's neck. "Besides, anyone can see that puppy belongs to you."

"Hey, Sheriff!" Ward had skated closer now, and he came to a sharp stop right in front of them. He was grinning wickedly. "I thought of a new slogan for my billboard! Right under that great picture of me, it'll say, Hide Out In Firefly Glen." He chuckled. "Get it? Hide out? Like a criminal." When Parker didn't smile, Ward scowled and tilted his head back arrogantly. "It's subliminal. I guess you have to be subtle to get it."

And then, with a cackle and a flourish, he skated nimbly away, his silver blades flashing in the sun.

Parker shook his head. "I guess the how-to book isn't working." He raised one eyebrow. "Or haven't you reached the chapter on incorrigible, stubborn old geezers yet?"

Worried, Sarah gazed after her uncle, stroking the puppy's soft fur for comfort. "He listens to me, but then he just goes ahead and does whatever he wants. He really seems to hate this Bourke Waitely fellow. Who is he?"

"Bourke owns the only hotel in town. He probably stands to make more money from the festival than anyone. He and Ward are enemies from way back. I've heard rumors, but that's all. Best I can piece together, Bourke used to be in love with Roberta, and, even though Bourke eventually married, he never quite gave up thinking he could steal her from Ward."

"Fat chance of that," Sarah said. "I never saw two people more in love than Ward and Roberta were."

"I know." Parker reached out and touched the puppy's nose softly. The little guy had fallen asleep under Sarah's rhythmic stroking. "They probably had the only truly happy marriage I ever heard of. They always gave me hope for the human race."

They didn't say anything further for several long minutes. Instead, they shared the simple pleasure of watching Ward's elegant skating, the way tiny, sudden rainbows would flash from the snow, the way his skates kicked out pinwheels of spun glass. And in the silence, they could clearly hear the tiny tinkling melodies made by the wind as it blew icy pine needles against each other.

Though she was so cold her nose was numb, and she ached all over from her many tumbles, Sarah found herself strangely contented. She liked the warm comfort of the puppy's weight against her chest and the easy companionship of the man next to her. In her experience, very few men were as good at silences as Parker Tremaine.

But she couldn't let this one stretch too long. She couldn't let herself grow accustomed to it.

"I really can't keep him, you know." She shifted the warm bundle without waking him. "I appreciate the thought, but—"

"How about Frosty?" Parker eyed the puppy appraisingly. He gave no indication that he had even heard her. "That's what we always call the king of the ice festival. And Frosty here seems to love the snow."

"Parker, I—"

"Look at him, Sarah. He's already adopted you." Parker touched the limp, sleepy paws with his knuckle gently. "Tell you what. Why don't you just hang on to him for a little while, just as long you're here? Then, if you really don't want to keep him, I'll take over."

Sarah looked down at the sweet, rounded head of the sleeping puppy. Wouldn't it be terribly difficult to have him for a little while, then have to give him up? And what exactly was this all about, anyhow? Could something else be going on here? Were strings attached to this gift? Why would Parker Tremaine buy Sarah a dog, unless he hoped that she…that they…

Perhaps it was time to get it all out in the open.

"Parker," she began uncertainly. "I feel as if there's something we need to get straight. I don't know if you're hoping—if you are thinking that maybe you and I…"

He looked politely curious, maybe a little amused, but nothing more. God, this was awkward. He hadn't ever even asked her out on a date, not really. There was just that one impulsive kiss in the jail cell. It might have meant nothing. She might be making a fool of herself.

"I mean. It's just that I don't want you to get the wrong idea. I don't think it's a good idea for us to…to see each other. Except as friends, of course."

"You don't? Why?" Parker cast a smiling glance toward the lake, where Ward was still grandstanding. "Because of the insanity in your family? I'm prepared to overlook that."

"I'm serious," she said earnestly. "It wouldn't work, really it wouldn't. I'm here for such a short time. A month at the most. And I need, well, I need to keep my life as uncomplicated as possible right now. I have a lot of things I need to sort out."

Slowly, as he watched her face, Parker's expression sobered. "Ward told me there used to be a guy back in Florida. Something that wasn't good for you, something that wasn't working. He mentioned a broken engagement." He watched her carefully. "Is that it? Is that what you have to sort out?"

"Kind of." She looked away. "Among other things. I just really don't need any emotional complications right now."

"Okay." Parker smiled. "No emotional complications. Not from me, anyhow." He glanced at the puppy, who was waking up, wriggling like a baby in her arms. "But I can't speak for Frosty here. I have an idea this little fellow is a real heartbreaker."

CHAPTER EIGHT

AFTER DINNER, when the cook had gone home for the night and Frosty had finally tuckered himself out and fallen asleep in his crate, Sarah sat with Ward in his workroom while he put a new finish on an old English carved chair.

He had offered to play chess with her instead, or even watch TV. But she had been happy to forgo those pleasures. Newly sensitized to the dangers paint fumes might present to an unborn baby, she made sure the exhaust fan was on, and she sat a little distant from the action. She loved to watch him work.

The chair itself was exquisite—part of Winter House's original furnishings. But it was Ward himself she enjoyed watching most. His gnarled hands were still so deft, and the way he swirled the brush was so graceful, sliding slow across the broad planks, following the curve of a scroll, then dipping delicately into the ridges of a fleur-de-lis.

"It's beautiful." She picked up an unused brush and feathered its bristles against the palm of her hand. "It's like being an artist, isn't it?"

Her uncle snorted. "*Hell,* no. I'm no artist. I'm just a drudge. Your aunt..." His hand paused. "Now *she* was an artist. She always knew what colors to pick, what pieces to put where. I was just the hack who carried out her orders. And considered it a privilege, too.''

Sarah smiled. She remembered that. Roberta could fuss over the placement of one picture, making Ward hold it first here, then there, then another inch to the left. Sarah had thought it silly back then. What was one picture in a house that possessed hundreds? But now she understood what a work of art Winter House was, and she realized that Roberta's careful attention had kept it that way.

Ward chuckled as he resumed his work. ''Me an *artist!* Your aunt would get a good laugh out of that one. She always said I had the decorating eye of a circus clown.''

''Aww.'' Sarah tapped her brush against his forearm sympathetically. ''Don't feel bad. You can always make a living as an ice-skating instructor.''

He glared at her. ''You scoff, madam, but sometimes the problem isn't the teacher. It's the student.''

''I know. I'm sorry. I'm hopeless.'' Her tailbone still ached from all those falls. ''Did you know Parker Tremaine was there the whole time? It was pretty embarrassing to discover I had an audience.''

''Oh, come off it. You know perfectly well that Parker Tremaine thinks anything you do is adorable. Although I bet he's never seen that face you make when you eat asparagus.''

Sarah looked over at her uncle quickly. ''Don't be silly,'' she began. He was still working, his gaze concentrated on the intricate carving on the arms of the chair, so she couldn't read his face.

"It's not silly. It's true. He's smitten." Ward glanced up suddenly, his brush poised in the air. "But I take it the feeling isn't mutual."

"Of course not." She beat the paintbrush nervously against her palm. "No, that didn't sound right. Parker is a very nice man. And I like him a lot. But he's just a friend. I don't think of him like *that*."

"Oh, yeah? Well, you'd be the first woman in Firefly Glen history who didn't." He went back to work. "That's how you'll go down in the record books, then. They'll say *She couldn't skate worth a damn, and apparently she was blind as a bat, too.*"

"Not blind," Sarah complained, half-laughing even though the subject made her a little uncomfortable. "I'm well aware he's handsome."

"Crazy, then? He's a fine man, Short Stuff. You could do worse." He grinned. "In fact, you *have* done worse. Don't forget the erstwhile Ed."

"I haven't forgotten him. In fact, that's why I'm not interested in Parker Tremaine, or anyone, right now."

"Nonsense. You fell off the horse, you get back on." He pointed the paintbrush at her, and a couple of dots of mahogany finish fell on her forearm for emphasis.

"Life's short," he said. He tilted his hand to look at his wedding ring, a simple, time-scratched gold band that she'd never seen him take off. "There are few enough years as it is. Ed's had three of yours already. How many are you going to let him steal?''

She squeezed the paintbrush in both hands, struggling with the decision about what to tell him. It didn't seem right to hide the truth any longer, not when he was obviously hoping that she might develop a romantic interest in his good friend Parker.

Besides, she would have to tell him about the baby sooner or later. Wouldn't it be more honest to do it sooner?

But she was a coward. She had never looked into her uncle's eyes and seen disappointment. She dreaded the day when she would. She hated the thought of losing his respect.

On the other hand, if she didn't speak up now, she was going to lose respect for *herself.*

''It's not just Ed,'' she said, drawing a deep breath. She sat straighter, taking her courage by the reins. ''There's something else, something important I've been wanting to tell you.''

He obviously heard the serious note in her voice. He put his paintbrush down slowly, resting it across the lid of the finish can. ''Okay,'' he said, giving her his full attention. ''Let's hear it, then.''

She didn't sugarcoat it, or lead into it with a meandering preamble. Ward was a blunt man who believed in meeting trouble head-on. And this was trouble with a capital *T*. He wouldn't admire her for trying to dress it up in a fancy hat and pass it off as anything else.

''I'm pregnant,'' she said simply. ''I'm going to

have Ed's baby later this year. He knows. He knew before we broke up. He would prefer that I get rid of it. He doesn't want me, and he doesn't want the baby.''

Ward looked grim. ''Man, this Ed guy just gets better and better.''

She lifted her chin. ''Well, that's the whole sad story, really. I'm pregnant, and I'm not going to be getting married. I'm going to have this baby, and I'm going to do it alone.''

Her uncle narrowed his eyes. ''That's it?''

She nodded. ''I'm sorry. I know what you must think.'' She swallowed. ''I know you're disappointed in me. But at least now you can see why I'm not in a position to date the sheriff or anyone else at the moment.''

''I can?''

She looked at him, confused. ''Well, of course. I'm pregnant—''

''I got that.'' To her surprise, her uncle was smiling. ''You're pregnant, and you're not going to marry the jerk. I think that's wonderful. Absolutely *terrific!* Now if you'd told me you were pregnant and you *were* going to marry the jerk, well, that would be bad news.''

''But I certainly can't be out dating—''

He shook his head woefully. ''God, child, you're about as Victorian as this chair. This is the twenty-first century, isn't it? What, you think you're damaged goods? Not fit company for any decent man? I think I read a line like that in *Jane Eyre,* or some equally

hysterical piece of antediluvian blather. But I've
never heard a real human being say anything that ridiculous.''

She could hardly believe his attitude. Where were
the questions, the recriminations, the lectures? Where
was the dreaded disappointment?

''But what about Parker? Surely if he knew about
the baby, he—''

''I just said he had a crush on you, Short Stuff. I
didn't say he wanted to marry you.''

She couldn't speak. She had imagined a thousand
reactions to her news. But never this…this uncomplicated pleasure. It still hadn't fully penetrated her
anxiety. But there, on the edges of the guilt that had
been smothering her, she glimpsed a thin border of
sunshine.

Ward was already back at work on the chair, smiling down at the scrolled arms and dabbing his brush
with new enthusiasm.

''Poor Parker,'' he said, chuckling. ''Oh, give the
guy a break, why don't you? He thinks you're cute.
He wants to take you to dinner.'' Ward tossed her a
grin. ''And I hate to rain on your hair-shirt parade,
Short Stuff. But even fallen women have to eat.''

HARRY HAD BEEN STOMPING around the department
like a snake-bit elephant all day, and Parker had just
about had enough of it. He didn't care if Harry was
Emma's husband. If the damn fool didn't start acting
civilized, Parker was going to take him out back and
introduce him to Miss Manners the hard way.

The telephone rang. Suzie was working this afternoon, and she answered it with her usual singsongy, fake upper-crust accent. "Good Ahfahnoooon. Fiahhfly Glen Sheriff's Depahhhtment." Parker tried not to cringe. She'd been doing this schtick ever since he had dared to tell her that "Hey, this is the cop shop" wouldn't quite cut it as a greeting.

She listened a moment, then she punched the hold button. "Harry," she said, pushing her glasses up on her nose wearily. "It's for you. Again. It's Emma. Again."

Harry shook his head without looking up from his paperwork. "I'm not here."

Parker felt his fingers making a fist without even consulting his brain. "That's odd, Harry. Because I could swear I'm looking right at your ugly mug right now." When Harry didn't respond, Parker jammed the button for the incoming line and picked up the telephone himself. "Hey, Em. I'm sorry. Harry's here, but he's sucking a lemon right now. Maybe you'd better call back later."

She didn't like that, but, as he had known she would, she accepted it rather than give Parker a chance to say anything further about Harry.

Parker put the telephone down and looked across the room, where his brother-in-law was glowering at him.

"Why don't you just stay the hell out of this, Tremaine?" The deputy's voice was crisp with bitterness. "This is not your problem."

Parker didn't blink. "I think it is," he said levelly.

"Yeah, well it's *not*." Harry was getting red. "And if you'd like me to prove it, I can—"

Suzie stepped between them, holding her hands out dramatically, like the referee in a prizefight.

"Gentlemen." She rolled her eyes. "And I'm using that term loosely. Gentlemen, in exactly thirty seconds, Troop 637 of the Firefly Girls is going to walk through that door. They are on a field trip. They're working on a law enforcement badge. So unless you think they'd enjoy watching two grown men brawl on the floor like hoodlums, maybe you'd better chill out."

"Hell, Suzie." Parker took a deep breath. "Why didn't you tell me they were coming?"

"I told you last Tuesday, last Thursday, yesterday, and again two hours ago." She tossed her dark hair in wounded hauteur. "But no one listens to me. I'm just the clerk, what do I know?"

Oh, great. Parker could hear Harry taking the same deep breath he had needed himself. The two men carefully avoided making eye contact as the front door opened and a blue stream of beanie-topped little girls poured in.

Parker summoned a smile. He had better overcome his frustration quick, or else when they went to bed tonight these kids would be having nightmares about the mean policemen.

He was steeling himself to handle Madeline Alexander's compulsive cheeriness, but to his surprise the last person through the door was Sarah Lennox. And then he remembered. Madeline had recruited Sarah as a backup troop leader.

Sarah hadn't noticed him. She was talking to Eileen O'Malley, tilting slightly toward the little girl, listening to her conversation as earnestly as if they were discussing quantum physics.

And Eileen was glowing under the attention. Parker could picture Sarah in her classroom, offering that same easy affirmation to any child who needed it. What lucky kids her students were though they probably didn't know it. They were too young to recognize how rare true emotional generosity was. When they got a little older and had been knocked around by fair-weather friends, selfish lovers, vain bosses and narrow-minded neighbors, then they'd appreciate Ms. Lennox, who had always made them feel good about themselves.

Parker felt his sour mood lifting. He turned to the children and said, "Okay. Who wants to see where we put the criminals?"

A dozen hands waved in front of his face like little pink flags.

"Well, let's see. Who can I trust with the keys?" He scratched his chin, surveying the eager faces, looking for the one who needed it most. If Sarah could do this, so could he.

He saw C.J. Porterfield standing toward the back. She had her hand up, but halfheartedly, as if she already knew she wouldn't be chosen. C.J. was the daughter of an Internet millionaire, and she was just as brilliant and hopelessly geeky as her old man.

Parker crooked his finger at her. "C.J., you look reliable. You come be the keeper of the keys. Deputy Dunbar is going to take you on a tour of the department, and when you get to the holding cell, you can unlock it for him."

C.J. took the keys solemnly, as if she had been handed a stick of dynamite. One of the keys was an antique, a big brass monstrosity that was more or less just for show. It had unlocked the jail cell Firefly Glen had used a hundred years ago, a cell long since torn down. Today, in this updated facility, the real cell key was small and silver and looked as if it might operate your mother's Honda.

You'd think a beady-eyed killer lurked in that cell right now, the way the other girls gathered around, eager for a chance to touch the brass key. And if Harry did his spiel correctly, they would get plenty of hair-raising stories about former inmates. Parker remembered from his own youth that field trips were considered a pathetic bust if they didn't include some blood and gore.

Luckily Harry had managed to rise above his mood, too. He took the kids away to show them the emergency radio. Parker had to smile, listening to him talk about mountain rescues at midnight, brushfires at dawn, coyotes caught snarling in the kitchen and fugitives caught streaking for the Canadian border.

Harry was good at this—he loved kids. He'd have them squealing and shuddering in happy horror before the hour was up.

It was a shame, really. Once, Parker had believed

that Harry would make a great father to Emma's children. But now he wasn't even sure Harry made a very good husband. Damn the man. What was *wrong* with him?

"So have you ever really had any criminals in your jail cell?" Sarah had wandered over to his side, and she was smiling. "Last time I was here, it looked more like a petting zoo."

"Of course we've had criminals," Parker said in mock indignation. "Once we held an escapee from the Albany prison for forty-eight whole hours. An *ax* murderer, no less."

She raised her eyebrows. "And that was—"

He chuckled. "Seventy-three years ago. But I haven't had a good night's sleep since."

"No sleep? Why, that must be just like when you have a new puppy," she observed, widening her eyes innocently.

He grimaced. "Uh-oh. You, too? God, I'm sorry. But I'm in the same boat. I took Frosty's brother, you know—he was the only one who hadn't been adopted. I swear that dog whines nonstop from dusk until dawn. Then, of course, he sleeps all day." He gave her a placating smile. "Good thing they're so darn cute, isn't it? Otherwise you might want to strangle the puppy and the guy who gave him to you, too."

"I'll try to control myself," she said. "Actually, I've found the answer. Frosty cries when he's in his crate, but if I let him sleep up on the bed with me, he's fine."

Parker held his face under control with a noble ef-

fort. "Really," he said politely, aware of all the little
ears around them. "How about that?"

Sarah shot him a suspicious look, but she didn't
comment. They watched Harry handling the kids for
a few minutes in silence. C.J. had just locked Eileen
O'Malley in the jail cell, and the other girls were
snickering.

"Well, you totally won't be able to escape," Daisy
Kinsale, a pretty blonde, was saying. "Not by squeez-
ing through the bars, anyhow!"

"But don't worry," Daisy's smug-looking buddy
Harriet piped in. "The bread-and-water diet will be
good for you!"

Parker felt Sarah's tension building. "Kids can be
such monsters," she muttered under her breath. "That
blond girl is Eileen's own stepsister, did you know
that?"

"Yeah, I did." Parker eyed Daisy Kinsale with annoyance. Brad Kinsale was a friend of his, and he
was a damn nice guy. Why didn't he teach his kid
better manners? "These mix-and-match families can
be pretty rough sometimes, can't they?"

She nodded. "Brutal. I have six stepsiblings, from
three different stepfathers. Believe me, I know all
about it."

He hadn't realized that Sarah's growing up had
been so turbulent. Though Ward had talked about
Sarah often, he had never mentioned this. Parker wondered if that might be what had made Sarah so aware
of other people's needs. Being forced to get along

with so many intimate strangers—it could either make you bitter as hell or intensely sensitive.

But what a rotten life for a kid. He wondered what on earth her mother had been thinking.

He sighed. "That's just one of the reasons I'm glad my ex-wife and I never had children. Divorce is always the hardest on them, isn't it? And it makes starting over so much trickier."

She didn't answer. She was staring at Eileen, apparently lost in thought. She looked so sad, as if she found Eileen's plight unbearable.

He suddenly wanted more than anything to make her smile. "I wouldn't worry too much about Eileen, though, if I were you," he said.

Sarah turned. "Why not?"

"Well, she doesn't know it yet, but she's undoubtedly going to turn into a wild Irish beauty, like every O'Malley woman for ten generations behind her."

He chuckled, remembering that Eileen's aunt, Deirdre O'Malley, had broken his own heart a couple of times during high school. "In a few years, every boy in town will be trotting around after her with their tongues hanging out. Including the boyfriends of every girl in this room."

"Good," Sarah said fiercely. Her chin was set in that special tight square she reserved for her most intense emotions. Watching her now, Parker realized that, for all her air of gentle fragility and her occasional mournful moments, Sarah Lennox was at heart a very strong woman.

Her appearance was deceiving. She wasn't as dramatic as the O'Malley women—those tall, athletic women with their fiery hair and their flashing eyes. Sarah was petite and slim. Her honey-blond hair was pale and translucent, like a halo around the narrow oval of her face. Her eyes were round, wide-set and kind, with none of the flashing arrogance that made the O'Malleys look like Celtic warrior queens.

Those eyes said Sarah could be easily hurt.

But that chin said she could take it.

Yes, he thought. He would take sweet, stubborn Sarah over the O'Malley firebrands any day.

If only she'd let him.

BY NINE O'CLOCK THAT NIGHT, when Parker was getting ready to go home, he was so tired he could hardly button his jacket properly. It had been a long day, but he had managed not to kill Harry, so in his book that meant it was a good day.

Harry had left first, five full minutes ago. Parker had stayed behind, leaving some final instructions with the graveyard deputy. He had thought it was smart to keep at least five minutes between him and Harry at all times.

But when he finally closed the department door and stepped out into the crisp, starry night, eager to get home to his quiet house, his warm fire and his annoying but adorable new puppy, he saw that Harry hadn't gone anywhere.

Instead, Harry and Emma were standing beside Emma's car. Their postures were so rigid they screamed hostility. Parker would have known he had

stumbled into a domestic disturbance even if he
hadn't been able to hear their arguments clearly.

Which, unfortunately, he could.

"You're a coward, Harry Dunbar. That's why
you've left. Because you don't have the courage to
stay and work things out."

"Think whatever you want, Emma." Harry's voice
was as jagged as broken eggshells. Parker stopped in
his tracks. He'd never heard Harry sound like that
before. "Say whatever you want. I don't give a damn
anymore."

"You never did." Emma was trying to yell, but it
came out hoarsely, as if her throat were raw from
hours of crying. "If you had *ever* loved me, you
couldn't give up on our marriage."

"That's right, Emma." Harry was trying to pull
away, but Emma was holding fast to his arm. "You
guessed it. I never cared."

"Hey." Parker moved into the circle of illumination cast from the streetlight. He went to his sister.
"What's going on here?"

"Goddamn it, Parker, this is none of your—"

"He's moved out," Emma broke in, turning to Parker. Her voice was hard and furious, but her swollen
eyes, streaming with tears, spoke of a dreadful an-
guish. "He hasn't got the guts to stay and work out
our problems, so he packed his suitcase and left me."

"Our problems can't *be* worked out." Harry had
finally extricated himself from Emma's clutch. "But
maybe you should remember that they are *our* problems. Not Parker's. Leave him out of this."

"Listen, Harry—"

"Shut up, Parker." Harry sounded like a total stranger. "Just shut up. Emma, go home. I'm not going to have this fight in the middle of the street, in front of everyone. It's *our* problem. Our private problem."

Emma drew herself up with an attempt at dignity, but she was shivering. She hugged her coat around herself like a little girl. Watching her, Parker felt his blood pounding in his temples. No one was allowed to treat Emma like this. *No one.*

"They stopped being *our* problems the minute you walked out the door, Harry," she said thickly. "They are *my* problems now. And I can handle them any way I see fit."

Harry stared at her, his mouth slightly open, as if he couldn't believe what she had said. "You'd tell him, wouldn't you?"

"You're darn right I would, if I thought it would help. At least he wouldn't just run away from the problem, like you did. At least he's not *weak.*"

Harry's head snapped back, as if from a blow. "You *bitch.*"

That was the last thing Parker clearly remembered. His vision blurred with something bright and red. He felt his arm go back, and then he felt the bones of his fist connect with the bones in Harry's jaw.

Harry must have been seeing red swirls, too, because he swung back like a madman, and before Parker could make sense of anything, he had slammed Harry's body against the wall. He had one forearm across Harry's throat, and his jacket bunched in the other hand. He swallowed, and he tasted his own half-frozen blood.

"Stop it, you crazy lunatics!" Emma was beside him now, tugging on his arm wildly. "For God's sake, stop it, Parker. Do you think it will help me if you kill him? *I love him,* you idiot. *I love him!*"

HALF AN HOUR LATER, Parker finally got home, but he didn't feel much like starting a fire or petting the puppy, which Emma had named Snowball. He was staring at the bunged-up thug in his bathroom mirror, wondering when he had become such a damn fool, when the telephone rang.

He started to curse, but the movement hurt his busted lip. It was probably just the new guy at the department, wondering how to handle some trivial little detail. But he couldn't risk not answering it, in case it was Emma. So he threaded his way around the scampering puppy and grabbed the bedroom phone on the fifth ring.

"Parker? It's Sarah. I'm sorry to call so late."

He plopped down on the edge of the bed, almost too tired to register his full surprise. Snowball began whining and trying unsuccessfully to leap up with him, but it was an old tester bed, and much too high.

"That's okay," Parker said, careful of his lip. "What's up?"

"I just wanted to say thanks for being so nice to the girls this afternoon. They had a wonderful time."

"Good. Me, too," he said politely. He waited, feeling sure she had something else to say. She hadn't called him at ten o'clock at night just to tell him that.

The hesitation on Sarah's side of the line was tense and expectant. He wondered if she was waiting for him to create an opening. But an opening for what?

"Anyhow," she went on finally. "I have also been thinking about what we said the other day."

Snowball began making a melodramatic racket, scrabbling at the bedclothes and whining, desperate to join him. Parker could hardly hear. So he reached over and scooped him up, one hand beneath his belly, and deposited him on the comforter. The puppy settled down instantly. He curled up against Parker's hip and rested his chin on his thigh, sighing blissfully.

"Don't get used to this," he whispered, his hand over the mouthpiece. Then he spoke into the phone. "And? What were you thinking?"

"That maybe I was being silly. You know, overreacting to the whole thing—the kiss, the puppy, the whole idea of dating. I meant to tell you this today, but the girls were always around and—"

"And?"

"And anyhow, I think maybe it would be okay. I'm not ready for anything serious, of course—and of course you aren't, either. But there's really no reason why we shouldn't have lunch, or see each other every now and then, if you want to."

She paused. "I mean, assuming you want to."

"Yeah," he said, softly stroking the puppy, who seemed to be asleep already. "I want to. How about dinner tomorrow night?"

She seemed taken aback. "Tomorrow?"

"Well, I'd say tonight, but it's a little late. You've probably already had dinner." He smiled. That hurt his lip, too, but he didn't care. "I'm calling your bluff here, Sarah."

"I wasn't bluffing," she protested.

"Okay, then. Dinner. Tomorrow night. Seven o'clock. Dress warm and come hungry."

CHAPTER NINE

JUST ONE DATE. Just for fun. Just as friends.

What harm could it do?

Reciting those simple phrases over and over, Sarah stood at the window of her bedroom in Winter House, waiting for Parker to arrive. She wished she could get rid of this edginess. It was a tight-chested, pins-and-needles anxiety, the kind you might feel right before a rough exam for which you hadn't studied nearly enough.

Maybe it was just the weather. All day long the sky had been heavy, riding low in the heavens like a boat with too much cargo. The cook had left early, complaining that her arthritis was acting up, as it always did before a snowstorm. Ward was eating out with Madeline, and Sarah would be with Parker, so the woman had nothing to keep her at Winter House.

Sarah's ears were tuned for the engine rumble of Parker's Jeep, so she almost missed the slight, silvery tinkling of sleigh bells. Even when the lovely sound pierced her consciousness, she didn't connect it with Parker. She thought at first, illogically, of wind chimes, like the ones on the balcony of her Florida apartment.

It wasn't until she saw the sleigh itself that she

understood. Drawn by an elegant gray horse, it glided across the snow like something from another century. The curving metal runners were elaborately filigreed, like fine calligraphy, and the graceful, roomy body of the sleigh was painted a festive green, with sparkling silver trim.

Parker brought the sleigh to a stop in front of the house as easily as if he drove one every day. The horse tossed his head and pawed the snow, setting the bells along his harness jingling merrily.

For a moment, Sarah didn't move. This was another world, a world she'd never seen before. And she was enchanted. Then, remembering that this magic carriage had come for her, she let the curtain fall shut, grabbed her coat, hat, muffler and gloves and lightly flew down the staircase.

She made it to the front door just as Parker was lifting the brass knocker. "Hi," she said, feeling a little giddy from hurrying. She glanced at the sleigh. "Nice car."

"Like it?" He grinned. "It's a 1920 model S. One horsepower."

When he smiled, she noticed a dark bruise that ran along the lower edge of his lip. She looked more closely. His lip was slightly swollen, too.

"Oh dear," she said softly. "That looks painful."

He worked the lip carefully, as if testing it. Then he smiled again. "Nope. Apparently it's not serious. Just showy."

"What on earth happened?"

He shrugged. "Nothing, really. Occupational hazard. Much too dull to bore you with."

She could tell he wasn't going to elaborate. And she didn't want to pry. So, giving up, she wrapped her muffler around her throat and walked down the steps. Up close, the sleigh was even more charming, the wood weathered with age but freshly painted and gleaming. The interior was piled high with rugs and pillows.

"Is it yours?"

He shook his head. "The horse and the sleigh belong to the town vet—he's a friend of mine. I told him I was going to try to impress Ward Winters's niece so that she'd help us persuade him to release all the sleighs for the festival."

She looked over at him, smiling. "So, is that what this date is all about? Trying to enlist my support against my uncle?"

"Oh, absolutely," he agreed, his face poker straight. "For myself, I have no interest in moonlit sleigh rides with beautiful women. None whatsoever."

She laughed at that and tried not to let the compliment warm her too much. She wasn't beautiful, and she knew it. She was cute—occasionally, when she was at her best, even pretty in a tepid, monochromatic way.

But maybe on a cold winter night, with sleigh bells tinkling and snow just starting to fall, all women looked beautiful.

He handed her up into the seat, which was surpris-

ingly comfortable. He arranged the rugs across her
lap, gave one last tug to secure her muffler, and then
he came around the front, offering the horse a friendly
pat, and climbed into his own position beside her at
the reins.

She didn't ask where they were going. She didn't
care. It was enough merely to exist in this moment of
extraordinary beauty. The heavy sky was like a silver
silk canopy over their heads, and the frost-sparkling
trees swept by like candles. The night was intensely
quiet, broken only by the whoosh of the runners over
the icy snow, the crunch of the horse's dancing
hooves, and the clear crystal ringing of sleigh bells.

It was cold, so cold that the air streamed white from
the horse's nostrils, and her cheeks burned under the
frigid fingers of the wind. But it was glorious, and
she never wanted it to end.

Finally, though, she saw a building, a low-slung
wooden cabin surrounded by trucks. Lucky's Lounge,
the neon sign out front read, at least sometimes. Occasionally the first *L* sizzled and disappeared, making
it look like "ucky's Lounge."

Sarah looked at Parker, a question in her eyes.

"I know," he said, one corner of his mouth tucked
into his cheek. "It looks awful. But it's got some of
the best pizza in town, and, most importantly, there's
a barn where I can stable the horse while we're eating."

She waited for him, reluctant to enter the lounge
ahead of him. *Someone* had driven all those trucks

here, and where she came from it wasn't always safe for a woman to enter a roughneck bar alone.

Besides, she liked watching him handle the horse, whose name was Dusty, it seemed. Parker murmured and stroked "—That's right, Dusty. You're a fine girl, sweetheart—" as he unhooked the harness and released the sleigh. Dusty nuzzled Parker's shoulder, blowing a soft snort, as if she understood and wanted to answer.

Finally Parker made sure Dusty could reach the hay. He arranged a blanket over the horse's back and turned to Sarah. "Okay. Now it's our turn."

The lounge was exactly what Sarah expected—smoky and low-lit, brimming with very large, unshaven men in flannel shirts who seemed able to simultaneously watch a football game on television, play pool and sing along with the country-western song on the jukebox.

Parker knew them all. He backslapped or was slapped by almost every man he passed. But somehow he maneuvered Sarah to a booth in the back corner, where the smoke was a fraction less dense and the sportscaster's excited voice was almost inaudible.

They had just barely placed their order—one large pizza, no anchovies; one beer, one bottled water—when a giant of a man came by with his hand out.

"You in?"

To Sarah's surprise, Parker pulled a five-dollar bill out of his pocket and laid it in the other man's huge palm. "Ninety-seven," Parker said.

The giant turned to Sarah. "You in?"

She looked at Parker for guidance. Obviously they were betting on something, but what were the rules? Should she, as an outsider, say yes or no? He was smiling, and he nodded subtly. She dug around in her pockets and found a five. "Okay," she said, depositing it in the man's hand.

"How many?"

"I beg your pardon?"

"How many yards?"

She glanced at Parker again, but his grin was so amused that she made up her mind to bluff this out on her own.

"A hundred and eleven," she said briskly. The giant nodded, made a note on a napkin and moved on.

Parker burst out laughing. "Do you have any idea what you just bet on?"

"Yards," she said, raising her chin. "And since he didn't look like a landscape designer or a dressmaker, I assume it must have something to do with the football game. Your guess of ninety-seven was too high for a spread. So I figured yards running. Yards passing. Something like that."

Parker's eyes glinted in the light from the neon beer sign on the wall next to them. "Darn. You're good. Where did you learn all that?"

She raised her eyebrows in polite disdain as she unfolded her napkin. "I have had my share of sweaty, muscle-bound boyfriends, sir." She chuckled. "Besides, I teach high school, remember? My kids don't know what I'm talking about unless I express myself in sports metaphors."

He laughed.

"But isn't betting illegal? Aren't they worried about doing it in front of The Law?"

"Technically, we're not betting. We're paying to watch the football game on television. The chance to win the pot is just, and I quote, a fringe benefit of paying the TV tax."

When she looked incredulous, he smiled and shrugged. "Believe me, this has been through the local judicial system. Judge Bridwell ruled that if it's a fee for the television, it's not betting. Presto-chango, it's legal."

It was beyond Sarah's comprehension, but she let it go. Joining the pool must have been the right move, because from that moment on she was one of the gang. Dozens of men came over to say hello, often bringing their wives and girlfriends.

When their pizza was finished, one of the guys at the bar bought her a new bottled water, having discovered that she didn't drink. Later a bearded man in a hat that said *Lumberjacks Do It Till You Fall Over* came by and gave her a dollar for the jukebox.

She was the only optimist who had guessed over a hundred, and when the quarterback threw his final touchdown, putting the total at one-o-seven, the whole bar erupted in a rich, throaty cheer. "Sarah, Sarah, Sarah," they chanted until she felt herself blushing.

She won five hundred dollars. With a huge, congratulatory grin, the giant dumped it in her lap, a hundred five-dollar bills, all crumpled and stained, some so worn they were held together with Scotch tape.

Embarrassed, she did the only thing she could think of. She bought a round for the whole bar. And the chorus went up again, this time even louder. "Sarah, Sarah, Sarah!"

All in all, it was wonderful—as cozy and welcoming as any group she'd ever tried to infiltrate. But, even so, she was glad when Parker tilted his head toward the door, indicating that it was time to make their escape.

"What nice people," she murmured, half-sleepy now that she was tucked into the rugs again. Parker was clicking Dusty along at a slow walk that set the sleigh into a rhythmic motion almost like the rocking of a cradle. She and Parker were fitted so close she could feel his body heat warming her from shoulder to thigh.

The clouds had moved off while they were in the bar, and the world looked just born, white and new and hushed. The sky had lifted, revealing a silent explosion of stars.

"Yes, they are," Parker agreed. He glanced at her. "And they certainly approved of you. They don't approve of everybody."

She smiled drowsily. "I'll bet they approve of anyone who buys them a round of beer."

"Well, maybe." He rode in silence for a minute. "Actually, I was thinking of my ex-wife. Once, when she came home with me for a visit, I took her to Lucky's. God, what a disaster. Tina sat there looking like someone had put a steel rod in her back, like she was afraid she'd catch something if she moved. And she had this bad-smell pucker on her face. After about ten minutes, not a soul in the place would speak to us.'' He shook his head at the memory. ''Tina wasn't a fan of small towns.''

Sarah looked over at him curiously. ''What *was* she a fan of?''

''Our life in D.C. It was the perfect town for her. Tina was a fan of power. Money. Excitement. She breathed glamour like other people breathe air.''

Sarah touched his arm with her gloved hand. ''And *you.* After all, she married you. She must have been a pretty big fan of yours.''

''Only when I was part of the power package.'' He shrugged. ''When she heard that I wanted to leave D.C. and come back here, she permanently resigned her membership in the Parker Tremaine fan club.''

''She divorced you because she didn't want to live in a small town?'' Sarah squeezed his arm, thinking what a fool Tina Tremaine sounded like. ''That must have been very difficult for you.''

Parker shook his head. ''Not really. Receiving those divorce papers was like getting a pardon from the governor. For both of us. Our marriage was the difficult part. For both of us. It was a terrible mistake, almost from the beginning.''

So Parker had moved away, leaving his ex-wife behind. Sarah felt a stirring of sympathy for Tina, which she knew was absurd, given what she'd heard about the woman. But Sarah had been left behind, too, and she knew how it felt. Was it possible that Ed and Parker had more in common than she had thought?

She shivered suddenly. Assuming the wind was bothering her, Parker reached over comfortably and wrapped his arm around her shoulders, pulling her more tightly against the solid warmth of his body.

No, she thought with an intense, instinctive defiance. Ed and Parker were nothing alike. Parker would have brought his wife, if only she'd been willing to come. Ed had made it clear that Sarah was not invited.

Gradually the streets they traversed became more and more populated, until they were in the thick of town. Parker slowed Dusty down even further, offering Sarah time to enjoy the view.

And what a view it was, especially for a little Southern schoolteacher who had never even seen snow before. Firefly Glen was like an enchanted village, with its snow-laden roofs, its smoke-plumed chimneys, its old-fashioned streetlights floating like neat rows of glowing golden orbs.

"Look over there." Parker suddenly drew Dusty to a standstill. "The Spring House—look!"

Sarah followed Parker's gloved finger, which was pointing toward a storybook Victorian mansion, all pink and white and dove-gray, with fanciful gables and ornate gingerbread woodwork. A huge porch wrapped around the entire house.

"Yes," she said, transfixed by the extraordinary feminine charm of the house. "My uncle showed me all four Season Houses when I came here years ago. It's even more beautiful than I remembered."

"But look," Parker said softly. "Up on the porch."

Sarah looked more carefully. And then she saw what he saw. Up on the wide verandah, pressing their noses against the honeyed warmth of a lighted window, were two large brown deer.

"They're cold," Parker whispered. "They want to go in where it's warm."

Sarah realized she was holding her breath. "They don't look real. Will they be all right?"

"Sure." Parker clicked his tongue softly, and Dusty began again to walk sedately down the tree-lined street. "The yard may be missing a few plants by tomorrow morning, but the deer will be fine."

Sarah watched the deer over her shoulder until she and Parker were too far away to make out the dark, still silhouettes against the golden windowpane. Then she settled back into the warm circle of Parker's arm.

"Did your uncle ever tell you how we got our Season Houses?"

Sarah thought back. "No. He just told me that Firefly Glen had begun as a tiny settlement of loggers and trappers, but that some millionaires from New York City discovered it around the end of the nineteenth century." She snuggled down into the rugs happily. "Why? Is it a good story?"

"It's a little unusual," he said. "Do you remember the Summer House?"

Sarah thought back. "Yes, I think so. A huge Italian villa? Seems to be deteriorating? Some crumbling mosaics, big empty swimming pool, long colonnades filled with leaves. I remember thinking it looked haunted.''

"That's the one. Well, that was the first mansion built here—almost a hundred years ago by Dr. and Mrs. Mark Granville, the darlings of New York society. Mark, they say, was tall, funny and kind. Moira, the story goes, was tiny and elegant and sweet. Anyhow, everybody wanted to do whatever the Granvilles did, so within a couple of years several other rich young couples had moved here, too. They built the Spring House, the Autumn House—"

"I remember that one, too," Sarah said eagerly. "Huge, out in the woods. Wood and glass and stone, kind of a ranch house."

"Yep." Parker grinned. "You have a good memory."

"The houses are fairly spectacular," she said. "And of course since my uncle lived in one of the Season Houses, I was extra curious about the other three."

"That makes sense. Anyhow, the Winter House was the last one built by the Granvilles' friends. After the Winter House, no new mansions were built here for thirty years."

Sarah turned to look at him. "Why on earth not?"

"That's where the story gets good. I guess a lot of women were jealous of Moira Granville. And suspicious, too. They didn't know anything about her family, about where she came from. In a small town, that's important. They investigated the heck out of her, and eventually they discovered something shocking. Apparently Dr. Granville had met his sublime young wife in a brothel in Boston.''

At Sarah's raised eyebrows, Parker chuckled. ''Yes, a brothel, where, by the way, an hour of her company had undoubtedly cost him considerably less than it did *after* the wedding.''

Sarah caught her breath. ''Oh, no,'' she said.

''Oh, yes. The judgmental old witches were furious. Jealousy happily switched to hatred, and Moira Granville was immediately ostracized.''

''How awful,'' Sarah said sadly. ''How cruel.''

''It's always struck me that way, too. But the women meant business. Have you ever noticed that half-painted ceiling in your uncle's house?''

Sarah sat up excitedly. ''Yes! Of course. But when I was here at thirteen, he said I was too young to hear the story of why it was never finished.''

Parker smiled. ''You *were*. Apparently the original Winter House wife came bursting into the parlor, frightening the poor artist half to death, demanding that he cease painting immediately. She was, by heaven, not going to live next door to a *whore*. She moved out the next day, and for thirty years the Granvilles lived in the Summer House alone, with only loggers and trappers and three empty mansions for neighbors.''

Sarah shook her head helplessly, almost unable to believe the story wasn't exaggerated, as legends often are. How unforgiving everyone had been! It felt almost shameful to be descended, however distantly, from such a judgmental woman. Sarah could only imagine the humiliation and loneliness the lovely Moira must have endured.

"Later, new, less finicky millionaires moved in— eventually even a descendent of that original outraged Mrs. Winters came back. There hasn't been a shortage of millionaires since." Parker laughed. "Now, as your uncle points out, the only problem is keeping them away."

But suddenly Sarah didn't feel like joining Parker's laughter. This was the other side of the small-town experience, the side she'd been forgetting. The narrow-mindedness, the prying eyes, the power to punish its members for sins real or imagined.

And how different was it in Firefly Glen today? Sarah had been here only a few weeks, but already she knew that the Glen was still essentially a small town, with both the small-town virtues—and the small-town vices.

Her uncle was open-minded and tolerant. But he was an acknowledged eccentric. What about the others? What about Theo Burke at the café, and the fussy, flowery Madeline Alexander? What about the mothers of the Firefly Girls, and the Daughters of the Revolution? What about the Junior League and the Altar Guild and the Garden Club?

What would happen when they found out that the newcomer, Sarah Lennox, was unmarried and pregnant and daring to date their darling favorite son, Sheriff Tremaine?

And at that moment, Sarah realized that she had been dreaming a dangerous dream. She had been dreaming that perhaps she could stay here, under the protective roof of her liberal-minded uncle, forever. She had been dreaming that this storybook town might embrace her, become her home.

And her child's home.

How ridiculous. She knew better. You couldn't hide from your problems forever, not even in Firefly Glen. She had to snap out of this daydream before it was too late.

Sensing that the rocking motion of the sleigh had ceased, Sarah looked up, trying to clear her mind. But her eyes were misty, as if the cold had stung them to tears.

"Sarah." Parker leaned over her, touching her face with soft leather-covered fingers. "You're awfully quiet. Are you all right?"

"I'm fine," she said, nodding firmly. But the motion caused the stinging tear to run down her cheek, where it instantly froze. "I'm fine. I'm just cold. It's getting colder, don't you think?"

"Maybe." Leaning across her, he pulled the largest, softest rug up, tucking it under her chin. He arranged her muffler so that it reached almost to her lower lip. Then he tugged down her white woolen hat, gently easing it so low on her forehead that her eyelashes brushed it when she blinked.

"Better?" he asked.

She nodded, watching him from her soft cocoon. His eyes were dark and soft, like moonlight. Yet deep in his gaze lay something else—something powerful but, for the moment, tightly leashed. It made her breath come shallow and fast to look at him.

"You're all eyes now," he said, slowly tracing the edges of her woolen hat, the rim of her muffler, with one gloved forefinger. Drawing a tingling line across the arch of her brow. "And they're so beautiful. All green-and-gold fire. I could lose myself in your eyes, Sarah."

She wondered if that were true, that her eyes were full of fire. She could feel something like that, deep in the pit of her stomach, something hot and sweet, like too much brandy.

"If you don't want me to kiss you, maybe you'd better say something now." He half smiled, but it had a ragged edge, as if it had been torn from something darker.

She was silent, except for her heart, which seemed to be drumming high in her throat. He drew closer. "Or now," he whispered, and his breath feathered out to brush against her cheek.

But she didn't say anything. And so, gently, he kissed her.

It should have been enough. That much would have been safe, or almost so. When her time in this enchanted village ended, she could take this one soft kiss with her as a reminder. A treasure pocketed against the poverty to come.

But let the kiss begin to burn—let it press and harden and catch fire—and it would no longer be mere memory. She would carry it forever as a scar.

She knew all that, and still she didn't stop him. She

let him take her into his arms, enfolding her with more rising, pulsing warmth than a thousand rugs of the finest wool. He groaned, low and hungry, and she answered with a small sound that would have been his name, except that, like a fire, he consumed the syllables before they could reach the air.

Oh, she was a fool, the worst kind of fool. But she no longer even wanted to resist. The magic of this winter night had crept inside her, filling her with hot, pointed stars and melting ice crystals of bliss.

Tomorrow, she thought hazily as she sank into the sweet heat of his lips. She would regret this tomorrow.

But tomorrow was on the other side of the stars, and it had no power here.

CHAPTER TEN

"SO WHAT DOES WARD THINK about you helping with the festival?" Madeline Alexander bit off the end of her white thread and started threading it expertly through the eye of her sharp silver needle. "Is he very angry with me for drafting you into the enemy camp?"

Sarah smiled. "He hasn't said much about it. He just commented once that it was a shame we were doing so much work for nothing, since there wasn't going to be any festival. He hasn't mentioned it since."

Sarah dug around on the sewing table, which was frothing with about fifty yards of white netting, fourteen bolts of cotton lace and nine spools of sequined ribbon. With any kind of luck, in three weeks this chaos would have become a dozen snowflake costumes for the Firefly Girls.

Right now, though, it was the hopeless mess in which she'd lost her scissors.

"Well, then I wonder why he hasn't come down to say hello?" Madeline cast another glance toward the staircase, which she'd been doing with increasing frequency over the past hour. "Are you *sure* he's not mad at me?"

Sarah was beginning to regret having agreed to let the troop leaders meet at Winter House. Madeline was doing very little sewing and a whole lot of mooning over Ward.

"I'm sure he'll be down later," she lied. Ward had told her he'd rather walk a tightrope naked over a crocodile pit than put one foot down those stairs while the Firefly Girl leaders were in the house. At least three of them, he said, had plans to chloroform him and drag him to an underground altar.

Finally having found her scissors, Sarah sat back and scanned the other women, wondering which three he meant. Madeline, of course. And maybe Bridget O'Malley, little Eileen O'Malley's grandmother—one of the most gorgeous sixty-year-old women Sarah had ever seen. She was about five-eleven and had eyes as green as shamrocks, dyed fire-red hair and a temper to match.

The third was probably Jocelyn Waitely, the hotel-owner's wife, though of course she'd have to divorce Bourke first. That little detail wouldn't stop her. Jocelyn was small and blond and smart enough to be darn dangerous. After knowing her only an hour, Sarah had decided she definitely wouldn't want to be standing between Jocelyn Waitely and whatever she wanted.

"Tell me, Madeline," Jocelyn said mildly, without looking up from the portable Singer she had set up on the parlor table. "Have you decided who you're going to vote for in March—Harry or Parker?"

Sarah's needle slipped, digging into the pad of her index finger. She whisked the finger away, popping it into her mouth before she could bleed on the white lace.

Looking up, she caught Jocelyn's sharp gaze on her, and she cursed her own clumsiness. Was she really so far gone that the mere mention of his name could make her twitch? Oh, brother. She was going to have to do better than this.

Madeline frowned over at her friend. "Parker, of course. Aren't you? It doesn't seem quite cricket, does it, for a man to run against his own brother-in-law?"

"I heard he may not still *be* his brother-in-law come March," Jocelyn said. Her tone was bland, but Sarah could see that her eyes were alight with an avid, rather unpleasant, curiosity. "He and Emma have split. I heard he moved out."

"That's just a temporary tiff, Jocelyn," Bridget O'Malley put in sternly. She had opinions as large and solid as she was herself. "Harry Dunbar and Emma Tremaine belong together, and they'll get over this. Everybody knows that."

This was news to Sarah. She and Emma and Heather had lunched together just two days ago, and, though Emma had seemed subdued, she hadn't mentioned anything as dramatic as a separation.

Of course, as much as Sarah liked Emma, she hardly qualified as an intimate of hers. Emma might well not talk of personal things around an outsider.

And Sarah was definitely still an outsider. She hadn't even known about the upcoming election. She wondered how Parker felt about it. He seemed so comfortable as sheriff, such a natural fit for the job. What would he do if Harry took that little gold star away from him?

"What does Parker think about it, Sarah?" Jocelyn's probing gaze was still on her. "Last night, when you two went to Lucky's, did he mention the election?"

Sarah stared stupidly. How did Jocelyn know that already? The Glen gossips obviously didn't work with anything as old-fashioned as grapevines. They must send their tidbits by fax.

She bent over her work, trimming a fluffy white-net skirt with silver sequins, cravenly glad to have something to look at other than Jocelyn's fox-sharp features.

"No," she said honestly. "He didn't."

"Oh." Jocelyn smiled. "I thought maybe he might have. After all, a sleigh ride is so cozy, isn't it? There's lots of time to talk...and so forth."

The other women must not have checked their fax machines this morning for the latest from the Glen Gossip Gazette. They seemed surprised. They closed in around her, or at least it felt that way, though no one actually moved. They peppered her with questions, determined to drag out every detail about anything as romantic as a sleigh ride.

For the next ten minutes, Sarah dodged questions that ranged from innocently curious to rudely speculative. She prayed she wouldn't blush. It was too soon to have to face such a grilling. She needed more time—time to think through what last night had really meant...to her, or to Parker.

And she definitely needed time to forget the feel of Parker's hot hands against her skin.

But somehow she managed to keep the details boringly generic enough: it had been quite cold; the pizza had been very good. Eventually the interest died down. Even Jocelyn seemed ready to move on to more fertile ground.

And then the doorbell rang.

Knowing that Ward would never let a mere doorbell lure him into the crocodile pit, Sarah got up to answer it. To her intense pleasure, followed by sinking dismay, it was Parker.

He looked wonderful. He was in civilian clothes, dark corduroy jeans and a black turtleneck that made his eyes blaze like blue fire. She felt herself flushing, weak-kneed all over again. Please, she prayed, don't let Jocelyn Waitely see her now. The gossip would race around and around the Glen, doubling over on itself, growing and swelling until it became a full-fledged scandal.

"Hi," she said, feeling ridiculously nervous. She hadn't slept with the man, for heaven's sake. She had just kissed him a few times after a pleasant evening out. They had been amazing kisses, yes. The kind that turned your legs to water and your mind to mush. But, as the song said, even a hot, mind-shattering kiss is just a kiss.

"Hi." He smiled.

The smile was enough to liquefy her bones all over

again. It was full of an intimate delight, as if they shared an intensely private and miraculous secret. Her insides did a tight, thrilling swoop under that look. She felt weightless and tingling, as if they had just joined hands and jumped off a very high diving board together.

As she fought to steady herself, she realized sadly that Ed had never looked at her that way. Not even after they had first made love. Not even when he had asked her to marry him. Not ever.

"Sarah," Parker said huskily, still smiling. "Kiss me."

She took a deep breath and fought the impulse to move toward him, mindlessly obeying both his words and her own body's primitive urgings.

"Don't be silly," she said in a half whisper, shaking her head firmly. "The house is full of people. The Firefly Girls troop leaders. They're probably all pressed against the parlor window right now, waiting to see what we do."

"So?" He tilted his head. The sun was bright today, and it caught one side of his face, illuminating his glossy black hair and sparkling on the clear blue of his eyes. "Kiss me. Let's give them something to talk about."

"They're already talking."

He didn't look impressed. "That's what bored old gossips do, Sarah. Let them." He took a step toward her. "I've waited twelve long hours to kiss you again, and I don't give a damn who sees me do it."

She resisted the urge to back up. "Perhaps not. But *I* do."

He stopped. "Oh." A muscle twitched in his jaw. "I see."

"Parker, I'm sorry. But I did tell you that I…" She lowered her voice. "I'm not ready to take on any emotional complications right now. I'm not ready to get involved with anyone. You knew that. Maybe I shouldn't have said yes to any date at all. But I thought you understood that it would just be as friends. Just for fun. Nothing…well, nothing serious. A few kisses can't change any of that."

While she talked, his smile had been sneaking back, one fraction of an inch at a time. "You sound as if you're working pretty hard to convince somebody of all that. Who, Sarah? Me? Or yourself?"

She forced herself to stand firm. "Both of us," she said with painful honesty. "I know we hadn't planned to end up…the way we ended up. I think it was just that everything had been so—oh, you know. The whole night had this strange kind of magic…. I know you didn't plan it that way."

He laughed. "Are you so sure? Maybe that's where I take all the dates I intend to seduce. Maybe after a romantic evening watching football at the Ucky Lounge, women are just putty in my hands."

Finally she had to smile, too. "I didn't mean Lucky's. I meant the whole package. The sleigh bells, the snow. The stars. The deer at the window. Even the way the sleigh rocked was…"

"Sexy?"

"Designed to throw us together." She shook her head, feeling again the searing awareness of his thigh sliding almost imperceptibly against hers as Dusty trotted unevenly down the fairy-lighted streets.

"It was like a conspiracy," she said. "On another night, with different weather, in a normal car, things would have been easier to control."

"Think so?" He grinned, as if she had provided the perfect opening. "Okay, we'll test that theory. As soon as I get back."

"Back?" The question didn't sound as casual as it should have. "Are you going somewhere?"

"That's what I came to tell you. I have to go to D.C. for four days. My ex-wife is having some legal problems, and she needs some advice."

Four days? That was a *lot* of advice. Somehow Sarah fought back the illogical twinge of jealousy she felt. Hadn't she just reminded Parker that she wasn't interested in him that way, that even last night's kisses had merely been the accidental by-product of a lethal concoction of sleigh bells and starlight?

So what difference did it make whether he spent four minutes or four days or four years with his ex-wife? None at all.

"That's nice of you," she said politely. "I hope it goes well."

"Me, too. But I'll be back on Friday, Sarah." He looked at her that way again, the way that made her weightless and falling, falling, falling.

"And Saturday night I'll take you on the most boring, completely unromantic date in the history of dating."

Still smiling, he leaned in and kissed her on the temple. He slid his lips lightly down to the flushing ridge of her cheekbone. For one, aching moment, his breath blew a soft warmth against her ear, sending white flashes of starlight through her veins.

"And then we'll see what happens."

"I DON'T FEEL LIKE being a Gravity Gladiator today," Emma whined as she looked over the menu at the Candlelight Café. "I feel like being a Calorie Coward. I say, open the floodgates! I'm going to have double-battered fish and French fries and a hot-fudge sundae. With *two* cherries."

Sarah and Heather exchanged a smile. Emma did this every time they got together. She always threatened to eat the most artery-clogging items on the menu, but when the moment of truth came, she ordered a salad. Heather said Emma was just letting off steam, so they never bothered to argue with her.

Today, though, she shocked them. When Theo came to their table, Emma ordered the fish and chips, extra tartar sauce, super-sized sundae on the side. Theo didn't bat an eyelash. She knew that in five-star restaurants the customer's choice was always the right choice.

But Heather had no such inhibitions. "That's about ten thousand calories, you know," she said when Theo had taken their menus and departed. "And about ten months off your expected life span."

Emma made a face. "Living forever is highly over-rated, especially if you can't have hot-fudge sundaes."

Heather's frown deepened. "Emma," she said quietly. "This won't help."

"Of course it will. I'll be in a carbo coma all afternoon, which will definitely help."

It was an uncomfortable moment. Obviously the two were communicating in some subtext that Sarah wasn't supposed to understand. Emma looked over at her guiltily, then seemed to come to a decision.

"Sorry, Sarah. We didn't mean to talk around you. It's just one of those boring personal problems, and I didn't want to monopolize lunch with it."

Sarah shook her head. "That's okay," she began.

"No, really. I want to tell you. You probably will hear about it before long, anyhow. The concept of privacy isn't recognized in the Glen."

Heather put her hand over Emma's supportively. Sarah could see that Emma's eyes were glittering, but she took a deep breath and when she spoke her voice was steady.

"Harry and I are going through a rough patch right now," she explained tersely. "So rough, in fact, that he moved out last week."

Sarah took Emma's other hand. "I'm so sorry," she said, aware of how useless the words were. "I'll bet he won't stay gone for long, though."

"Of course he won't." Heather looked fierce, and Sarah could tell how much she cared about her friend's happiness. "Harry can be a bullheaded mule sometimes, but he's not dumb. He'll be back.'' She lifted one eyebrow. ''Unless, of course, you eat ten thousand calories at *every* meal.''

Emma, flanked by support, seemed to gather strength. She gave a squeeze to her two hand-holders, then extricated herself and took a swig of white wine. ''Okay, ladies. This self-pity party is officially over. I don't want to talk about me. I want to talk about Sarah and Parker.''

Sarah froze, her water glass halfway to her mouth.

Emma grinned. ''Yes, my friend, the rumors are flying, but I don't know which ones to believe. Some people say you and Parker spent the night in the barn when you returned the horse to the Autumn House. Others say you just parked the sleigh in front of the Spring House for a couple of hours and did some heavy duty getting acquainted.''

Sarah sighed. But Emma wasn't finished.

She wiggled her eyebrows. ''Another rumor says you won five hundred dollars at Lucky's lap-dancing with the loggers before Parker got jealous and beat a bunch of them up.'' She turned to Heather. ''I don't believe that one, do you? Parker would get jealous long before that.''

Sarah covered her eyes with her hand. ''This is crazy,'' she said. ''One date. Just one innocent date. How can people read so much into so little?''

''It comes from living in the frozen North,'' Heather put in wryly. ''All those long winters with nothing to do, no one to talk to, nothing to think

about. Survival favors people with overactive imagi-
nations.''

"Well, that's what's happening here," Sarah said
emphatically. "We had one date. It was very nice,
but it was nothing worth gossiping about. We're
friends, that's all. Chances are we won't even go out
together again."

"Oh, yes, you will," Emma said. "Parker is already talking about it. Although I have to warn you,
it doesn't sound that great. He was pumping me for
ideas, and he wanted to know what some of my very
worst-ever dates had been.''

Theo arrived with the food, and Sarah busied herself tossing her chicken-breast salad carefully, cutting
up her meat into tiny chunks. She hoped Emma would
be distracted by her own high-calorie feast, which,
Sarah had to admit, looked fabulous.

But of course she couldn't be that lucky. Emma
went right back to the conversation, like a homing
pigeon.

"So I said to him, are you sure you wouldn't rather
hear about my *best* dates? But he said, no, he was
putting together the all-time most terrible date."

Heather was scowling at the greasy food, so Emma
stuffed a huge French fry into her mouth defiantly.
She wrinkled her nose at Heather before turning back
to Sarah. "The worst date ever? What gives with
that?''

"He's just pulling your leg," Sarah said. "It's just
this...this dumb joke."

"Well, I figured maybe he was kind of testing you

a little. Or maybe testing his own feelings. You know what I mean? I told you how hung up he is on finding the perfect woman. Well, maybe he's trying to be sure he's not reacting to the date itself, you know? Trying to be sure you're the perfect woman even if all the other conditions are awful.''

Heather made a scoffing sound. ''Of all the convoluted ideas you've ever come up with, Em, that may be the weirdest.''

But Sarah was amazed at how close to the truth Emma had actually come. She put down her fork.

''If that is what he's doing,'' she said, ''I could save him some time. I'm *not* the perfect woman. The perfect woman doesn't live a thousand miles away, for one thing. The perfect woman doesn't come with a lot of baggage, like an ugly engagement ended only weeks ago. The perfect woman doesn't come with…''

She caught Heather's eye across the table. But Heather had on her most professional face, and Sarah couldn't extract any guidance from her expression. She let her sentence disappear into a swallow of water.

Emma looked thoughtful. ''I don't know about all that,'' she said. ''The perfect man wouldn't be, as Heather so vividly put it, a bullheaded mule. The perfect man wouldn't be trying to steal your brother's job. The perfect man wouldn't pack his bags and move to a motel when the going gets rough. And yet Harry is definitely the perfect mule—I mean *man*—for me.''

Sarah stared at her friend. "This is different," she said helplessly.

"Maybe." Emma smiled. "But Parker doesn't think so."

PARKER PULLED HIS Jeep off the road, put the gear in neutral, yanked on the emergency brake and killed the engine.

"Here we are," he said, turning to Sarah with a poker face. "I hope you are good with a wheelbarrow."

Sarah wasn't quite sure how to react. The empty lot in front of them looked like the ruins of a bombed-out building. Several heavily bundled people were walking back and forth, doing something that looked a lot like dismantling the edifice.

"Our date is *here?*"

Parker surveyed the scene with a hint of smug satisfaction. "Right. I asked around and, working with details from several different sources, I put together a composite of the world's worst date."

She waited. He was enjoying himself thoroughly, and she found his amusement ridiculously cute.

"Here's how it goes. First, I make you do something only *I* care about—fix me dinner, clean out my garage, carry my golf clubs while I play eighteen holes, stuff like that. In this particular edition of The Date From Hell, I've brought you to the site where we usually put the ice castle for the festival. This year, we'd just begun to build the frame when the property owner decided to withdraw his permission to use the land.''

Oh, dear. Her instincts told her this involved Ward. She squeezed her eyes shut, hoping she was wrong. ''My uncle?''

''You guessed it. Anyhow, now we have seventy-two hours to clear our mess off his land. You get to help. But that's only part of our horrible date.''

She raised her eyebrows. ''There's more?''

''Yep. While you're getting bored and tired and dirty on my behalf, I spend most of my time talking to my friends, ignoring you. If I do talk to you, I talk only about myself. I drink too much and completely forget to feed you anything. Then I take you home and maul you like an animal, blindly assuming you've had as much fun as I have.''

She had to laugh. She'd had a couple of dates like that in her time. They were always first dates. And last.

''Okay,'' she said. ''That should definitely kill the magic.''

But it didn't.

The Date From Hell turned out to be even more fun than their first.

She loved his friends, who ranged from seventeen to seventy and who were unfailingly polite and welcoming to her. She loved hearing him talk to them, and she loved hearing him talk about himself. She learned more about Parker Tremaine in three hours out here than she had in the entire three weeks she'd been in Firefly Glen.

And she liked everything she learned. He was witty, self-effacing, hardworking and well liked. He gave credit to others, took very little for himself. He was quick, well-informed and tolerant. He didn't get annoyed when people around him messed up. He laughed off small mistakes, and he pitched in to help remedy big ones.

She couldn't have found a more striking contrast to Ed, with his petty, tyrannical perfectionism and his limitless ego.

She worked hard, but she didn't mind that. It was fun being part of a team, and everyone was eager to show her how to pull out nails safely, or how to stack broken boards so they wouldn't topple over. The hours flew by, and though she definitely got dirty, she couldn't say she ever got bored.

According to the bad-date rules, Parker couldn't feed her, but when the sun started to fall on the horizon, he quietly instructed someone else to bring her a thermos of soup and a mug of hot chocolate.

Plain food…but delicious. It was warm and salty, rich and nourishing.

She sat on a large red cooler, watching Parker over the rim of her steaming mug. He had taken off his jacket, hard work providing its own heat as he muscled a large plank of wood onto someone's truck.

He caught her watching him and, brushing his tousled hair back from his damp brow, he smiled.

Oh, that smile, she thought with a sinking sense of doom. He didn't need romance and music and starlight, did he? He had that smile, and it warmed her from head to toe, in spite of the snow that had just begun to fall around them.

A few minutes later, he came over and sat down on the cooler next to her, a thermos of coffee in his hand. "We're going to have to call it a day soon," he said, gazing up into the darkening sky. "Because of the snow."

He tugged off his work gloves with his teeth, then turned to her. "You okay?"

She sipped her chocolate to hold back a grin. "Hey. That's against the rules. You're not supposed to care."

He shook his head helplessly, then he reached out and pulled free a strand of hair that had been caught on her cheek. "Maybe not," he said softly, tucking the hair behind her ear. "But I'll be damned if I can stop myself."

She opened her mouth, ready to offer a flip rejoinder, but she found herself without words. Gazing into his tired, dirty face, she realized that Parker Tremaine was a far greater threat than she had ever imagined.

Oh, she had known from the start that his sex appeal was nearly lethal. She had expected resisting him to be a challenge. Later, when they were alone, the sparks between them might flare up again, creating a fire that would be difficult to douse.

That would have been trouble enough. For a woman in her condition, falling in lust with this man, with *anyone,* would be vulgar and stupid. Unthinkable.

So she had given herself an ultimatum. Resist him,

or tell him it's over. If she succumbed to even one of those dangerous kisses, she would end it here, tonight.

But suddenly, as if she had been running through a field that abruptly ended, just beyond the tips of her toes, in a sheer free fall down an open cliff, she saw the much greater danger.

And she knew she had to end it anyhow.

Falling in lust was the least of her worries.

She was in danger of falling in *love*.

CHAPTER ELEVEN

AS PARKER DROVE toward Winter House, he wondered whether maybe he'd gone a little too far with this Date From Hell business.

Although Sarah had entered into the day with a willing tongue-in-cheek enthusiasm, for the past hour or so she had been polite but stilted, growing more and more subdued. Hell, ever since they got in the car, she'd been practically mute.

He backtracked over the afternoon, wondering when the change had hit her. Had someone offended her? Had he said something stupid?

Maybe she was just tired. She had worked too hard. She couldn't be used to that kind of bruising labor, especially at these altitudes.

He glanced at her out of the corner of his eye as he steered his Jeep toward her uncle's house. She did look pale, with smudges of exhaustion under her eyes. He was reminded suddenly of how weak and vulnerable she had looked that first day, on the mountaintop, leaning up against a tree, as if she needed its strength to help her stand.

For a dreadful moment, he wondered if she might be sick. Really sick. But Ward would have told him, wouldn't he? And most of the time she was so glowing and sensual, he couldn't take the idea of illness very seriously.

Probably, like a fool, he had just let her wear herself out.

He pulled into the driveway of Winter House and stopped the car. Sarah looked so far away over there in her bucket seat, with the gearshift sticking up between them like some chrome-plated techno-chaperone.

Suddenly he wished he had the damn sleigh back. He clearly had been too cocky, believing he could make magic for her without any romantic bells and whistles. Sarah didn't look like a woman caught in anybody's magic spell tonight. She looked tired and remote and—just his luck—still so desirable he could hardly breathe.

He would have given every penny in his pocket for one lousy trickle of starlight.

He reached over and gently tugged a wood shaving from her hair. He ran the back of his finger along her cheek. "Tired?"

"A little," she said quietly. "I guess I should go in."

He wanted so much to take her in his arms. Damn these intrusive gear shifts. Who had invented them? The Society for the Protection of American Virgins?

"Sarah," he said, letting his finger touch the corner of her mouth. "Sarah, look at me."

"I have to go in," she said, still in an exhausted monotone. "Maybe we should wait and talk tomorrow."

He leaned over, ignoring the bite of the gearshift into his side. He put his finger under her chin and turned her face toward him. She did look sick, he thought suddenly. She was in some kind of trouble, some kind of pain.

"Sarah. Sweetheart. Tell me what's wrong."

"Nothing's wrong," she said, and for a minute she rallied. She turned the corners of her mouth up, as if she were a puppet controlled by strings. It was sweet, but it damn sure didn't feel real. He preferred no smile at all to that saccharine pretense.

"Honestly, nothing is wrong. It's just that I..." She swallowed and started over, doing a little better with the smile this time. "I had a lovely time today, Parker. I always have fun when I'm with you. But, even so, I think we should stop seeing each—"

She never finished the sentence. From the direction of Winter House, a loud, smashing noise exploded into the quiet evening air. It was the sound of glass shattering. And it was followed by the rapid pounding of someone's footsteps running across the hard snow of the estate's grounds.

"Oh, my God!"

Though Sarah looked immediately toward the house, Parker's gaze flew instinctively toward the running footsteps, just in time to see a hooded figure fleeing into the dark stand of trees.

"My uncle!" With one hand, Sarah was shoving open the car door, the other pulling frantically to release her seat belt. Parker reached over, flipped her belt open, then addressed his own.

Reluctantly he abandoned any thought of chasing the hooded figure. He couldn't let Sarah go up to the house alone, not knowing what she would find inside. What if the fleeing man hadn't been the only one here?

So the two of them raced up to the big front door alone. Parker was dialing 911 on his cell phone. Sarah already had her key out and, in spite of her obvious anxiety, her fingers didn't fumble. As the door swung open, she was already calling, "Uncle Ward! Uncle Ward! Where are you? Are you all right?"

They found him in the library, which was growing very cold as the evening wind blew snow in through the large, star-shaped hole in the beautiful stained-glass window. A small white layer of powder already dusted the dark green leather top of the library table.

Parker scanned the scene quickly. Ward lay in a tangle on the carpet, pieces of gold and red glass rayed out around him. A deep, ugly cut on his forehead was oozing blood that had reached the floor and was mingling with the intricate flowers of the Oriental rug.

Frosty sat by his shoulder, obeying his guard dog instincts, but the frightened puppy in him was whimpering softly and shaking all over.

When he saw Sarah, Frosty ran to her, ears flopping. She scooped him up, murmuring comfort, and held him tightly as she rushed to her uncle's side.

It didn't take long for Parker to size up what had happened. Just beyond Ward's head, a large rock lay near the carved leg of the table. It had clods of frozen dirt stuck to it, obviously having been dug recently, probably from the Winter House grounds. It was roughly the size and shape of a football, though distorted with sharp, jagged edges. A piece of paper had been tied around the rock with a rubber band, and big black letters had been scrawled on the paper.

"Butt out, Grinch. Leave our festival alone," it said.

Parker wasn't surprised. He had been afraid something like this might happen if Ward persisted in his sabotage of the festival.

It probably hadn't been intended as a physical attack, but with horrible, blind accuracy, and the world's worst luck, whoever had lobbed this rock through the stained-glass window had hit Ward Winters on the head, hit him hard enough to knock him from the chair where he'd been reading.

Parker bent over Ward, checking his pulse. *Thank God.* It was faint but steady. Sarah had set Frosty down and was kneeling on the other side of her uncle, brushing away enough blood to get a good look at the size of the cut. Parker heard her abrupt inhale, and he knew it must be deep.

She cradled her uncle's head in her lap, elevating it to slow the bleeding. She turned dark eyes toward Parker. "Can you get me a clean cloth from the kitchen? Something I can hold against this? Please. I don't want to leave him."

Parker was on his feet before she finished her question. "I'll be right back," he said. "I've already called the medics, so if you hear someone at the door, don't worry. I'll let them in.''

He was almost certain no one else was in the house. The hole in the window was too jagged and awkwardly placed for anyone to have entered there, and all other points of entry seemed secure. Plus, his instincts told him this was merely a threat. It was a coward's trick, that nasty little note wrapped around an anonymous missile. The imbecile who had thrown it was undoubtedly the same punk Parker had seen scuttling into the woods.

Still he quickly checked rooms as he passed on the way to the kitchen. Everything looked normal.

By the time he got back with the cloth, he heard two very welcome sounds—the crunch of the ambulance pulling up the driveway, and the loud, fussy rumble of Ward's voice complaining that he was perfectly fine, leave him alone, for God's sake.

Parker pulled open the door, motioning the medics to come in, and then he led the way to the library, where Ward was now sitting up in the upholstered armchair nearest to the table. Blood was dripping down over his eye, but that didn't keep him from looking as energetically bad tempered as usual.

He glared at Parker and the medical technicians as they entered the library.

''Damn it, it's just a little nick. Who the hell called in the army?''

Sarah put her hand on her uncle's shoulder. ''Uncle Ward, calm down. They're just going to take you to the hospital—''

"The hell they are!" Ward lunged forward, but was held in place by Sarah's restraining hand and, probably, his own discomfort. "I'm not going anywhere."

Parker handed the clean cloth to the older man.

"You know, Ward," he observed placidly. "I think your brains may have fallen out of that gash on your head. You're talking like an idiot."

Ward chuckled, then grimaced as the motion clearly caused pain. "Insult me all you like, Sheriff. This is my home, and I'm not going to be driven out of it by any rock-tossing jackass."

The arguments took forever. The debate was far from balanced, with Parker, Sarah and the two medics on one side, and Ward alone on the other. But in the end they compromised—as Parker could have predicted they would—by letting Ward win. He would not be going to the hospital.

He did agree to let a doctor come to the house and stitch him up. Parker arranged that, and while he was out of the room, he also called Harry. He told the deputy what had happened, then gave him a few fairly simple instructions: catch the vandal, and catch him tonight.

Two hours later, the doctor finally had Ward back in one piece, though it had taken eleven stitches to do it. Ward also had several bruises, and a sprained elbow, which he'd fallen on as he tumbled from the chair. Somehow, using all her persuasive skills, Sarah had coaxed her uncle into bed, though he had expressed a strong desire to storm out into the night, find the stone-throwing jerk and teach him a lesson.

But Sarah had deposited Frosty on the bedspread beside her uncle, and that had done the trick. Ward was a fool for the puppy already, and Sarah had warned Parker that Frosty probably wouldn't be moving out of Winter House any time soon. Which was fine with Parker. One puppy was enough to handle.

And anyhow, it was starting to look as if Ward might be better off with a dog in the house.

While Sarah had been tending Ward, Parker had cleaned up the broken glass. He found some large pieces of heavy cardboard and taped them over the hole in the library window. He wondered if the moron who threw that rock realized how expensive a stained-glass window like this was to replace. This wasn't like scrawling something rude on a bathroom stall, which could be erased or painted over. This was big-time vandalism, and there would be hell to pay.

"He's asleep." Sarah's voice came from behind him. She sounded exhausted.

With a sigh, she plopped onto the library sofa. She had bloodstains on her white sweater, and blue circles under her eyes. She looked even more tired than she sounded.

"Thank you, Parker," she said, smiling over at him with obvious effort. "I don't know what I would have done without you here."

"I'm glad I was." Parker set the tape down on the refectory table and came over to join her on the sofa. He unbuttoned her sweater, helped her ease it off and, folding it up so that the bloody stains didn't show, tossed it aside.

He gathered her into his arms and held her close, rubbing his hands along her arms to keep her warm. The library was still half-freezing.

"You should go to bed now, too," he said.

"I can't." It was a clue as to how exhausted she was that she didn't try to pull away from his embrace. He was well aware she had decided to put an end to whatever had been developing between them. "I have to check on him every two hours. The doctor suspects a concussion."

"You sleep. I'll do the checking," Parker said, resting his cheek against her hair. The motion pressed her head onto his chest. She didn't resist that, either. "I'm planning to stay down here tonight, anyhow. Just in case the fool who did this gets any more dumb ideas."

She shook her head, but there was almost no force behind it. "I can't let you do that. You've done too much already."

"It's my job," he said softly. "Protect and defend, all that stuff. Besides, I want to. He may be your uncle, but he's my friend, too."

"What about Snowball? He's been alone all day."

"No, he hasn't. While you were up with Ward, I called Emma. She's going to take him home with her. She adores him. I think she'd secretly like to steal him from me anyhow."

He felt her lips curve up in a smile, though she didn't move a muscle. "We'll do it together, then," she said. "I'll stay down here, too, and we'll take turns."

He shook his head. "It's too cold for you, with the window broken. Too uncomfortable. You'll get sick."

"I never get sick," she said sleepily. "It'll be fine. It'll be like camping out. I could light a fire."

Yes, he thought, looking down at her graceful curves, folded like a butterfly up against him. She certainly could.

But he resisted the urge to follow that train of thought. He looked around the room. The sofa near the fireplace was roomy, overstuffed and covered with pillows and soft satin throws. He might be able to make it comfortable enough.

He sighed and gave up. It was too tempting to resist.

"All right. But I will take the first shift. That's not negotiable."

She nodded, her head moving softly against his shirt. "Yes, Sheriff."

"And you have to promise me that you'll get some sleep."

But there was no answer to that. He felt the butterfly softness of her body go limp, relaxing against him in utter innocence.

She was already asleep.

SARAH WOKE SLOWLY, registering where she was with her senses rather than with her mind.

The sweet-ash smell of wood burning. She was

close to a fire, so close she could see its amber shadows dancing against her eyelids. So close she could hear the hiss and simmer of the logs as tongues of fire licked them.

She was in the library. But why, and why was it so chilly? She burrowed deeper into the warm comfort of satin wrapped tightly around her body. It was warm in here, but out there, beyond the satin, it was not. Her cheeks and ears were tight with cold.

She opened her eyes, peeking at the fire between her lashes, wondering if the heater was broken.

And then she remembered. Her uncle. The smashed window. Parker.

She sat up, holding the comforter around her shoulders. The fire provided the only light in the room, but it was enough. She found Parker easily. He was dozing on the Queen Anne armchair, his feet stretched out, long and graceful and utterly still, toward the fire.

She rubbed her eyes hard, wondering how long she had been asleep. Had she missed her turn to check on Ward? Carefully, so that she wouldn't disturb Parker, she eased out of the tangled comforter and stood, hoping her socks would muffle her footsteps. He must need sleep desperately. She certainly had.

But Parker wasn't sleeping. As soon as she moved toward the door, he opened his eyes. "It's all right," he said quietly. "I checked on him an hour ago."

She stopped beside him. "Is he okay? Did you wake him? The doctor said we have to make sure he's coherent, and that his eyes are focusing correctly."

Parker raised his eyebrows without lifting his head.

"Oh, I woke him, all right. The first two times he was almost civil. This last time, he suggested—perfectly coherently—that I should pay a visit to the devil."

He shut his eyes again. "By the way, he said if we wake him one more time tonight, he's going to shoot us."

Sarah chuckled. "He probably won't, though."

"No," Parker agreed, smiling. "Probably not."

Sarah checked her watch, squinting at it in the volatile orange firelight. To her surprise it was almost five in the morning. It would be dawn soon.

"I must have missed my turn more than once," she said guiltily. "I'm sorry about that."

"I'm not." Parker opened his eyes and looked at her appraisingly. "You look much better now. You needed the sleep."

That probably was true. The drama of the evening had been exhausting, and Heather had warned her that the baby might sap her strength a little, leaving her more easily tired than usual.

She put her hand to her stomach instinctively.

But Parker was watching her, his eyes unreadable in the strange, shifting light from the fire. Suddenly self-conscious, Sarah tugged her shirt a little farther down over her jeans, as if it might be possible for someone else to recognize the slight swell of her waistline.

It wasn't possible, of course. Not yet. She couldn't even see it herself, not by looking in the mirror. It was only when she ran her hand over her stomach that she sensed something different. Something new.

Still she felt vulnerable. She crossed her arms against the sudden cold that slipped through Parker's cardboard shield.

"It will be light soon," she said. "No one is going to come back and cause trouble now. Why don't you go on home and get some real sleep?"

The fidgety restlessness that had come over her didn't seem to have affected him at all. He sat in complete repose. He hadn't taken his eyes away from her.

"Is that what you want?" He spoke without pressure, as if whatever she answered would be all right. "Do you want me to leave?"

It seemed ungrateful to say yes, after all he had done for her. How could she explain that his presence here, in the notoriously weak willed hours before dawn, felt somehow dangerous?

"It's just that I want you to get some sleep," she equivocated. "And trying to sleep here doesn't seem very…"

"I won't be able to sleep at home, either," he said gently. "Either place, I'm just going to lie awake. I'm just going to lie there thinking how much I want to make love to you."

She turned her head away. "Parker. Don't."

"Why not?" He reached his hand out and captured hers. Gently he tugged her toward the armchair, until her thighs were pressed against the upholstered arm.

She tried to pull away, but he held her easily.

Slowly he fingered the palm of her hand in a subtle massage. He tilted his head, as if reading her response to the touch.

"Why are you fighting this so hard, Sarah? You know you feel it, too. Would it be so awful if we just let it happen?"

She breathed hard, concentrating on ignoring his clever fingers. "I told you. I can't get involved right now. Just a month ago I—"

"I know. You were engaged to another man. You might be on the rebound. The timing is terrible. Okay, let's say all that is true. What should you do, lock yourself in a deep freeze until the appropriate amount of time has passed? What is the acceptable mourning period for a bad engagement, anyhow? Two months? Six months? A year?"

He shook his head. "I can't wait a year, Sarah. I won't."

"It's not just the engagement," she said, knowing that he wasn't going to give up this time, not until he pushed her all the way, right to the final, fatal admission. "It's much, much more complicated than that."

"What?" Narrowing his eyes, he sat up a little straighter. "You're not still in love with—what was his name, anyhow? You never told me his name."

"Ed." She half swallowed the syllable. "His name is Ed McCutcheon."

"Ed." He repeated the word with clipped distaste. "Okay. You're not still in love with Ed, are you? You can't be. The way you kissed me..."

"No." She looked down at their hands. She was

holding on so tightly, as if he were the only thing that kept her grounded. She realized how easy it would be to come to count on that hand. To believe it really could save her from danger. It couldn't, of course. Because *he* was the danger.

"No," she repeated numbly. "I'm not in love with Ed anymore. I'm not sure I ever was. Not really."

He took a deep breath. "Okay. Good. Then whatever it is, we can get through it." He leaned toward her, running his other hand along her arm, up to the elbow. The touch sent shivers through her from shoulder to toe.

"We can make this work, Sarah. I know we can. You just have to give it a chance."

"You don't understand. That's still not all." She continued to stare at their hands, at his strong fingers wrapped around her fragile wrist. "I never loved Ed. But I *made love* to him, Parker."

He made a low, furious sound. "Do you think I give a damn about that?"

"Yes. I think you will. Because I may not love Ed McCutcheon, but I am going to have his child."

She finally looked up at him, at his blank and staring eyes. "It's true, Parker," she said softly. "I'm pregnant."

CHAPTER TWELVE

SARAH HAD NEVER SEEN a living hand so still. Not even her uncle's hand earlier tonight, when he had lain unconscious and bleeding on the floor. Parker's hand was more like that of a painted statue. Even the fitful firelight couldn't give it the illusion of life.

She pulled her own hand free of the frozen fingers and turned away. She wasn't disappointed, not really. Because she had always known it would be like this. She had always known that Parker's interest in her couldn't survive the truth. She hadn't ever allowed herself to hope.

Not really.

"So now you see why I've been trying to avoid any new complications." Rather than look at his stunned, expressionless face, she busied herself folding up the satin comforter that had cocooned her just moments ago.

She plumped and settled the pillows, until no one could have guessed she had ever been there. "Obviously I can't even think about starting a new relationship right now. I have to concentrate on the baby, on getting my life back in order."

And, as she said the words, she realized that they were absolutely true. She needed a new plan. A new, detailed life plan, to replace the one that had been tossed in the trash can, along with all the little pink *x*'s.

Yes, a new plan right away: that was the answer. Without a plan, she had been like a ship without a rudder, and any wind had been able to blow her off course. This one had blown her into Parker Tremaine's path, and straight toward a collision of the heart.

"But why didn't you tell me about this sooner?" Parker's voice was strangely rough. "God, Sarah. Why didn't you tell me right away?"

Was he angry? Surely he wouldn't dare. What right did he have to be angry? It was he who had pushed this relationship. She had always hung back, insisting that it must not, could not, be.

She turned and looked at him. "Because I wasn't ready to talk about it to anyone," she said stiffly. "Because it wasn't any of your business."

He frowned hard, a straight line driving like a gash between his brows. "It wasn't," he repeated slowly, "any of my business?"

She stood very straight. "No. It wasn't."

They stared at each other across the cold room, the silence somehow just as unpleasant as a quarrel would have been. Perversely, part of her wanted to quarrel. At least then she could release some of this emotion pressing against her chest. It was such an unbearable weight, as if the burden of losing him were something physical she would now have to carry from place to place, like a rock.

But that was ridiculous. *Losing* him? How could you lose something you never had?

"I'm going to check on my uncle now," she said, picking up her bloodstained sweater. She didn't even remember taking it off. "I do thank you for all your help tonight, Parker. You know the way out, so—"

Suddenly there was a rapping on the front door. Sarah's breath stalled, and she realized that she must be even more unnerved by the night's events than she had understood.

And why shouldn't she be? Her uncle had enemies out there, hiding in the freezing black shadows.

All at once, she was intensely aware of how odd this mansion was, how isolated and deep an Adirondack winter could be. And she realized that, if Parker hadn't been in the room with her, she might have felt true fear.

Ashamed of what seemed a foolish weakness, she tried to mask her thoughts. She didn't want him to think her a coward. She *wasn't* a coward.

She lifted her chin and made a motion toward the hall. But Parker was already standing.

"I'll answer it," he said firmly. "You stay here in the library."

She obeyed, but she followed him as far as the doorway. She needed to see who it was.

It was Parker's deputy sheriff, Harry Dunbar. And he was holding someone else by the scruff of the neck. A teenage boy, it seemed. Sarah edged forward. Yes, a nice-looking teenage kid. Dressed all in black, but red faced and miserable.

"Here's your criminal," Harry Dunbar was saying. He sounded disgusted. "Although why I should have to drag my ass out of bed in the middle of the night to track down a stupid punk like this..."

Parker was shaking his head. "Mike? I can't believe it. Of all the people I expected to see—"

"God, Sheriff. I'm sorry." The kid's voice was terrified. He ran his hands through his dark hair over and over, as if he wanted to pull it straight out of his head. "I'm so sorry. I didn't mean to hurt anybody, honest I didn't. I did it for Justine. For her father. I was just supposed to send the message—"

"Shut up, Frome." Parker sounded as tough as nails, completely unmoved by the misery before him. "I don't want to hear any excuses out of you. There is no excuse. Blaming other people isn't going to help. You're in more trouble than you have ever seen in your whole sorry life, buster."

"What do you want me to do with him?" Harry still had hold of Mike Frome's jacket collar, which forced the kid to bend over at a strange, tangled-puppet angle.

"I'll take him," Parker said tersely.

He looked back at Sarah, who was still standing in the doorway, wondering how on earth this apparently nice, normal teenage boy could have done so much damage here tonight, and why?

"I have to go back to the department," Parker said. "We'll have to sort this out—talk to Mike's parents, for starters." The kid groaned, but Parker didn't so much as blink in reaction. "It'll take a while. Will you be all right?"

She nodded. "We're fine," she said carefully.

He paused, and she could tell that he wanted to say more but was constrained by the presence of Harry and the boy Mike.

"I'll call you later," Parker said finally. "About how Ward is doing. And about—that other matter."

That other matter. She shook her head. "No, that's not necessary. You'll be busy. And I think we've really discussed it pretty thoroughly."

"No, we haven't," Parker said grimly as he grabbed the boy's arm and steered him toward the waiting car. "Not even close."

HE DIDN'T CALL THAT DAY, or the next.

At least not to talk to her. He talked to Ward several times, updating him on the investigation into poor, red-faced Mike Frome. But he never asked to speak to Sarah, and of course she wouldn't have dreamed of asking to speak to him.

What would have been the point?

Mostly, Sarah tried not to think about it. And for the most part she was successful. She was busy, and that helped. The news about her uncle had gone out with the speed of a microchip, and as soon as the sun was fully up, Madeline Alexander had come bustling into the Winter House, eager to play Florence Nightingale. Ward was a terrible patient, crotchety and demanding. It took both of them to keep him placated and in bed.

And then there was the matter of replacing the broken window, which required hiring glaziers to put in a temporary glass, and a dozen calls to artisans around the country, requesting bids for a new design. The estimated price was in the thousands, and in spite of herself Sarah felt sorry for the teenager who had made such a costly mistake.

On the third day, she found a flyer shoved through the Winter House mail slot, alerting everyone to an emergency session of the Firefly Glen City Council, that night at seven o'clock. Final Festival Vote: Cancel or Continue? it read. No further details were provided.

Sarah didn't show it to her uncle until almost seven o'clock, fearing that he would insist on attending. The doctor had told him to keep calm and close to home for at least a week. But to her surprise, Ward merely snorted when he read the flyer, crumpled it into a ball and lobbed it into the nearest trash can.

"Let them meet until they're blue in the face," he said, turning his attention back to the chessboard, which Sarah had transplanted to Ward's bedroom. "Those morons at City Hall can't regulate Ward Winters into submission."

He looked up and grinned as he captured one of Sarah's pawns. Frosty, who sat next to him on the bed, grinned, too, his tongue hanging out cheerfully.

"I am far too clever and devious for them." Ward puffed out his chest and leaned back against his pillows. "I am an outlaw now, my child. I live by a different code. Like Zorro."

Sarah responded by taking her uncle's bishop. "And what code would that be? Do we find it in the *Mischief Maker's Manual? The Gray Panther Guerilla Guidebook?*"

He frowned, then leaned forward to study the board grumpily. "We don't find it in *Make Anyone Do Anything—A Primer of Persuasion,* that's for sure."

Sarah looked up, startled.

"Didn't know I knew about that, did you?" Ward looked extremely self-satisfied. His bandage, which angled over his right eye from his hairline to his temple, merely intensified his rogue charm. "I guess you and your beloved sheriff aren't quite as clever as you think, isn't that right, Short Stuff?"

Sarah almost fell for it. She almost jumped in with a denial. *He's not my beloved sheriff.* But she caught herself in the nick of time. Ward was just fishing for an excuse to open that topic again. She wasn't going to give it to him.

"That's right," she agreed evenly, moving her queen two spaces to the right. "But you may not be, either. I think that's check, Mr. Zorro, sir."

Ward didn't like to lose, so after that he concentrated harder on the game. He had finally escaped her clutches, regrouped and managed to turn the tables when Madeline, who had been downstairs puttering around in the kitchen, suddenly showed up in the doorway.

"Parker is here to see you, Ward," she said. Though she was dressed as cheerfully as ever in a pattern of fluffy pink peonies, she looked nervous.

She twisted a blue dish towel tightly between her hands. "He says he has news from the meeting. Shall I show him up?"

Sarah glanced at her uncle. He appeared completely serene, pulling slowly and rhythmically on Frosty's ears, sending the puppy into a trance of joy.

He moved his knight. "Sure. We're through here." He gave Sarah a smug smile. "Checkmate."

When Sarah made a motion to stand, Ward stopped her. "I might need you," he said with a plaintive tone that Sarah recognized as one hundred percent fraudulent. He touched his bandage pitifully. "In case I feel faint."

Sarah gave him a dirty look, but she sat back down. She could hear Parker's footsteps in the hall. It was already too late to escape.

Ward apparently needed only one glimpse of Parker's face to guess the outcome of the meeting.

"They're going ahead with it, aren't they?" With a low curse, he collapsed back against the carved headboard of his bed. The drapes of the canopy cast his face in shadows, but the annoyance in his voice was crystal clear.

Parker nodded. He seemed unfazed by such an unconventional greeting. "Hi, Sarah," he said politely. Then he turned toward the older man. "Of course they are, Ward. The vote was unanimous."

"Those greedy morons." Ward growled. Frosty looked up at him quizzically, thumping his tail. "I can't believe it."

"Why not?" Without waiting for an invitation,

Parker sat on one of the armchairs near the fireplace. "You didn't think a few pranks could destroy a tradition that's almost a hundred years old, did you? They held the festival the year spring came early, melting the ice castle faster than they could build it. They held it right after the blizzard of '33 killed more than thirty Glenners. They held it during the Depression. They held it during the war." He smiled gently. "Did you really think you could stop it?"

Ward was silent a moment, his fingers fidgeting irritably with the fine Egyptian cotton bedclothes. "Where are they going to put the castle?"

"In the square. It will have to be smaller, of course. Medford is going to draw up new plans tonight."

"The decorated sleigh parade?"

"Those who have privately owned sleighs will use those. The rest will make do. Cars, sleds, trucks. Whatever."

"What about Bourke Waitely?"

Parker hesitated for the first time. "Reservations at the hotel are down by fifty percent. Not much the city council could do about that. Looks as if he's going to lose a lot of money."

Ward laughed. "Well. At least there's that."

"Yep. There's that. You annoyed the heck out of Bourke, Ward. Congratulations. And it only cost you...what? Ten grand and a busted head?"

"It was worth it," Ward said acidly. "Meddling old bastard."

Sighing, as if he gave up on the whole thing, Parker

stood. "I need to get going. Sarah, any chance I could talk to you for a minute?"

She looked at her uncle, who didn't seem as distressed as she had expected by Parker's news. Had he known all along that the festival would survive his attacks? Or did he have something else up his sleeve?

"Didn't you hear the sheriff, Sarah?" Amazingly, Ward's voice was as mischievous as ever. "He wants to talk to you."

"I'd better not leave you," she said sweetly. She touched her forehead. "You know. In case you feel faint."

"I'm much better now," Ward said irritably, pulling Frosty closer and stroking him, as if to say that at least *someone* in the room was sweet and agreeable. "Parker, take Sarah away. Clumsy, ungrateful sarcasm makes my stitches hurt."

PARKER LET SARAH LEAD the way. On the surface, she appeared completely composed. She walked smoothly down the wide staircase in front of him, her slim hand pale but steady on the banister. Her hair was tied back neatly with a green ribbon that matched perfectly the green wool dress she wore.

But he knew she was edgy. He could see it in the tight set of her jaw.

It was ironic, wasn't it, that he could read her so well after such a short acquaintance? Ironic, too, that he found the simple, tailored green dress on Sarah sexier than the skimpiest lingerie would be on any other woman?

Yes, it was ironic, all right. In a hundred ways she seemed to be the perfect woman. The one he'd been looking for, dreaming of, ever since the fiasco with Tina.

They could still hear Madeline in the kitchen, so Sarah turned left. She avoided the library, too, though they passed right by it. Instead she took him to Ward's personal den, a small room with an alcove formed by the square front bay window.

During the day, Parker knew, that alcove was brilliant with a gold and green light, which streamed in through the stained glass panes. At night, though, the windows were black, and the only illumination in the room came from several small Tiffany-style reading lamps.

He knew she had chosen this room for privacy, and because it was as close to the front door as she could get without actually throwing him out of the house. He felt her tension growing by the second. This was going to be a tricky conversation. He hoped he could find the right words to say what he needed to say.

"My uncle tells me that he isn't going to press charges against the boy who broke the window." Sarah had started talking even before they were fully in the room, obviously rushing into a topic that would keep the conversation safely impersonal. "I'm not sure I understand why."

"I'm not sure I do, either. Mike Frome could use a good scare. He says he threw that rock because he thought it would impress his girlfriend, Justine. She's Mayor Millner's daughter. The mayor's whole family

is furious that Ward has tried to sabotage the festival.
I guess they like the idea of ruling an ever-expanding
kingdom.''

Sarah frowned. ''So Mike thought what? That a
little vandalism would enhance his stock with this
Justine?''

''Apparently. And the worst part is, I think maybe
he was right.''

''Sounds as if Mike could use a different girlfriend.''

''Definitely.'' Parker sighed. ''Or a couple of days
in court. Ward likes Mike, though. We all do. Maybe
that's part of the problem. We've always cut the kid
a lot of slack.'' He shrugged. ''So anyhow, Ward is
going to make Mike work off the window, but otherwise his record will still be clean.''

She nodded. She stood awkwardly in front of
Ward's big floor globe. Parker thought he could
safely assume that she'd rather be anywhere on that
globe right now than here in this room with him.

She seemed to be out of small talk. She looked at
him, and she swallowed, squaring her jaw even further.

''Listen, Parker, maybe I should start. I want you
to know that you don't need to feel uncomfortable
around me. I know you're not interested in getting
mixed up in anything this complicated. I never expected you to. You're a very nice man, but please,
don't worry about how you're going to explain it to
me. I already understand.'' She smiled. ''And it's really okay.''

He looked at her, helplessly caught in an inner debate. He ought to just nod his head and walk out of here. He'd spent two whole days trying to persuade himself to do exactly that.

Because Sarah Lennox was *not* the perfect woman. Not even close.

And he knew from experience how miserable two badly matched people could make each other. He knew that once the initial fog of sexual chemistry burned off, all the molehill flaws in the relationship stood out like mountains.

He wasn't going to do that again. He'd rather be single forever. That was a simple, unchangeable fact.

And yet he couldn't walk out of here right now.

That was a fact, too.

He couldn't explain it, but something in Sarah spoke to him. Maybe her beautiful face, or her gorgeous body. Maybe her passionate empathy for the underdog, or her stubborn loyalty to her uncle. Maybe the way she made friends everywhere, whether it was with boozing loggers, gossiping matrons or his own insufferable sister. Maybe her Madonna grace when she cradled a sleepy puppy, or her circus-clown clumsiness when she crawled, laughing and unashamed, toward him across the ice.

Which was all probably just another way of saying that Sarah Lennox was full of love, and full of life. Was it any wonder that her amazing vitality had found a physical expression? Could he really be surprised that someone so brimming with life was in the process of creating life, as well?

"I need to ask you two questions," he said. "If you don't want to answer them, you don't have to. But I have to ask."

She looked at him, a question in her hazel eyes. "All right," she said.

"Do you still love the father of this child?"

She lifted her chin. "No. I already told you. No."

He took a deep breath. "Okay. One more. Do you think that, even without love, there's any chance you and he will get back together? For the sake of the baby?"

He hated to ask. He could see the hurt flicker behind her eyes. "No," she said quietly. "Not because I wouldn't try. I might. I might try anything to make a good life for my child. But Ed isn't interested. He made that perfectly clear."

Parker tried not to be relieved. He tried not to put his own personal desires ahead of needs of this innocent life. But he *was* relieved. He had been so afraid she would say yes.

"Then I can't give up," he said. "I can't stop wanting to see you."

She looked at him. "But Parker, we—"

"I know it doesn't make any sense," he interrupted. He didn't want to hear her answer yet. Not before he had made his case. "But I can't just give up on us. Not without at least trying. Not without doing everything we can to see if we can make it work."

She shook her head. "We can't."

"You don't know that." He took a step closer to

her. She backed up, but she hit Ward's armchair, and there was nowhere else to go. "There's something happening between us. Something powerful."

She was still shaking her head. "Yes, it's called sex. We're attracted to each other, Parker. It would be nice if I could stop being a woman just because I'm becoming a mother, but apparently I can't. When you kiss me, I..." She looked away. "It's just sex."

"You're wrong. It's sex, all right. But it's not *just* sex. Believe me, I've been there. This is different. This is more."

She couldn't put any distance between them, but her head was tilted away from him, and the dragonfly light from the Tiffany lamp spilled across her hair, onto her cheek. She was breathing raggedly under that soft green wool.

"You want the perfect woman, the perfect family," she said, her voice roughly trembling. "And why shouldn't you? I wanted that, too. Everyone does. But that's not what I am, Parker. I'm definitely not the perfect woman."

"Then I don't want her anymore, whoever she is. I want you, Sarah. I need you." He touched her cheek. "Give me a chance to see if I can be what *you* need."

She turned toward him. Her eyes were bright, as luminous and trembling as dragonfly wings.

"I'm not sure I can trust my own feelings right now," she said. "My body—my emotions—what if I'm just feeling unbearably vulnerable? What if I'm just a coward? What if I'm trying to trap someone into helping me, into being a substitute father for this baby?''

He smiled. ''You're not a coward.''

''I am.'' Her eyes widened. ''I'm scared, Parker. Sometimes I'm so scared I can hardly breathe.''

''I think that's normal,'' he said, feeling his heart-beat quicken with the need to comfort her. ''But you are certainly not trying to trap anyone. Look at yourself. For weeks now, you've been trying desperately to keep me at arm's length. And yet you can't, not quite. Doesn't that tell you something, Sarah?''

''Yes.'' She took a ragged breath. ''It tells me I'm in danger. It tells me I could get hurt.''

''We both could,'' he said simply. He put his hands on her shoulders and met her gaze with a straightfor-ward honesty, trying not to think of what he would do if she gave the wrong answer.

''It's a risk. A big risk, one I probably haven't got any right to ask you to take. But I am asking, Sarah. I don't know what lies ahead for us. I don't know if what we feel is—enough. But I want to find out. I want to keep seeing you, even knowing that one of us, or both of us, could get hurt. Will you take that risk with me?''

She stared without speaking. He could see the questions hanging between them like a cloud. He couldn't answer them. He didn't have the answers yet. So, almost without breathing, he waited.

She studied his face. Finally she nodded slowly.

''Yes,'' she said, lifting her chin in that way so like her uncle's. ''I will.''

CHAPTER THIRTEEN

AT THE CITY COUNCIL MEETING, the citizens of Firefly Glen had taken a solemn vow to create an ice festival, no matter what dragons stood in their way. And so, beginning the very next day, they went about keeping that vow with a vengeance.

The streets were suddenly full of bustling purpose. Signs advertising the event hung in every window. Ballot boxes for King Frosty and his Snow Queen stood in every store. That contest quickly eclipsed the Parker-Harry showdown as the most entertaining election in town.

And, overnight, everything turned white. White garlands replaced the green ones from Christmas, looped between streetlights, across storefronts, around the central town square. Frog's Folly Children's Fashions displayed an enchanted window of white velvet dresses and suits, ivory hats and alabaster muffs, amid a flurry of silver snowflakes.

With the costume ball only two weeks away, the fabric store had a run on white satins and silks. The craft store ran out of silver glitter, opalescent sequins and seed pearls. Sewing machines hummed as everyone rushed to create snowmen, snowflakes, snow queens, ice fairies and polar bears.

And behind it all, from sunup to dusk, and sometimes late into the night by spotlight, the hammers
pounded as workmen hurried to build the frame for
King Frosty's magnificent ice palace.

Though Ward still refused to admit he had lost,
Sarah had to agree with Parker. Nothing could stop
this festival from coming.

Meanwhile, Sarah and Parker had their own vow
to keep, the vow to give this relationship, whatever it
was, whatever it might become, a chance. During
these two weeks, they honored their vow, too. It was
as if somehow, that night, they had stumbled onto the
magical phrase that caused the wall of resistance between them to blink and vanish. They hesitated...they
smiled...they touched, and then they abandoned
themselves completely to the sheer joy of being together.

For the whole fourteen days, she didn't sleep much,
and neither did he, as if they resented any hours apart.
They lunched at the Candlelight Café, holding hands.
They borrowed the green sleigh from the Autumn
House and took it into the woods in search of wide-
eyed deer. They played chess with Ward, but even
two against one they always lost because they
couldn't concentrate on anything but each other.

One snowy afternoon, Parker taught her how to eat
thick, sweet icicles cut from the Winter House cor-
nices. They fell laughing onto the snow and made
angels.

Parker even tried to teach her to skate, though after
a few minutes he realized it was hopeless and decided

he'd rather sit on the bench and kiss her until the heat they generated nearly melted the three feet of lake ice down to nothing.

And they talked. They talked about everything—work and family, friendship and food, politics and pirates and porcupines. But they didn't talk about tomorrow. She had a ticket on her dresser back at Winter House, a seat on an airplane that left the day after the ice festival ended, winging its way back to Florida, where it was already eighty degrees and sweltering. Parker knew about the ticket. She knew he knew. But neither of them mentioned it.

For the first time in her life, Sarah didn't try to look ahead. Instead, she accepted each day as if it were an ice crystal, a thing of beauty shot through with deep rainbows, but so fragile she had to cup it carefully in both hands and speak softly in its presence.

Even at such a glorious time, Parker did occasionally have to work. And then, slightly guilty, Sarah would finally attend one of the Gravity Gladiator meetings. These were rarely held at the exercise class anymore. It was too cold, and everyone felt too torpid, lulled into a semi-hibernation by the weather.

More often, the women met for lunch at the Candlelight Café and seriously considered changing their name to Emma's earlier suggestion: the Calorie Cowards.

''Well, what an honor!'' Emma grinned as Sarah sat down that Thursday, the last day before the festival officially opened. She picked up Sarah's left hand. "Why, Heather, look. It's a miracle! They were able to surgically remove Parker's hand from Sarah's!"

Heather chuckled. "Leave the woman alone, Emma. We were just saying how nice it was to see *someone's* romance working out, remember?" She raised her water glass in a welcoming salute. "I'm glad you were able to come, Sarah. We've missed you."

Nice to see someone's romance working out? That didn't sound promising. Sarah squeezed Emma's hand before she let it go. Then, as she unfolded her napkin, she quickly scanned the other woman's face. Emma looked thinner, and the sparkle in her blue Tremaine eyes had all but disappeared.

"I guess that means Harry hasn't come back," Sarah said softly.

Emma shook her head. "He's the stubbornest man alive. I've just about decided to kidnap him from that stupid motel room and tie him up in our cellar until he comes to his senses."

Theo came by, and Sarah placed her usual order. When they were alone again, she turned to Emma. "I know it's not really any of my business, but…is there anything I can do?"

"No." Emma's voice was uncharacteristically harsh, and she toyed with her wineglass in a way that suggested it might not be her first today.

"No," she said again. She sighed from the bottom of her diaphragm and turned her tense, drawn face toward Sarah. "Not unless you can convince dumb

Harry Dunbar that a woman marries a *man*. She doesn't marry a goddamn sperm count.''

Heather's eyes widened. ''Well, okay.'' She dragged the word out in a wry drawl. ''I guess that got right to the point. But now let's see if we can employ some civilized euphemisms here, Em. Just for the sake of the other customers, who might be trying to eat.''

Sarah kept her eyes on Emma. ''You mean you and Harry can't have a baby? Is that what you're saying?''

''I'm saying *Harry* can't. As he's forever pointing out, *I* could, with someone else.'' She closed her eyes and tilted her head back, breathing deeply. ''Only problem is, I don't *want* to. Not with someone else.''

Sarah didn't know what to say. This problem was bigger than she had imagined, and far beyond the reach of mere friendly advice.

However, the irony of their two dilemmas didn't escape her. Here Sarah sat, struggling to cope with the fact that she would be a mother much too soon. And next to her, Emma, who was trying to cope with the possibility that she might never be a mother at all.

Mute with distress, Sarah met Heather's gentle, understanding gaze across the table. And she knew that the irony had occurred to her, too. Heather shook her head once, solemnly, and raised her shoulders, as if to say, *Life!*

''Okay, no more wine for you.'' Heather slid the glass toward the center of the table. ''Don't get drunk, Em. Get mad. Go kidnap that handsome husband of yours, like you said. And when you've got him all trussed up in the basement, just keep saying one word to him, over and over.''

"Oh, yeah? What word is that? *Homicide?*"

"No." Heather smiled. *"Adoption."*

Emma shook her head. "I've said that word a million times. Frankly, I like *homicide* better."

"Hello, ladies. Sorry to interrupt, especially just when the conversation was getting interesting. Who are you going to kill?''

Sarah looked up, a little sunburst of warmth spreading through her as she saw Parker. She hadn't noticed him come in, though he must have taken a while winding his way through the crowded café to their table at the back.

"Oh, good grief." Emma tossed up her hands, looking thoroughly disgusted. "I thought we finally got rid of you.''

"I'll just be a minute." He didn't even look at his sister. He kept his eyes fixed on Sarah. "I think I may have left something here," he said, smiling.

"Well, what? Get it and go. We're having some quality girl time.''

"What did you leave?" Sarah tilted her head.

"This." Parker leaned over and kissed her, a soft touch of heat that made its way through her veins like slow white wine.

"Oh, give me a *break!* Heather, have you ever seen anything so sappy as my idiot brother?''

But Parker just kissed Sarah again, waving Emma to silence with one hand. Sarah heard her two friends begin to chuckle, but she couldn't help herself. She hadn't kissed Parker in hours, and she simply couldn't resist.

"Damn it, Sheriff," a man's voice broke in suddenly. "I've been looking for you. What the heck is this? Aren't you supposed to be on duty?"

Parker let go of Sarah reluctantly. As he straightened and turned, she could see the man who had come up so rudely behind them. He was short and snub-nosed, probably in his early seventies, with a few sparse white strands of hair combed desperately over a large pink scalp. He reminded Sarah of a Pekinese dog. His eyes were black and shiny and small, and he was obviously so mad his face was holly-berry red.

"Hello, Bourke," Parker said mildly. "As you can see, I'm at lunch right now. If you've got an emergency, take it to Dunbar."

So this was Bourke Waitely. Sarah had been wondering about the man behind the name—a name her uncle couldn't even utter without a growl of fury. Parker had told her that the two old men had been feuding for so long no one could quite remember why. Something to do with Roberta, he thought.

And suddenly she remembered where she had seen this man before. On her first day in Firefly Glen, in the coat store, talking to Parker. Warning him to get Ward Winters under control.

"I'm talking to *you,* Tremaine. I want you to do something about Winters once and for all. It's criminal, the trouble he's causing. And all to spite me. You know what's really wrong with the old coot, don't you?"

Parker looked impassive. "Why don't you tell me, Bourke?"

"This is his first festival without Roberta, that's what. He can't stand the thought of it. He can't stand it because he's eaten up with guilt. He knows he killed her."

Sarah half rose, nearly knocking over her water. *"What?"*

Parker put his hand on her shoulder. "What the hell are you talking about, Bourke? Roberta Winters died of pneumonia. You know that."

The little man's face was so dark it looked downright dangerous. Sarah wondered if he might be going to have a stroke.

"I know that's what the death certificate says. But Ward is responsible, you can be sure of that. If he hadn't driven their car into a ditch that night, she wouldn't have broken her hip. And if she hadn't broken her hip…"

He took a few deep breaths, as if he had to push back the emotion a little before he could go on. "He killed her, all right. And I told him so."

"When?"

"Over Christmas. He got to talking all big about how much she had loved him, and…well, anyhow, he's been after me ever since. That's what this festival thing's all about. I told him the truth, and now he hates me for it."

Sarah was on her feet.

"Let me get this straight." Parker's voice was

darkly controlled. "You told Ward Winters that he killed his wife?"

Bourke nodded, pulling out his handkerchief and wiping his half-bald head, which was covered in perspiration. "Yes, sir," he said belligerently. "I damn sure did."

Parker and Sarah exchanged glances.

She picked up her purse blindly, touching Parker's arm with her other hand.

"It's okay," she said. "I'll go to him."

HER UNCLE WAS STANDING at the upstairs oriel window, staring out onto the undulating white landscape below. It had begun to snow again, light but fast. The chaotic flakes flew crazily past the window, in all directions at once.

Sarah came in behind him quietly. On the ride home, she'd been trying to come up with something useful to say.

He heard her, but he didn't turn around. "Hi, Short Stuff," he said. "You finally finished fraternizing with the enemy?"

She put down her purse on the marble-topped table. "I was having lunch with Emma and Heather," she said. She paused. "But while I was there, Bourke Waitely came by."

Her uncle's head half turned, but then he stopped himself and continued gazing out the window. "I guess that was enough to ruin your appetite."

"He seemed pretty upset. He said some...some ridiculous things."

Ward snorted. "Well, that could have been predicted. Every time Bourke Waitely opens his mouth, something ridiculous comes out."

She moved up behind him, and put her hand on his arm. "You know what I mean," she said. "He was talking about Aunt Roberta. And you."

His arm was as tight as a brick. "You know, I think I'll sue the bastard for slander." He nodded firmly. "Yeah. I'll sue him for every penny he has. That would be amusing."

Sarah's heart twisted. "You don't need to do that," she said quietly. "Everyone knows he's talking crazy." She put her head on the back of Ward's shoulder. "Parker says Bourke was in love with Roberta once, too. But she married *you*. So the things he's saying now—everyone knows they're just a bunch of bitter, jealous lies."

Ward was silent for a moment. Then, still without turning around, he reached over and patted Sarah's hand. "He *was* jealous, poor devil. It made him just about crazy to lose her." He shook his head slightly. "I can't blame him for that. I would have gone crazy, too, if she'd chosen him."

"But she didn't." Sarah tightened her grip on his arm. "She chose you. And she never regretted that choice. Never."

"No, I really don't think she did, Short Stuff. I think she was happy with me." He inhaled raggedly. "But does that make it any better, if I killed her at the end? If she died because I made a stupid mistake at the wheel?"

Sarah felt her heart wrenching. So much pain lay behind that question. And what could she say that would help? She hardly even knew the details of the accident. It had been last winter, the final night of the festival, and Ward had been at the wheel. That was all she'd ever heard. But winter driving was always tricky....

"Well, what did *she* say?" Sarah wished her uncle would turn around. She wanted to judge from his eyes the depth of his guilt. "Did she blame you?"

He laughed harshly. "Of course not. It wasn't in your aunt to be cruel. She never said one word about it."

"Right." Sarah smiled, remembering her aunt's warm, perceptive concern for everyone she met, including her little thirteen-year-old great-niece, who was so morose and unlikable that summer. "And if she didn't want you to be unhappy, if she didn't want you to feel guilty, don't you think you owe it to her to be happy? In a way, haven't you dishonored her memory by suffering over it so much?"

He turned, then. His shaggy eyebrows were thrust down hard over his intelligent eyes. "That's a pretty low blow, Short Stuff. Tell me. Are you trying to manipulate this pitiful old man into something here?"

She grinned at him. "Chapter Twelve of *Make Anyone Do Anything*. How to get your great-uncle to drop that heavy load of unnecessary guilt and get on with being happy. As happy as his wife would have wanted him to be. As happy as she spent her whole life trying to make him."

To her shock, Ward's eyes suddenly were moist and gleaming. She held her breath, disbelieving. Never, never had she seen her uncle shed a tear.

And apparently today wasn't going to be the first time. He cleared his throat and scowled at her in the old, familiar way. He seemed to have forced the moisture back in place with a sheer, stubborn will.

"I knew it. Throw that ridiculous book away, Short Stuff. I told you it was garbage."

She met his gaze and, with relief, she recognized the old-time twinkle. "Yes, sir, " she agreed meekly, holding back her smile. "Yes, I suppose you're right."

He grumbled under his breath, but the words didn't matter. She knew it was going to be all right. She gave him a quick kiss.

"I'd better get back to work," she said. "I've still got two snowflake costumes to finish."

He nodded absently. She was almost out the door before he spoke again.

"Hey, Short Stuff," he said gruffly.

She paused. "What?"

"I've been thinking. Why don't you stay?" He asked the question casually, as if it were as unimportant as a query about the weather. "Why don't you just tell them down in Florida to take that teaching job and shove it? Have your baby here. At Winter House. We could use a little life up here in this frozen hole we call a town."

Sarah was strangely paralyzed. Everything she considered as an answer seemed to lodge in her throat like pebbles clogging a stream. She looked at him, trying not to let the ache in her chest reach her face, where it would become visible, and he would know how much she wanted to say yes.

"So why not?" He shrugged. "I mean, what do you need to go back for? So you can find another constipated jerk like Ed? Hell, no. You fit better here, Short Stuff. Can't you feel it?"

"Here?" The word sounded tight and thin, as if it came from someone else's mouth. "In Firefly Glen?"

"Right." His brusque, no-nonsense tone helped her to stay in control. "It's small, and it's colder than God's basement, but it's never boring. You could live here with me. Winter House is a creaky, weird old mansion, but it's seen a lot of love in its day. I'm going to leave it to you eventually anyhow, so why wait till I'm dead? As far as I'm concerned, it's your home now, Sarah. And the baby's. If you want it."

Home.

She fought back a strangled sound. Did he know, she wondered, what mystical, aching power that word held for her? Did he know how many years she had longed to find a place that could deserve that hallowed name?

All those terrible childhood years. As her mother had tugged her from one house to another, from one stepfather and stepfamily to another, she had searched in vain for "home." That paradise other people seemed to take for granted.

But "home," she had discovered, was more than

a bed, a warm meal, an address. It was even, to her surprise, something more than love.

It was a complicated concept built on a foundation of the completely unconditional, the wholly reliable, the intangible, unchangeable something you knew you could always trust, no matter what.

She looked at her uncle. Was it possible that finally, after all these years, she was standing on ground firm enough to support such a concept?

"Well, come on, Short Stuff. What do you say? Will you think about it, at least?"

"Thank you, but I—"

She stopped.

"I—"

She swallowed back the jagged pebbles and took another risk.

"All right," she said. "I'll think about it."

THE SNOW STOPPED FALLING at eight in the morning the first day of the festival, as if under orders from the Firefly Glen City Council. The weather held its breath at a crisp, clear, blue-skied and perfect twenty-eight degrees.

Bravely Sarah offered to stay at home with her uncle, but he shooed her out of the house, saying Parker would never let him hear the end of it if he allowed Sarah to miss a single event.

She couldn't remember ever having so much fun. On Friday, she cheered as Parker's team won the hockey game, and the sleigh from Autumn House won the decorated sleigh rally, in spite of stiff competition from Theo Burke's Candlelight Camaro.

And she got her first look at the finished ice palace. It was simple but beautiful, a square building with a tower at each end. Its pure, translucent walls caught the sunlight and fractured it into a million prisms, so that the entire structure seemed to sparkle.

But Saturday was the most important day of the festival. Sarah woke that morning with a bubble of excitement that nothing could pop, not even knowing that her efforts on behalf of the Firefly Girls had prevented her from creating a costume of her own for tonight's ball.

When her uncle joined her at breakfast, Frosty trotting at his heels, he carried a large, flat box with him. "From your aunt," he said tersely, setting it down beside Sarah, then turning his attention to his cereal and his newspaper.

Sarah opened it slowly. Inside, shimmering like a sheet of ice crystals, was the most beautiful dress she'd ever seen. A simple, ankle-length sheath, with a fur-trimmed ballerina neckline and long, fitted sleeves, it was made of white velvet encrusted with seed pearls and clear glass beads.

Sarah was speechless.

"She wore it years ago, when she wasn't much older than you," her uncle said without looking up from the sports page. "It's supposed to be an ice angel. It should fit." He sneaked a sly glance at her. "Of course, *she* wasn't pregnant at the time."

Sarah laughed, holding it up against her breast with

a deep, inarticulate joy. It was exquisite. She could imagine how beautiful her aunt had looked in it. And how her uncle's eyes would have glittered with pride when he looked at her.

She kissed her uncle softly. "Thank you," she said. "It's perfect."

He fidgeted, as if the kiss annoyed him. "There's a white fur coat in the upstairs closet. I had it cleaned. And she did this thing with her hair—" He waved his hands around his head hazily. "You know, powdered it, or glittered it or—" He frowned, realizing that this wasn't "men's" talk. "Hell, I haven't got a clue how women do that. Your aunt looked great, that's all I know."

From then on, Sarah counted the dragging minutes until nine o'clock, when Parker was going to take her to King Frosty's ball. It was the highlight of the entire festival, with music and dancing inside the ice castle, which would be lit by dozens of swirling multicolored spotlights.

She got through the day somehow. She walked with the Firefly Girls in the children's costume parade, and then she manned the giant snow slide for several hours, until her ears were ringing from the high-pitched squeals of delight and terror.

Finally darkness fell. Still buoyed by that bubble of anticipation, she went home, bathed and dressed. She was glad to discover that the slight thickening of her waistline didn't prevent her from wearing the ice angel costume. Finally she rummaged through the scraps from the snowflake costumes to find tiny silver sequins to arrange on her softly powdered hair.

Her uncle stopped in his tracks when he saw her. "I wouldn't say you're more beautiful than Roberta." He cleared his throat roughly. "But you're a close second, Short Stuff. A mighty close second."

If she still had any doubts, Parker's reaction told her all she needed to know. It wasn't what she expected. He didn't smile with misty pride and compliment her effusively. Instead, as he looked at her, his mouth tightened to a fierce hardness. His eyes glinted, and suddenly his face looked intensely male, and hungry.

"I'm not letting you out of my sight all night," he said as he helped her into the car. "You look so gorgeous it's damn dangerous."

She smiled. He looked fairly amazing tonight himself, though he wasn't technically wearing a costume. Emma had warned her that most of the men compromised by pretending to go as lumberjacks, which meant they could use their everyday clothes.

Parker wore a thick, white Irish wool sweater over black slacks. And he looked as sexy as any man she'd ever seen.

"You may have to let me out of your sight," Sarah said. "What if you're elected king? You'll have to sit on the throne beside your queen. And I'll be left to dance with whoever takes pity on me."

Growling, he took her in his arms. "You won't dance with anyone but me."

"But I've heard people talking. They think you'll be elected king, and then you—"

He shook his head. "I won't be."

"How can you be—"

He put his finger over her lips. "Trust me. I won't be. And if I were, I'd give up my throne. I won't leave you, Sarah. How could I ever leave you?"

He was so close his breath misted white against her mouth before he kissed her. She felt herself melting as his arms closed around her, and his chest pressed hard against hers. The temperature might have fallen to nineteen degrees outside the car, but in here her body was practically on fire.

But they were expected downtown in a very few minutes, so somehow they pried themselves apart, and Parker started the car.

They arrived just in time for the ritual storming of the palace by the new king and his army, a mock battle that included fireworks and a homemade cannon that fired snowballs at the castle walls.

Hundreds of spectators, many of them visitors from neighboring towns, had gathered to watch. Emma rushed up to join them just as Mayor Millner prepared to announce the royal ice court. "Found you," she said triumphantly.

Emma had told Sarah she was coming dressed as the moon queen, and her silver-and-blue costume couldn't have been more lovely.

"Hey! I thought you weren't going to have a costume," Emma said as she hugged Sarah warmly. "Darn. That was the only hope I had of outshining you." She knocked Parker on the chest. "Hi, bro," she said playfully. "Love *your* costume!"

Parker shushed her. "They're about to announce the queen. Show some respect."

"Sorry," Emma said, making a face. "No can do. Wrong queen."

The name was announced over the microphone with a flourish. *Justine Millner.* Emma growled as the blond, smiling mayor's daughter accepted her crown from her father with a graceful, but not entirely convincing, display of surprised humility.

Justine was beautiful, Sarah thought, but she looked like trouble. Poor Mike Frome. He was going to get his heart broken, she suspected.

The king was next. *Harry Dunbar.* Sarah applauded vigorously, surprised but delighted. She looked over at Emma, who was clapping harder than anyone.

In contrast to Justine, Harry looked utterly stunned. He glanced around him at the others, as if to say there must have been a mistake. But the crown was placed upon his head, his people cheered, and he was told to give the order to storm the castle.

Sarah looked at Parker, wondering if he minded losing, especially to Harry. But Parker was studying Emma, who was watching her estranged husband with a proud, protective, bittersweet smile.

"You knew," Sarah whispered. "You knew it was going to be Harry."

Emma turned to Sarah with damp, happy eyes. "It's called stuffing the ballot box, my friend. It's a time-honored tradition in Firefly Glen." She rested her head on her brother's shoulder briefly. "Besides,

Parker actually would have won, and he wouldn't have accepted the crown, so..."

She looked up at Parker. "Thanks, bro," she said.

"No problem, sis," he responded lightly. "Now how about you scram? I'm trying to have a date here."

With Emma gone, Parker put his arm around Sarah and drew her close, warming her as they watched the mock battle raging in front of the ice palace.

This was the first time Sarah had seen the palace at night. She hadn't thought it could be any more beautiful than it was in the daylight, with the sun setting it on fire. But tonight it was like something out of a dream.

Its icy profile seen by moonlight was infinitely romantic, deeply mysterious. Its two towers rose into the starry night like knives of flashing crystal. Its clear, frozen walls undulated with color from the constantly turning spotlights.

When the fireworks exploded overhead, signaling the victory by the king, the crowd roared its pleasure. King Harry led his men inside the gates, and hundreds of fairies and princesses followed, each escorted by a rugged lumberjack or a white-velvet prince. The costume ball was officially underway.

Sarah and Parker danced for hours, under silver streamers and pearly white balloons. As he had promised, he never left her side, not even once. They talked to friends, sampled the delicious buffet, drank wine and admired the elaborate ice sculptures, but they didn't ever allow more than an inch of distance between them.

As the night grew late, Sarah gradually began to realize Parker was seducing her with the music, with the movement, with his warm, strong body.

He held her more tightly with each song. His cheek brushed hers softly, came away, and then dipped to hers again. His hand drifted low, his fingers finding the sensitive hollows of her back. She moaned, but he didn't let up. He tightened his hands. He kissed her ear, her bare neck, her shoulder. And all the while he moved, subtly, to the music she only barely heard.

Soon she was a live ember in his hands, glowing for him, aching for him. Her skin felt too tight to hold all the glittering desire she had inside. She could hardly lift her head from his shoulder.

What if he made it happen right here, out on the dance floor? What if this shimmering thrill she felt inside simply exploded like a silent, internal firework? Would everyone know? Would he hold her up, intact? Or would she fracture like a spray of silver confetti and collapse in his arms?

"Sarah," he whispered. "It's time."

She had to breathe deeply to find enough air to speak. "Time? I don't know what you—"

"Yes, you do." He tilted back and smiled into her eyes. That smile alone was almost enough to undo her. She clutched his arms and tried to find her legs, which had suddenly begun to tremble.

"You see, Sarah? Your body is telling you, too. We've waited as long as we can, sweetheart. It's time to take another risk."

CHAPTER FOURTEEN

THEY RETRIEVED Sarah's coat and walked to the Jeep without saying much. The temperature must still be dropping, she thought, trying to shrink inside her coat. She was like someone with a fever. Burning up and shivering at the same time.

Every parking space was filled, and cars lined the road, nose to bumper as far as the eye could see. Many had license plates from as far away as Pennsylvania and Quebec. It would take an hour to get out of here.

But Parker obviously wasn't in the mood to be patient. When he found his exit blocked, he cut across the snow, the Jeep bumping over the curb and across the corner of the square. Finally he reached the road again, and his way was clear.

He took Sarah's hand and held it tightly on the seat between them, his finger stroking her palm with a slow, deliberate warmth. She closed her eyes and let the rhythm move through her.

They had been driving several minutes, apparently following the moonlit curve of the lake, before she said anything.

Finally she spoke. "Where are we going?"

"I thought I'd take you home," he said. "My

home.'' He glanced at her, his eyes flashing in the darkness. ''Would you like that?''

''Yes,'' she said simply.

He had never suggested taking her to his house before. They had needed time to get to know each other better before they rushed into anything serious. But they also knew their willpower had limits, so they had forced prudence on themselves by staying out in the open, in crowds, in public. Even at Winter House, someone had always been just around the corner, preventing them from taking this one final, oh-so-dangerous risk.

The house was silent and mostly dark as they came up the driveway, but Sarah fell in love with it instantly. It was a large, two-story modern Adirondack cabin that hugged the western shore of Llewellyn's Lake. It was made of smooth, symmetrical red-pine logs and rose from the surrounding woodlands with a comfortable sense of belonging.

One golden light shone above the gleaming wood porch, and in one of the upstairs windows another light burnished the curtains with a welcoming glow.

It was so quiet out here that Sarah could hear the wind moving through ice-covered pine needles with that haunting, glassy tinkle of wind chimes. It was a sound she'd hear in her dreams forever, she thought. Whenever she dreamed of Parker.

He opened the door and flicked on the interior lights. The entire first floor seemed to be one room, one rich, red-pine room with cool green accents: a hunter-green leather sofa pulled up to a huge, river-rock fireplace, a green-and-red Oriental carpet spread across the floor; a glossy green philodendron cascading from a built-in bookshelf.

"It's wonderful," she said. She thought it might be the most peaceful room she'd ever seen. "You can forget, living at Winter House, that simplicity like this still exists in the world."

He smiled as he draped her coat over a wooden tree, then moved toward the fireplace. The logs were already arranged and ready. He simply drew a long, thick match from a box and struck it against one of the stones.

The kindling caught immediately, and a sweet, smoky smell wafted into the cool, clean room.

"Well, if I had your uncle's income to hire a housekeeping staff, I might buy more knickknacks," he said, tossing the spent match onto the logs. "On a sheriff's salary, I prefer to keep things low maintenance."

She shook her head. "This wasn't done on a sheriff's salary," she said. She had just noticed that the eastern wall was entirely windows, two-stories tall, and they overlooked the lake.

"You'd be surprised how well Firefly Glen pays its employees," he countered lightly. "These millionaires have forgotten how to think in terms of minimum wage. But actually, you're right. I was a lawyer for several years, and I worked in Washington for a while, too, so I was able to save some. Plus, I was very lucky. I inherited enough money to live comfortably."

That made sense, looking at this sophisticated room. Its delicate balance of ease and elegance had been achieved by a trained eye, by someone accustomed to living around quality and beauty.

"And yet you work so hard. Why?" She thought of the grief he put up with from the querulous Glenners, the long hours, the freezing nights squaring off against coyotes in people's kitchens. "Why work at all?"

He shrugged. "I work because my folks believed in it. I guess I believe in it, too." He smiled. "And besides, I'm no good at crossword puzzles, and I hate to fish. What would I do with my time?"

They had been talking to ease the tension, to lower the temperature that had risen so dangerously between them while they danced. But suddenly, with that innocent question, the flame shot once again into brilliant life.

He came over to her. "Of course, now that I've found you, I can think of a few things."

He put his fingers under her chin and tilted her mouth toward his. A silver sequin tumbled from her hair, sparkling as it fell.

"Maybe I should let Harry have the job. He wants it bad enough. And suddenly I can imagine spending all day, every day, doing nothing." He smiled. "Nothing but touching you. And looking at you."

She let her eyes drift shut, the sound of his voice like warm water washing through her.

"And making love to you," he said softly. He took

a long breath. "God, Sarah. I'm falling in love with you. Do you know that?"

She opened her eyes and looked into his. "Yes," she said. "I know that."

"And you are falling in love with me. Do you know that, too?"

She nodded carefully. Her whole body felt as if it were dropping into some terrifying, bottomless space, and yet she knew she hadn't moved an inch.

"Yes," she said. "Yes, I know that, too."

"Then this isn't wrong," he said, his voice suddenly fierce. "It's right, damn it. It's so amazingly right, and it's going to be beautiful. I want you to believe that. I want you to stop being afraid."

"I'll try," she said around the swollen beating of her heart. "I'll try."

He unzipped her costume with one hand, still holding her chin with the other. She felt the velvet fall apart from her shoulders to her thighs, exposing her naked back to the cold moonlight that streamed in through the windows.

He slid his hand around, the movement pulling the dress from her shoulders. Silver sequins caught the firelight as the velvet slithered over her skin and fell to the floor.

She wore almost nothing beneath, and she suddenly felt more vulnerable, more insecure, than ever before in her life. She didn't really know her own body anymore. The pregnancy had finally begun to change her, subtly still, but unmistakably.

She wondered if the new contours would make her less desirable to him.

But his face was as tense, as focused and hungry as ever. He finished undressing her, and then he lay her on the carpet, close enough to the fire that she could hear it crackling and feel its fingers of heat reaching out to stroke her.

The rug was thick, scratching softly at her back. Closing her eyes, she wrapped one hand across her stomach, the other across the unaccustomed fullness of her breasts.

She heard him remove his own clothes, but she couldn't watch. It seemed impossible, but she already felt the deep, warning clenches of climax moving through her, like the early readings of an earthquake. She was afraid that, if she saw him now, she might not be able to wait.

And then, with a slow animal grace, he stretched himself out beside her. Finally she looked at him, at the bronze, ribboned muscles, the glowing satin skin. She followed the line of firelight and found the beautiful, shadowed power of his erection. Her whole body spasmed once, in unbearable anticipation.

He unwrapped her hands carefully, one at a time. "You have nothing to hide," he said, bending over to touch his lips to her tingling breast. "Every inch of you is perfect, Sarah. I have never wanted a woman more than I want you now."

He ran the palm of his hand across the small, hard swell of her stomach, learning it. Loving it. He trailed gentle kisses from one side to the other, and she groaned, fighting off the waves of climax that threatened to crash over her. It was too soon, too soon. She wanted this to come slowly and last forever.

He paused, obviously registering the tension that rippled through her limbs. "Look at me, sweetheart. What's the matter? Are you still afraid?"

"Not of you," she said, trying to smile. "I'm a little afraid I'm about to spoil everything. I'm—" She found that her lungs were moving so shallowly she could hardly speak and breathe at the same time. "Things are happening pretty fast. I may not be able to wait for you...for you to..."

He laughed softly. "Then don't wait," he whispered, bringing his lips to her aching breast once again. "Just let it happen."

She could hardly think now. He had let his hand drift down, and she was spinning in a private darkness that disoriented her. And the waves kept coming closer. "But I...we..."

"We will. I promise." He slipped his fingers inside her, and she felt herself tighten helplessly around him as the tide completely overtook her. "It's only the first time you'll feel like this tonight, sweetheart, not the last."

THE DAWN WAS PEACHES AND HONEY. It had spilled onto the pillow, mingling with the tangled gold strands of Sarah's hair. And reluctantly Parker had wakened her with a kiss.

He had to take her back to Winter House, though the idea of having her more than an arm's reach away from him was almost unbearable. He didn't ever want to open his eyes again, and not see her lying beside him. He didn't ever want to breathe and not find the small flower of her perfume in the air.

But she had to go home. Her uncle would worry. And, though he didn't give a damn what the gossips said, something told him that Sarah wasn't ready for what would happen when the town found out about the change in their relationship.

She had never lived in a small town. She couldn't imagine how intensely connected everyone felt, how entwined their lives, how useless any attempt to keep a secret.

But he knew. He'd lived here too long to delude himself about the gossip that was coming. As his grandfather used to say, Glenners would gossip the tread right off their lips.

When they learned that Sarah was his lover, they would start. And when they learned that she was already pregnant by another man...

Well, even Parker couldn't quite imagine what would happen then. He simply knew that he didn't care. Sarah had brought happiness back into his life, and a sweetness he had stopped believing in years ago. He hadn't ever thought to see it again.

He wanted that sweetness. He wanted Sarah Lennox in his life. In his bed. And as soon as she was ready, he was willing to stand on the top of the Congregational Church steeple and announce it to the world.

But it wasn't that easy. Her life was in Florida, and

she still had an airline ticket for tomorrow morning to prove it.

Tomorrow.

The realization hit him like an electric shock. She planned to go away tomorrow.

What a fool he was. For the past two weeks, they had been living in a fantasy. Their own secret ice kingdom, where the real world didn't intrude. But it was time to come out now. He couldn't dawdle in this haze of smug sexual satisfaction. It was time for discussions and decisions.

Big ones.

"Sarah, we need to talk," he said. They were almost at Winter House now, though he had driven as slowly as the Jeep would go.

She nodded sleepily, stirring from her drowsy nest against his shoulder.

"I know," she said, rubbing her eyes. "But not right now. I need to see my uncle. I need to let him know I'm all right. He might be awake, and he might have been worrying."

"He knew you were with me, Sarah. He hasn't forgotten that much about being young."

She smiled. "Still." She ran her fingers through her hair, sending one last rain of sequins onto the black leather of the seat. "I need a nap. I want a bath. And I want some time to think. Last night was..."

"Amazing."

"Yes." She rubbed her arm, as if the mere mention of last night had raised goose bumps. He knew, because he felt the same way. "But it was also confusing. Sex can cloud your thinking, Parker. We need a few hours to clear our heads before we talk about anything serious.''

"Sex *is* serious,'' he said. ''That kind of sex is, anyhow.''

She smiled over at him placatingly. ''Six hours? Just until noon? I promise we will talk then.''

He couldn't deny her anything when she smiled like that. Oh, hell, he couldn't deny her anything ever.

"Okay,'' he said, taking one last kiss as payment. He deepened the kiss and he heard her small whimper as the easy fire caught. He was glad. If he had to suffer, she should suffer, too.

"Just wait,'' he said, pulling away, ''until you see how long six hours can be.''

BUT IT WAS ONLY TWO HOURS, really.

Two hours until everything blew up in his face, as if fate had planted one of last night's ice festival fireworks squarely in the middle of his naive little portfolio of happily-ever-after blueprints.

Parker had picked up his puppy from Suzie, who had agreed to keep him while Parker was on twenty-four-hour call for the festival. Then he had come home, showered, redressed and finally passed out on the sofa.

The phone had probably rung a dozen times before he heard it. The puppy was sitting next to the sofa, whimpering to get his attention. Parker put one hand on the puppy's head and reached over his shoulder with the other one, fumbling for the receiver.

It was Sarah.

"Hi," she said too brightly. "I'm sorry to wake you up. I just wanted to let you know there's been a little hitch. I won't be able to meet you right at noon."

He shouldn't ever try to sleep during the day. It left him muddy headed. At first he didn't even have the sense to be alarmed.

"Why not?" He raised himself to a half-sitting position. "Is everything all right?"

She hesitated. And in that tiny silence, Parker's internal alarms finally began to go off. No. The answer was no. Everything was *not* all right.

"Sure," she said, though her tone was a neon sign that announced she was lying. She was a terrible liar. "It's just that…"

Another pause.

"I've heard from Ed," she said in a tense, unhappy voice. "He's here. He wants to see me. He wants to talk about the baby."

CHAPTER FIFTEEN

"DAMN IT, GRIFFIN. Can't you be a little more convincing?" Emma broke off her kiss and scowled at the sinfully handsome man sitting next to her in the window seat of The Paper House. "Surely they wouldn't call you Playboy Cahill if you couldn't seduce a woman better than this."

Griffin Cahill's elegant, tanned face looked wounded. "I'm not accustomed to *pretending* to seduce women, Emma. Apparently I'm not at my best unless my feelings are sincere."

She rolled her eyes. "Hogwash. You haven't had a sincere interaction with a female in ten years. Just pretend I'm one of the bimbos you date every weekend."

"The bimbos I date aren't *married* bimbos," he pointed out reasonably. "And we aren't actively trying to get their husbands worked into a dangerous lather." He glanced out the window. "Are you sure this is, at heart, a particularly intelligent plan? As I recall, your husband carries a weapon."

Emma sighed. "What, you're afraid of a little gun?"

"Well, yes, Emma, as a matter of fact, I am. I

forgot to wear my bullet-proof codpiece this morning.''

She had to laugh. She *was* asking a lot, but Griffin, with his blond hair, blue eyes and shockingly white teeth, was the best-looking man in town. One of the richest, too. Harry had always secretly been a little jealous of him, all the way back to high school. Emma intended to exploit that as much as possible. This was war, and she needed every advantage she could get.

So it had to be Griffin.

''Look. He's not going to shoot you, damn it,'' she said. ''He might throw a punch or two, but—''

''Emma.'' Griffin held up one long, graceful hand. ''If we're going to do this, let's just do it. You said he'll be here at noon, so unless you want him to walk in on us arguing—''

''No. You're right.'' Emma positioned herself to be thoroughly romanced. ''Let's go.''

This time Griffin was significantly more effective. Emma's disappointment was almost intolerable, therefore, when the next person to open the door was not Harry, but Jocelyn Waitely.

At the sight of Emma Dunbar in Griffin Cahill's arms, the prissy woman looked shocked to her dyed-blond roots.

''Oh!'' Apparently she was shocked speechless, which was a first for Jocelyn, Emma thought waspishly. ''Oh, dear.''

Emma exhaled irritably. ''We're closed, Jocelyn,'' she said. ''I forgot to turn the sign.''

Jocelyn's eyes had begun to glitter unpleasantly,

and Emma noticed that she didn't have to be asked twice to leave. She could hardly wait to get out and start spreading the dirty word.

Sighing, Griffin watched her go. "Not that I'm complaining, Emma, but how many takes do you expect our little scene to require?"

"One more. I promise. Just one more." She hoped that was true. Maybe Jocelyn's appearance had been a blessing in disguise. If blessings *could* come disguised as witchy old bats with filthy minds.

But maybe, if for some reason Theo had forgotten to send Harry to The Paper House at noon as planned, Jocelyn would do it for her. She was probably making a beeline for the sheriff's office right now.

Five minutes later the door opened again. Griffin must have great ears, Emma thought, because he swept her into his arms just in the nick of time and began kissing her so passionately she thought her eyelashes would catch on fire.

Wow, she thought. And then again, stupidly. *Wow.*

From there, things began to happen quickly. The door slammed, someone cursed fiercely. And suddenly Griffin was thrown to the side. When Emma caught her balance, Harry was standing between them, his whole body tense and threatening.

"Get the hell off my wife, you bastard." He whipped his furious face around to Emma. "What in hell do you think you're doing?"

"You know what I'm doing," she said calmly. "I'm doing exactly what you told me to do."

"The hell I did."

Griffin was standing now, and he looked superbly in control, just smug enough to goad Harry into a real temper. Emma was glad she'd picked somebody smart, because her pre-scripted dialogue would only go so far. Sooner or later Griffin would have to improvise.

"Listen, Dunbar. Maybe you'd better not talk to your wife that way."

Harry made fists. "And maybe you'd better not say one more goddamn thing about how I should handle my wife." He jammed a forefinger into Griffin's expensive silk-and-cotton shirt. "*My* wife. Hear that? *My wife.*"

"Well, maybe you should start treating her like your wife, then. In my experience, and I've had plenty, well-tended wives don't go around looking for other men."

Emma could have kissed him all over again. That was the perfect thing to say. Harry would never be able to endure having Griffin Cahill suspect he might be a lousy lover. It was pure locker-room mentality, but weren't all men boys at heart? Especially her foolish, darling Harry?

"Get out, Griffin," Harry said between clenched teeth. "I need to talk to my wife. Alone."

Griffin looked toward Emma. The man deserved an Oscar. Though she knew he could hardly wait to be tossed safely out of this ridiculous situation, he managed to look reluctant, tenderly protective.

"Emma? What do *you* say? Does he have the right to tell me to go?"

She thought for a minute. Then she turned slowly to face Harry, her hands on her hips. She had worn a new dress for the occasion, and she knew she looked great. Plus, her hair was probably all tumbled, and her lipstick smeared, so she probably looked pretty sexy, too. Harry had that look, as if it was driving him crazy to see her like this.

Thanks, Griffin, she said silently, mentally blowing him a kiss. He was such a terrific kisser, it probably would be a mistake to ever try that again.

"I don't know. Do you have the right, Harry? A husband who loves his wife, who is *living with* his wife, has the right to tell her she can't kiss other men. A husband who is living at the Firefly Suites doesn't have any rights at all."

She paused. "At least that's the way I see it. What do you think, Griffin?"

"Seems eminently logical to me," Griffin said conversationally. "Though I might also say—"

"Shut up, Cahill." Harry was looking at Emma with an expression she recognized. He might, just might, have begun to see through her charade, she thought. But maybe it didn't matter. He still knew he hadn't liked seeing her kiss Griffin. And he knew he wouldn't ever want to see it again. "I'm going to tell you one more time. Get out."

Griffin, bless his chivalrous heart, still hesitated. "Emma?"

She smiled up at her husband. She was glad she had worn her prettiest slip, because she had a feeling this was going to be her lucky day.

"Go ahead, Griffin," she said without taking her eyes from Harry. "And lock the door on the way out, would you, please? Harry and I don't want to be disturbed."

IT TOOK SARAH ten minutes to find a parking space. Though this was the last day of the festival, plenty of activities were still going on. The judges were handing ribbons to the winners of the ice sculpture contest, the broomball tournament was in full swing, and the polar bear dip for charity would begin in another hour or so. The town square was teeming with people, and the streets were clogged with traffic.

So, by the time she got out of the car and began walking the length of Main Street back to the Firefly Suites, she was already late. And she hadn't forgotten how Ed hated for anyone to be tardy. She felt a tightening in her chest. She was dreading this encounter more than she could ever have imagined.

"Sarah. Sarah, wait." Out of the dense crowd, Parker appeared at her side. His breathing was slightly irregular, as if he'd been running to catch her. Maybe he had seen her from the sheriff's department windows, which overlooked the municipal parking lot.

"Come." He took her elbow and steered her toward the secluded walkway between Theo's café and Griswold's Five and Dime next door. "I need to talk to you."

She glanced at her watch. "Parker, I'm late." Fifteen minutes late, in fact. Ed would be livid.

"I know." Parker looked drawn, as if his sleepless

night had cost him. She wondered if she looked equally exhausted. "I called Winter House, but Ward said you'd already left. I wanted to tell you..." He shook his head. "Damn it, Sarah. Don't go."

She frowned. "You know I can't—"

"Why should you meet him? What right does he have to come back now, asking to see you?" His mouth was tight and grim. "I don't want you to go."

His frustration was so intense it was like a physical presence between them. She tried to smile, hoping she could defuse his tension by being relaxed, by acting as if this were not the end of the world.

"I have to," she said as calmly as possible. "You know what right he has, Parker. He is the baby's father. I can't ignore that fact just because I don't like it. Or because you don't."

"Yes, you can." Parker's hand on her arm tightened. "He did."

"I have to go," she repeated numbly. "Try to understand. This is Ed's baby, too. I tried to run away from that fact, but I can't keep running forever. Reality has to be faced."

"Then let me come with you. I'll explain it to him. I'll tell him that you and I..."

She shook her head. If Ed met Parker, he would be illogically jealous, no matter how little he wanted Sarah himself. He was like that, petty and insecure, and vindictive. No telling what he would do if he thought another man was sniffing at the crumbs he'd left behind.

"It's better if I go alone. Really."

Parker backed away two steps, holding up his hands. "So what do you want me to do, Sarah? Be noble? Stand back politely while this bastard comes in and stomps all over our future? Last night we—" He stopped. Cleared his throat. "We made love, and—"

"I know," she broke in softly. "But the fact that you've become my lover does not make you the baby's father. You know that. He has rights, Parker. Legal rights. Moral rights. Biological rights. I can't wish them away so that you and I can make love happily ever after."

He was silent. With a sinking heart, she watched the struggle in his face. Oh, how he hated this, as she had always known he would. He hated not being the first, the real, the only.

She realized then that he hadn't ever honestly faced the messy truths about her pregnancy. He had simply created a light, manageable scenario in which, because he loved her and loved the baby, he could step in cleanly and, by virtue of his higher moral ground, essentially *become* the baby's father.

Ed's reappearance was his wake-up call. This was the moment when Parker had to accept that his fairy tale could not survive even one strong blast of reality. That standing on high moral ground didn't, in the end, protect you from much of anything.

Even worse, this was the moment she had been dreading ever since she had first kissed him. The moment when he realized that loving her, loving a woman who was about to bear another man's child, was simply too messy and painful and complicated.

It was simply too hard.

"Do you know what I really think, Sarah? I think you want this meeting with Ed." Parker's tone was rough, suddenly, and his eyes had darkened until no blue remained. Sarah flinched, though with some part of her mind she understood that this was just his jealous misery scraping the smooth surfaces from the dialogue. "You *want* to see him."

He didn't mean that. He didn't believe that.

"In a way, I guess I do," she said carefully. "I want to face him, because he must be faced. That's all. I want to know what I'm up against as I try to piece together my new life."

"He'll want you back. He'll want his child." Parker shook his head, a deep line of anger slashing the skin between his brows. "What man wouldn't?"

She smiled at his innocence, at the profound goodness he possessed that made him believe such things. "This man didn't, Parker. His first reaction was to tell me to get rid of it."

"But he's had time to think. Time to come to his senses. He'll want his child." He wiped his hand over his eyes, as if he could wipe away his visions. "And you'll say yes, won't you, Sarah? For the baby's sake, if not your own. You'll say yes, and then the three of you will be the perfect little family."

Oh, God. Parker, don't.

She felt her throat close up as she turned away from him.

"The perfect family is *your* fantasy, Parker. Not mine."

THE MINUTE SARAH SAW ED, standing next to the bar, his body rigid with annoyance that she had dared to keep him waiting, everything about this terrible meeting suddenly became shockingly simple.

She didn't have to struggle with the moral dilemma of what to do if he had, as Parker feared, come to try to win her back. She didn't have to wrestle with her conscience, didn't have to weigh her own selfish desires against her deep commitment to provide the best possible life for her baby.

She didn't have to search her soul, trying to determine whether she was, by rejecting Ed, making her child pay the price for the mother's sins.

There was no struggle to find an answer, because there was no question.

She could never go back to Ed. And it wasn't because she had fallen in love with a more-rugged face, a sweeter nature, a sexier body. Even if she had never met Parker Tremaine, she could never have returned to the miserable, one-sided relationship she'd endured with Ed.

She had changed, in these few weeks. She had grown. She had learned a lot about herself, and a lot about love.

She didn't love Ed, and a family without love was the worst life any mother could offer a child. And Ed, petty, vain, tyrannical Ed, would be the worst father, much worse than no father at all.

So it simply didn't matter what he had come to say. She would never, ever go back to him.

With at least that much of the burden lifted from her shoulders, she found herself able to walk up to him serenely.

"Hi," she said politely. "I'm sorry I'm late."

"Damn, Sarah." Ed stared at his watch, as if he simply couldn't believe what the hands were telling him. "I've got a plane to catch. Won't you ever learn how to get anywhere on time?"

She looked at him evenly. "If you're short of time for this meeting, Ed, maybe you shouldn't waste any more of it complaining about how late I am."

He did a small double take. She had never talked like that to him before. But he covered it quickly. She could almost watch the progression of thoughts across his handsome features. He wanted to be indignant, but he realized it wasn't prudent.

So that must mean he wanted something. He obviously didn't feel that he occupied the power position in whatever discussion he'd come here to have. Selfish need was the only thing that ever forced him to moderate his temper.

"Sorry," he said with an obvious but not very successful attempt at being gracious. He gestured to one of the lounge tables. "Shall we sit down?"

She accepted the chair he held out for her. But he didn't sit right away himself. She thought he might be staring at her waistline. The dress she wore had, over the past few weeks, grown a little bit too tight. Soon she would have to buy maternity clothes.

But he wasn't. She followed his gaze, and she saw that he was clearly eyeing her noticeably larger breasts.

She found herself flushing with anger. She hated having his gaze on her. How had she ever tolerated his hands? Her stomach tightened, and she felt a brief, vicious return of the morning sickness she thought she'd left behind.

When he realized that she had caught him staring, he glanced away. "You look well," he said awkwardly. "Are you?"

"Yes," she said, setting aside her annoyance. "The morning sickness only lasted a few weeks. I'm fine now. I've seen a doctor up here. The baby is fine, too."

He didn't respond. He just shifted in his seat and looked anywhere but at her, as if any mention of the baby made him uncomfortable. But she didn't allow herself the luxury of hating him, of despising his cold, selfish denial of this helpless child he had fathered.

She couldn't afford to think about that. She was determined to keep this civil. He had a right to know the basic details.

"I may have miscalculated the due date at first. The doctor up here says I'm about five months pregnant now. The baby will probably be born in June."

He toyed with his napkin.

"Really," he said, obviously struggling to say the right thing, strike the right attitude. "That's good. I guess." He looked up, his eyes tense. "I'm sorry, but I still think you were wrong, deciding to go through with it. It would have been so much simpler if you would just have—''

''Not for me,'' she said with enough unyielding emphasis to make him look away again.

She leaned back in her chair and gazed at him steadily, amazed at how angry the suggestion could still make her. He had no concept of how real this baby had become to her, did he? To him, it was still a *problem,* a *thing.*

''Ed, let's get to the point. Why are you here? You do know, don't you, that it's far too late now to be hoping I'll agree to any procedure.''

''Of course I know that.'' He offered her his best half-profile, his most wounded expression. ''God, Sarah. I'm not really a monster, you know.''

She let her silence speak for itself.

He flushed. ''You've really turned into a bitch, haven't you? I saw this change starting in you even before we broke up. Once, at the beginning, you were such a sweet woman, Sarah. So easy to get along with.''

Once, at the beginning, she had been such a fool. So easy to push around. So grateful that a strong, steady man wanted to make a strong, steady life with her. So relieved that she was not going to end up like her mother, bouncing from one weak, faithless man to another like a marble in a pinball machine.

Ed had liked that needy, insecure woman just fine. What bully wouldn't?

But she didn't say any of that to him. What was

the point in needling each other? She just wanted to get this over with. It was giving her a headache.

"You know, I had hoped that when we met again you wouldn't be bitter, Sarah. I had hoped you might have taken time to see this from my perspective. To see how I've suffered, too, because of what's happened." He tugged on his cuffs, sniffing slightly to show his disappointment. "But apparently I overestimated you."

"No, I think you overestimated *yourself,* Ed. And your so-called suffering."

He bristled, offended. He set his chiseled lips into an unforgiving line. Touching her aching temple with her fingers, Sarah sighed, sorry that she had risen to the bait yet again.

"Look," she said quietly. "This is pointless. Why don't you just tell me why you've come to Firefly Glen?"

He tossed his napkin onto the table in a weary gesture of resignation. "Okay. Here's why. I want to know what it will take—" he paused "—to keep this quiet."

She had been prepared for many things, but not this. She couldn't even be sure what he was talking about.

"To keep what quiet?" She narrowed her eyes, trying to figure it out. "I don't see how I can keep people from learning that I'm having a baby. A baby has a way of making itself known, especially after it's born."

"No." He tightened his mouth. "I mean my involvement. My involvement in your problem."

She tilted her head. "I think you'd better be more specific," she said carefully.

"All right." He folded his hands on the table, the picture of rational male patience face-to-face with unreasonable female emotion. "What I want to know, Sarah, is exactly how much money it's going to take to make this problem go away for me. How much you are asking for your silence."

She didn't trust herself to speak. She just looked at him, feeling a strange pity for the woman she used to be, all those light-years ago. How could she ever have been so weak as to think this man was strong?

He fumbled in his pocket and pulled out a long, narrow brown envelope. "I've had the papers drawn up. All that's left is to fill in the numbers and write the check."

He finally noticed the look of quiet disgust on her face. Alarmed, he pulled out his most-reliable weapon. His charming, wheedling tone, the one she'd heard him use so many times with difficult parents.

"The truth is, I'm hoping to get married soon, Sarah," he said with a boyish candor. "I've fallen in love. She's the most wonderful woman. But she's very young. Very innocent. She's the daughter of the chairman of the board. It's a terrific chance for me. If he—I mean, *she*—ever found out about you and me…"

He spread his hands, as if surely she could appreciate the dilemma. "It's a very high profile family. If they find out that I have a pregnant ex-girlfriend who could show up at any moment, making headlines, causing trouble—''

Sarah almost laughed, but with effort she controlled herself. Did Ed have delusions of grandeur now—did he really think that their tawdry affair and illegitimate baby would make ''headlines'' anywhere in the world? They wouldn't even make headlines here in Firefly Glen.

''What is this wonderful woman's name?''

''Melissa,'' he said cautiously. She noticed that he carefully omitted the last name. ''Why do you ask?''

Without answering, Sarah took the envelope from his hands. She opened it and scanned the brief legal document that lay, in triplicate, within. It was almost obscenely simple. For X amount, Sarah Lennox absolved Ed McCutcheon of any responsibility for the child they had conceived.

Probably, she thought, she ought to turn it over to a lawyer. Most people would say that she was a fool. Here was her chance to take him for every cent she could get. Just scrawl in a few nice, round zeros after her favorite number and...

But she didn't want anything from Ed.

Except her freedom.

For extra convenience, the envelope even held a pen. She pulled it out, clicked it open and boldly wrote ''One dollar'' on the empty line. Then she signed her name, pulled off a copy for herself and handed the document back into Ed's limp, disbelieving hands.

He looked at the papers, then at her, with a kind of bewildered anxiety in his eyes, as if he suspected a trap.

"One dollar?"

"That's right." She stood. "Don't just sit there with your mouth open, Ed. You're free. Put the dollar on the table. We'll leave it as a tip for the waitress. And then go on back to California."

He kept frowning at the contract, turning it over again and again, as if he thought she might have used disappearing ink to scribble in some diabolical trick.

She began to walk away.

"Sarah, wait." He caught her arm, stalling her. "Are you planning something? Why did you want to know Melissa's name?"

She looked down at his blunt-fingered hand, so alien now against her skin.

"Because," she said, a cold distaste turning her voice to sheer ice. "I'll be mentioning the poor child in my prayers tonight. If she's really going to marry you, Ed, she's going to need all the help she can get."

CHAPTER SIXTEEN

IN THE CLEAR DELFT-BLUE SKY overhead, the winter sun looked as pale and thin as a white dinner mint. But its appearance was deceptive. As the afternoon wore on, that anemic-looking sun managed to muscle the temperature up to almost fifty degrees.

The tourists took off their sweaters and tied them around their waists. Worried officials inspected the ice palace, checking for weak spots. The ice sculptors huddled in anxious clusters, fretting that their creations would not last the day.

The only people who welcomed the heat wave were the Firefly Glen United Charities volunteers, who stood shivering, waiting to make their heroic dip into the freezing water of Llewellyn's Lake.

Sarah didn't care about the weather at all. For the past hour, ever since she left her meeting with Ed, she had been wandering through the exhibits at the ice sculpture contest, only half seeing anything, just hoping to buy enough time to sort out her muddled thoughts.

The theme this year was "People We Love." And the sixty-five entrants had, as usual, interpreted the theme in sixty-five different ways. One artist had chosen Scooby-Doo, another had carved a bust of Shakespeare, and a third had, in a fit of amusing candor, sculpted a six-foot replica of himself.

Sarah was standing in front of an anatomically correct sculpture of Marilyn Monroe when she spotted Harry and Emma walking by. They seemed so contentedly absorbed in each other, she almost didn't speak. Harry's arm was around Emma's shoulders, and her fingers were hooked casually over the edge of his back pocket. It completed a simple, magical circle.

Sarah would have let them pass. But they saw her first.

"Sarah!" Emma dragged Harry over, though he clearly would rather have been alone with his wife on a planet all their own. "How are you?"

Sarah dug through the ashes of her mood and salvaged one real smile for Emma's joy. "Great," she said. "I guess I don't have to ask how *you* are."

Emma grinned. "It shows, huh?"

Sarah caught Harry's eye. "A little. You're pretty much glowing like a lightbulb, Emma."

"Well, here's my special secret. A rip-roaring fight does wonders for the circulation." Emma grinned. "And making up afterward is good exercise, too."

Harry was flushing, so Sarah took pity on him and changed the subject. "How's Mike Frome doing? My uncle says he donated some of Mike's restitution hours to the city. Has he started working yet?"

Harry nodded. "He's been painting Parker's office. Nothing too hard, but we'll keep him busy, I guess.

We considered the chain gang, busting rocks, but then we thought, no, the kid can't be trusted with rocks.''

His brown eyes twinkled, and finally Sarah could see why Emma was so crazy about her husband. He had a lot of laughter in those eyes.

"But Mike's worst punishment," he went on, still smiling, "is having to put up with Suzie. She's our clerk, and she's a pistol. She never shuts up. She rags Mike about Justine Millner so bad the kid's going to get a complex. But he's getting his eyes opened about Justine, so maybe it's worth it."

Emma snorted. "I don't know how you get to be eighteen whole years old without already having your eyes opened about Justine Millner, but hey, maybe the kid's slow." She glanced wryly at the Marilyn Monroe ice sculpture. "Or maybe—" She jerked a thumb toward the amazing translucent breasts, which hadn't melted an inch, even in all this heat. "You know."

Sarah laughed. Emma looked around, as if noticing for the first time that Sarah was alone. "Hey. Where's Parker?"

"Parker? I'm not sure," Sarah answered, as normally as she could.

"You're not sure? You two have been breathing the same square inch of air for two weeks straight. And now you're not sure where he is?"

Sarah shrugged casually. "I think maybe he had to work."

Harry shook his head. "No, we put a temp on call today so that everyone could..."

But Emma had caught on. She glared at Harry, who finally got the message, too.

"I don't know, though," he amended awkwardly. "Maybe he had to go in."

Sarah smiled. "Maybe," she agreed. Harry was a very nice man.

Emma touched her arm. "Hey, we were going to go get a hot chocolate over at the elementary school. Want to come?"

"No. I'm fine." Sarah nodded firmly. "Really. You go ahead."

"Well, okay." Emma looked worried. Then she grinned. "But remember what I said, girlfriend. Sometimes a good argument is the sexiest thing you can do for a relationship."

Sarah shook her head and waved Emma away with a laughing smile.

But when they were gone, her smile faded away quickly. She moved on down the rows of sculptures numbly. She had the strangest feeling of needing to see everything today, needing to commit to memory all the special sights and sounds of Firefly Glen.

The snow banked up against the buildings, like piles of glittering white sequins. The laughter of children, carrying clear across the crisp air. The tattered brown lace of bare tree limbs, waving against a powder blue horizon. The ice palace, wetly gleaming, already dissolving by microscopic degrees under the rays of that powerful white disc in the sky.

It was as if she knew her hours here were numbered. And she wanted strong, clear memories to take with her, to pack and unwrap at home.

She tried to keep her spirits from sinking too far. She would survive. And somehow, someway, she would create a home for her baby. That was the only thing that really mattered.

In fact, it was actually much better that Parker had been forced to face the problems now. No real harm had been done in these two weeks of romantic fantasy. They had made love once, and the rest had been achingly innocent. They had been like children, willfully oblivious and naive but not wicked.

Just children. Playing house in the mouth of the volcano.

But they had been lucky. They could walk away now, and know that they had not permanently damaged anyone. How much worse it would have been if he had found out later, found out two, three, four years from now that he simply couldn't stay the course.

Later his defection would have been truly terrible. Later, when her child knew him. Depended on him. Loved him, just as Sarah had so foolishly allowed herself to do.

She tried to tell herself that she was lucky she hadn't made another terrible mistake. Lucky that these risks she'd foolishly taken hadn't led to real disaster.

She took a deep breath. She knew now what she needed to do. Once she got home, once she got past the worst of this, she would sit down and make a new plan. She would map out a safe life for herself and her baby, down to the minute, if possible. She would think it through carefully. She would accept only complete control, total security. She would depend on no one but herself. She would, if she could, eliminate all risks.

She was almost at the end of the last row of sculptures. Only one exhibit remained ahead of her. Her car was in the other direction, but she decided to go look at it. At least she could truly say she had seen them all.

And then she would go back to Winter House, and tell her uncle her decision. She would be flying back to Florida tomorrow.

It wasn't the biggest sculpture she'd seen today. Or the showiest. But it was, perhaps, the most beautiful. Only about two feet tall, it was a magical butterfly carved in the act of rising from a rose, its icy wings catching rainbows in the brilliant winter sunlight.

It had been carved with great delicacy, and it was unusually thin, almost mystically transparent. In today's unseasonable temperatures, the tips of the wings had already begun to melt.

The artist, who was sitting on a folding chair beside his creation, didn't seem at all disturbed by the fact that his sculpture was doomed. Sarah watched his peaceful face, turned up to catch the rays of the sun as if he were a surfer in Malibu, with no thought but enjoying the warmth.

"Hi," she said impulsively. "I just wanted to tell you that I love your butterfly. It's very beautiful."

He opened his eyes without straightening up. His eyes were beautiful, too, ringed with thick black lashes. Extremely sensitive eyes. And extremely intelligent.

He smiled broadly. "Hey, man, thanks. I liked that one, too."

She noticed that he was already referring to it in the past tense. She watched helplessly as one shining teardrop of water dripped from the butterfly's wing. It made her feel, absurdly, like crying. She wanted to catch the drop and hold it, put it back, make it stay. She wanted to stop this dying by degrees.

"Don't you mind?" She knew she ought to just move on, but she couldn't. She wanted to understand where he found this serenity, this amazing acceptance of the inevitable. "Don't you feel..." She searched for a word. "Cheated? Cheated to have worked so hard on something so ephemeral? Something that simply can't last?"

He glanced over at his butterfly. "Not really," he said pleasantly. "It's the rules of the game, you know?"

"No. I'm not sure I understand."

"Well." He scratched his two-day growth of beard. "I don't know. It's just that all the best things in life don't last very long, right? Thunderstorms. Rainbows. Bird songs. The perfect hamburger. Great sex."

He grinned. "They kind of streak through, and if you're lucky enough to be in the right place at the right time, you reach out and touch 'em. But you can't hold on. It ruins stuff like that if you try to hold on."

Sarah was temporarily unable to think of a sensible response.

"But, hey." He raised his brows. "I guess you know all about that, huh?"

How did he know that? She wondered if her heartache was as clear on her face as Emma's joy had been on hers. "What do you mean?"

He gestured toward her stomach. "I mean, well, excuse me for getting personal, but you're going to have a baby, right?"

She hesitated, shocked to discover that her "secret" could be visible to a discerning stranger. But suddenly she realized that she was glad—that it felt lovely and healthy to discuss her baby openly. A baby now. Not a secret.

She nodded. "Yes, I am."

"So what can be more ephemeral than that? The baby will be like your very best ice sculpture, but it won't be yours for long. You'll make it, and you'll take care of it, and then, when the times comes, you'll have to let it go."

Sarah swallowed hard. And then she gasped softly. She put her hand on her stomach, feeling for the first time a tiny quiver inside her, like the sleepy beat of butterfly wings.

He grinned again, and then he leaned back, closing his eyes, returning to his mindless basking in the sun.

"So yeah," he murmured absently. "Beautiful things are like that."

SHE COULDN'T FIND PARKER, though she practically ran from one end of the square to the other. She went to the Sheriff's Department, the café, even back to the Firefly Suites, in case he had been looking for her there.

She checked everywhere, asked everyone. But no one knew where Parker had gone.

Finally, almost exhausted, she drove back to Winter House. She would rest a little, then renew her search by telephone.

As she pulled into the driveway, she saw his Jeep. Her heart stumbled. It felt a little like a miracle, and she had been afraid she was out of miracles.

But he was here. He had been here, at Winter House, all along.

He was coming down the steps from the house, his hands jammed into his jacket pockets, heading toward his car. He still looked tired, she thought. His hair was tousled and his head was bent as he walked in the face of the wind.

She yanked hard to engage the emergency brake and scrambled out of her car as fast as she could release the seat belt. He looked up when he heard her. "Sarah?"

She began to run. His face changed, and then he was running, too. They met somewhere between the two cars, colliding awkwardly, all desperation and no grace.

"Sarah!" He pulled her into his arms, kissing any part of her his lips could reach—her hair, her chin, her eyes, her mouth. "Oh, my God, Sarah. Tell me you didn't go back to him."

She spoke against his lips, the words half-distinct. "I didn't go back to him."

He let out a low groan. "Thank God." He tilted her head so that he could look into her face. "Sarah. I'm so sorry. Can you ever forgive me?"

She could hardly speak. She had run only a few yards, but her heart was racing as if the distance had been a marathon.

"No," she said. "I mean yes, oh, God, you know there is nothing to forgive. Parker, I was such a fool—"

"No, *I* was." He closed his eyes on a deep, ragged breath. "I was terrified, Sarah. I was so afraid that I was going to lose you. You must have loved him once, and I was so afraid that if you...if he—"

He couldn't finish. Infinitely touched, she reached up and pushed a strand of his dark, silky hair out of his eyes. "I told you I never loved him. That was true. Until I met you, I didn't even know what love was."

He looked at her with a gaze that was equal parts hope and fear. His eyes were so blue, she thought. They were as blue as the sky above them right now. She felt a sudden, distinctly maternal urge to take every fleck of fear or pain out of those wonderful, beautiful eyes. She wanted to leave only the hope. And the love.

"Can you forgive me, Sarah? You had every right to meet him today. I understand that. I always did understand it. I was just so damn scared."

"I know," she said. "I know."

"I want you to know that I understand he's going to be a part of your life forever. I can't promise to like it. But I *can* promise to stop being such a possessive, jealous jackass."

"Oh, really? You can promise that?" She smiled. "What if Ed and I need to confer daily about the baby?"

He hesitated. "On the phone?"

She laughed softly. "I was thinking over lunch."

He gritted his teeth, but he managed to nod. "Even then. I don't want to share you. But if I have to, I will. I meant it, Sarah. I *will* stop being such a possessive, jealous jackass."

She squinted thoughtfully. "What if Ed needs to spend the night occasionally, to help see the baby through an attack of colic?"

But now he knew she was teasing. He tightened his grip around her waist. "The man can move into the downstairs bedroom and play tiddlywinks on my dining room table, for all I care." His voice was husky with emotion. "Just as long as you're in the upstairs bedroom with me."

"Liar." She rested her cheek against the soft warmth of his leather jacket. Her breath misted against the gold star.

"But you don't have to promise me anything," she said. "That's what I wanted to tell you. You don't have to promise me anything at all."

He had begun to stroke her hair. It was as if, after their desperate race to touch, to speak, to explain, they had found their way to the other side and entered a place of profound peace. "I don't?"

She shook her head, a tiny movement that he probably barely felt. "No, you don't. It's enough that you love me today, that you want me today. I've never understood that before. But I do now. I have learned a lot in the past few weeks, Parker. From this odd, wonderful little town. From the baby. And from you."

He didn't jump in to contradict her. He obviously sensed that she was saying something that mattered a great deal to her. And he was listening. She loved him more than ever, just for that sensitive silence.

"I've spent so much of my life trying to control the future," she said. "From the time I was a little girl, I've been practically obsessed with it. I've made elaborate, detailed plans that somehow gave me the illusion of safety. I think I wanted to believe that I could take a pencil and paper and plan away any risk of failure or pain."

He tightened his grip and put a kiss on the crown of her head.

"But I've finally realized that trying to control the future is absurd. And arrogant. Because if you think you can decide what the future *will* be, that means you think you know exactly what the future *should* be. And no one ever knows that."

She closed her eyes against a sudden sting of tears. "This baby, for instance. I didn't plan this baby, and yet it's one of the most wonderful things that ever happened to me."

She lifted her face to his, though she knew her eyes were moist and aching with love. "And you. I could never have planned you."

"I didn't plan you, either." He gazed at her with eyes warm with kisses to come. "Although I think I might, on one of my loneliest winter nights, have *dreamed* you."

Somehow she managed not to kiss him. She had just one more thing to say.

"So here's my promise to you." She put her hands on the lapels of his supple jacket. "I promise to stop trying to plan the future. I'll let it unfold in its own way, in all its terrifying, wonderful mystery. Things could go wrong. Someday you may find that you can't really love a woman who carries another man's child. But that doesn't mean we can't have today."

"Sarah—"

"I promise it, Parker. No more plans. Just today. I promise to cherish the way you feel about me today, without asking whether it will last forever."

He smiled. "I guess we both think we sound like very reasonable, mature adults, don't we? But let's see if I've got this right. I'll try to live with my fear that you might stop loving me. And you'll try to live with *your* fear that I'll stop loving *you*."

She looked at him. It did sound a little ridiculous, put that way.

"Essentially, yes. We'll both accept a level of fear and insecurity we were never willing to accept before."

He put his hand under her chin.

"Or maybe this would be easier," he suggested. "How about if we just go inside, tear up your plane ticket, tell your uncle we're getting married next week, and then drive back to my house and make love to each other until we can't breathe, or talk or even think? Until there's no room in our hearts for anything as foolish as fear."

She felt her pulse begin to race. Her eyes filled with sweet, fiery tears.

"Now that," she said softly, "is a plan."

EPILOGUE

THEY WERE MARRIED two weeks later, on election day.

Parker said he felt he owed the town something exciting to do that day, since he had denied them the thrill of a dramatic, family-feud race for sheriff.

To everyone's surprise—except maybe Emma, who guessed, and Sarah, who had been in Parker's arms when the decision was made—Parker announced that he would not seek a second term in office, leaving Harry to run unopposed.

Shortly thereafter, Parker told his closest friends that he planned to set up his own law practice, in the big brick professional building at the opposite end of Main. He said he was pretty sure he could make a decent living defending Ward Winters from defamation lawsuits alone.

The gossips in town were almost sick from all the delicious, gooey news, like children let loose in a bakery. Emma Dunbar had been seen kissing Griffin Cahill. Harry Dunbar had nearly killed Griffin with his bare hands. Inexplicably, Emma and Harry were living together again. Parker Tremaine was going to marry Sarah. Sarah was going to have a baby. *And,*

*oh, my heavens, have you heard, Parker's not the
father!*

Sarah knew that Parker made sure she never heard
the worst of it. And by the time the wedding came
around, it was all fairly old news. Glenners liked Parker Tremaine, that was the bottom line. And if Parker
could live with the mystery baby, they supposed they
could, too.

And besides, they did love a wedding.

Winter House, filled with flowers and music and
hundreds of smiling, weeping people, had never
looked more beautiful. Its eccentric, Gothic-
monastery charm, Ward explained wryly, was the perfect stage for anachronistic tribal rituals of high
drama.

Sarah remembered very little of the ceremony,
which had passed in a blur of confused joy and trep-
idation. She remembered best the steady feel of
Ward's arm under her fingers as she walked down the
aisle, and then the familiar, comforting thrill of Parker's hand in hers.

But she knew that she would never, never, forget
the reception.

Everyone was there.

Madeline Alexander had stayed up every night for
two weeks, sewing Sarah a wedding dress, so of
course she was there, coming by every few minutes
to adjust a pearl button or tug at a ruche of lace.

Harry and Emma came, too, of course. Emma was
the matron of honor, beautiful in blue, and Harry wore

his shiny new star with a rather endearing, grateful pride.

Eileen O'Malley had been the flower girl, and as she stood beside Sarah, so serious in her blue velvet, her red hair a fire of curls around her pudgy shoulders, Sarah had caught her first, breathtaking glimpse of the beauty to come.

Heather Delaney came, too, though she wore her pager and had to leave halfway through the reception to deliver a baby. She and Sarah exchanged glances as the beeper went off, and Sarah knew they were both thinking the same thing. Someday that little electronic sound would call her to Sarah's side, to bring her child into the world. Heather kissed Sarah as she left and hugged her, too, something the ultra-contained young doctor rarely did.

Theo catered the food, which was served in the dining hall by candlelight, of course. No wedding feast had ever been more visually enticing, or more delicious, and yet Theo had stayed in a constant agony of embarrassment, sure that she hadn't lived up to her own standards.

Even Mike Frome was there, working off some restitution hours by serving hors d'oeuvres to the guests. Sarah winked at him as he went by, handsome in his tuxedo. He'd worked off about one square foot of a fifty-foot window so far. Poor Mike, Sarah thought. He was going to be working for the Winters family for years.

Actually, everything started well. Sarah and Parker

danced the first dance, posed for pictures, shared champagne and cut the cake.

And then the trouble began.

Justine Millner walked by, wearing a bright red gown made out of approximately three-quarters of a yard of silk. Watching her, Mike Frome tripped on something—Parker later suggested it might have been his tongue—and sent a plate of hors d'oeuvres flying into the library window, which broke.

Ward, who simply couldn't believe it, yelled something rude, to which Mike's grandfather, Granville, took offense. The two old men began shoving each other, and several of the younger men started circling them, trying to find a safe way into the fray.

Madeline Alexander began to cry, wailing that surely her beloved Ward was going to die. And at that Bridget O'Malley reared up like the warrior queen she had been born to be, and announced that Madeline had better stop acting as if she had dibs on Ward Winters, which she didn't.

Jocelyn Waitely, who had knocked back too much champagne, joined in the debate, announcing loudly that *she* was the one Ward liked the best, which caused her husband Bourke to dash his drink into the fireplace, causing a semi-spectacular explosion that sent the rest of the guests screaming for the exits.

Sarah watched in mesmerized horror as her lovely reception turned into a scene from an Irwin Allen movie. Somehow, just as the chaos reached its peak, Parker came to her rescue.

He took her hand, pulled her into the one remaining

quiet corner and, looking deeply into her eyes, asked
huskily, "So, Mrs. Tremaine. This is what you've
married. Want an annulment yet?"

She settled into his arms. "Nope," she said. "How
about you?"

"Well, no," he answered, kissing her nose. "But,
then, this was my town already."

"And now it's mine." She put her hands on either
side of his face. "I love Firefly Glen, Parker Tremaine. And I love you."

He grinned. "As much as Madeline Alexander
loves your uncle?"

She considered it carefully. "I don't know," she
admitted. "I still wouldn't set myself on fire for
you."

"Then come with me," he said, pulling her to her
feet. "Let's get out of this insane asylum and go
home. Perhaps I can start that fire myself."

This November 2001—
Silhouette Books cordially invites you
to the wedding of two of our favorite

YULETIDE BRIDES

A woman gets stuck faking happily-ever-after
with her soon-to-be ex-husband—or *is* she
faking?—all the while hiding their baby-to-be,
in **Marie Ferrarella's CHRISTMAS BRIDE.**

A man hired to bring back a mogul's lost
granddaughter goes from daring detective to
darling dad, when he falls for the girl *and*
her adoptive mother, in **Suzanne Carey's
FATHER BY MARRIAGE.**

Because there's nothing like
a Christmas wedding...

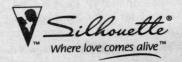

Silhouette®

Where love comes alive™

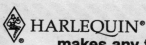

*H*ugh Blake, soon to become stepfather to the Maitland clan, has produced three high-performing offspring of his own. But at the rate they're going, they're never going to make him a grandpa!

There's *Suzanne*, a work-obsessed CEO whose Christmas spirit could use a little topping up....

And *Thomas*, a lawyer whose ability to hold on to the woman he loves is evaporating by the minute....

And *Diane*, a teacher so dedicated to her teenage students she hasn't noticed she's put her own life on hold.

But there's a Christmas wake-up call in store for the Blake siblings. Love *and* Christmas miracles are in store for all three!

Maitland Maternity Christmas

A collection from three of Harlequin's favorite authors

Muriel Jensen
Judy Christenberry
&Tina Leonard

Look for it in November 2001.

WITH HARLEQUIN AND SILHOUETTE

There's a romance to fit your every mood.

Passion

Harlequin Temptation

Harlequin Presents

Silhouette Desire

Pure Romance

Harlequin Romance

Silhouette Romance

Home & Family

Harlequin
American Romance

Silhouette
Special Edition

A Longer Story
With More

Harlequin
Superromance

Suspense &
Adventure

Harlequin Intrigue

Silhouette Intimate
Moments

Humor

Harlequin Duets

Historical

Harlequin Historicals

Special Releases

Other great
romances
to explore

PLEGEND01

CALL THE ONES YOU LOVE OVER THE HOLIDAYS!

Save $25 off future book purchases when you buy any four Harlequin® or Silhouette® books in October, November and December 2001,

PLUS

receive a phone card good for 15 minutes of long-distance calls to anyone you want in North America!

WHAT AN INCREDIBLE DEAL!

Just fill out this form and attach 4 proofs of purchase (cash register receipts) from October, November and December 2001 books, and Harlequin Books will send you a coupon booklet worth a total savings of $25 off future purchases of Harlequin® and Silhouette® books, AND a 15-minute phone card to call the ones you love, anywhere in North America.

Please send this form, along with your cash register receipts as proofs of purchase, to:
In the USA: Harlequin Books, P.O. Box 9057, Buffalo, NY 14269-9057
In Canada: Harlequin Books, P.O. Box 622, Fort Erie, Ontario L2A 5X3
Cash register receipts must be dated no later than December 31, 2001.
Limit of 1 coupon booklet and phone card per household.
Please allow 4-6 weeks for delivery.

**I accept your offer! Enclosed are 4 proofs of purchase.
Please send me my coupon booklet
and a 15-minute phone card:**

Name: _____

Address: _____ City: _____

State/Prov.: _____ Zip/Postal Code: _____

Account Number (if available): _____

---

097 KJB DAGL
PHQ4013